Gutted

TONY BLACK

Gutted

preface
publishing

Published by Preface 2009

10 9 8 7 6 5 4 3 2 1

Copyright © Tony Black, 2009

First published in Great Britain in 2009 by Preface Publishing
1 Queen Anne's Gate
London SW1H 9BT

An imprint of The Random House Group

www.rbooks.co.uk
www.prefacepublishing.co.uk

Addresses for companies within The Random House Group Limited
can be found at www.randomhouse.co.uk

The Random House Group Limited Reg. No. 954009

A CIP catalogue record for this book is available from the British Library

Hardback ISBN 978 1 84809 052 1
Trade Paperback ISBN 978 1 84809 051 4

The Random House Group Limited supports The Forest Stewardship Council (FSC),
the leading international forest certification organisation. All our titles that are printed
on Greenpeace-approved FSC-certified paper carry the FSC logo. Our paper
procurement policy can be found at www.rbooks.co.uk/environment

Mixed Sources
Product group from well-managed
forests and other controlled sources
www.fsc.org Cert no. TT-COC-2139
© 1996 Forest Stewardship Council

Typeset in Times by Palimpsest Book Production Limited,
Grangemouth, Stirlingshire

Printed and bound in Great Britain by Clays Ltd, St Ives PLC

For Madeline

Chapter 1

ON THE HILLS AT NIGHT, you hear screams, you start running. I don't care what your name is – you do it. Instinct, adrenaline, whatever, it kicks in and you tank it. Sensible people run the opposite way. Mentallers like me chase the screams.

My heart was pounding as my legs stretched out beneath me through the gorse, it was Corstorphine Hill, for Chrissake . . . not exactly fairway territory. In my current condition, wedded to a bottle of scoosh and smoking forty, scrub that, sixty a day, I had five more minutes of this before a massive coronary kicked in.

I slipped, landed on my arse. Was wet below, was Scotland, c'mon . . . it's in the contract. 'Fuck me!' I yelled, my palms scratching on the hard, gnarled roots of a tree. Stung like a bastard. As I tried to get up I took another flyer, cracking my head soundly on the tree's bole.

'Oh, Jesus hellfire . . .' I touched my temple. Found blood on my fingers, couldn't figure if it came from my head or my scratched hands. Both formed their own pain brigade, marching through me in time to my fit-to-burst heart.

The screams came up again. Louder now. I was closer. The ground I covered, skitting down the hill on my arse, must have been in the right direction. I didn't know whether to be grateful or not. The noise seared me. Real pain. Suffering. And, if I wasn't wrong, laughter . . .

Someone's up to no fucking good.

I tried to get a look about but there was little or no light, save the moon, just the thin crescent job, and half covered by cloud at that.

I strode on, tracked the wails. Felt my teeth itch with each new burst of anguish. Someone, or something, was in serious trouble. As if I needed any confirmation of this, the tormentors upped the ante.

As the first shot rang out, I thought: That's it.

Game over.

I waited for a cry, a scream, something to seal the deal.

What I heard was . . . nothing.

I stood stock still. Only the breeze moving all around me in the silence of the wood. I felt the veins in my neck thumping like pistons. I strode forward, branches lashing at my face, caught a log below and it hurled me down a steep slope. As I fell, my pocket-bottle of Grouse escaped and rolled away.

I could hear movement below, voices, more shots, then . . . the screams again.

The ground hit me like a Mack truck. I stopped dead by the edge of a clearing. There was light now. A pimped-up Corrado with the full beam on. I got myself upright, spat out a mouthful of muck, checked my bridgework was still in place and tried to focus.

C'mon, Gus, get a fucking grip!

My eyes smarted. I wiped away the long grass my hair had trapped and waited for my vision to settle. It didn't take long; I wished it hadn't come back at all. *This* I did not want to see. I was ready to kill. There's a phrase, hear it all the time, *I'll swing for you* . . . That's where I was at with these bastards already.

I looked about for a weapon, rock, stick, anything. Found nothing. Was gonna have to be old school. Didn't faze me. I ran in, fists balled.

'Right, y'bastards!' I wailed, like a nuthouse on meds night. Grabbed the first body I could, a young ned, say seventeen tops, and put a sledgehammer jab through his puss. He dropped like a wet sandbag. It took the other three a time to turn around; the howls from the dog they had tied to the tree drowned out everything. They were taking potshots at it with air rifles; when they spotted me their target changed.

'Get that cunt!'

I felt a crack on the side of my head, then a thud at my shoulder. There seemed to be a few seconds before the almighty agony of hot pain burnt at both these points, but when it did, I cuffed it aside, like swatting flies.

I took my own aim, on the one nearest the dog. He was tall, a six-footer, but a string bean – all coat hanger shoulders and skin pebble-dashed with acne. He wore a white hooded top that was an easy grab in the dark. I quickly hoyed his face down onto my boot.

'Taste that, shithead.'

I must have got a good few kicks in before I felt two lightning bolts strike my back, right between the shoulder blades. I dropped the lanky streak of piss and flung up my hands.

I'll give them this: they were hardy. Grabbed my arms and laid into me with fists. I'm guessing they were no strangers to the odd pagger. The fists came quick and sharp, jabs, interspersed with the odd kick. It took me a while to roll over, but I got there, just in time to catch the big one aiming to jump on my head.

I pulled back. He missed, rolled over on his backside.

The other two watched him fall and I took my chance to get upright again. On my feet I cracked some quick rights, pegged one of them out.

The two on the ground scuffled backward on their arses.

I stood in front of the car lights. 'Right, you sick little fuckers, want to meet the daddy of pain?'

I picked up the rifles, smacked them over their heads. There were wails, shrieks. 'Not so fucking hard now, eh?'

3

'Ah, mister, fuck off.'

'That's me – Mr Fuck-Off . . . How do you fucking do?'

The dog whimpered. I heard it struggle to free itself, blind with panic.

I took the gun barrels, bent them under my Doc Martens and flung them down. As I went over to the dog, I tried to lower my threat level; the animal was in a state of abject fear. The wounds didn't look too serious, but Christ, I was surprised it hadn't died of sheer terror.

I bent down, offered an open palm. 'It's okay . . . it's okay, boy.'

I got to within inches of the dog when I felt a heavy thwack on my spine.

'Think you're hard, eh? Think you can mess with the likes of us?'

The second strike knocked me into the undergrowth. I seemed to roll a bit, five maybe ten yards, then came to rest under a tree. I thought I'd landed in shit – smelled like it. I turned over, put my hands behind me, tried to push myself up, but I was slipping on something that felt wet, slimy.

As I made a last attempt to ease myself up, the string bean appeared before me, holding up a branch like a club, ready to knock seven bells out of me. I felt my hands slip again, fail to find any purchase. I thought that was it, I was a goner.

'Holy fuck,' said the yob, 'holy fucking shit!'

He lowered the branch and then his pals appeared at his back. 'C'mon, let's get out ay here.' They tugged at his white hoodie, grabbed his arms.

'Is he dead?' he said.

'Aye, course he is . . . look!'

They seemed to be looking at me. Problem was, I didn't feel dead. Was this dead? Never. It felt too much like life, which was depressing to contemplate.

I struggled to free myself again. As I did so, I slipped back. Seemed to slide off whatever I'd landed on. I heard the yobs

4

scampering away through the bushes as I turned over and lifted myself from the ground.

When I looked down things suddenly made more sense.

I'd been rolling about on a corpse. I had the blood of a dead man all over my hands.

Chapter 2

I FELT A STAB IN my guts. A heave, then I bent like a hinge, chucked up all over the corpse. There was more where that came from, but I battened a hand on my mouth, fought the urge.

As I stared down, my instinct was to scrunch eyes, look away.

'Holy shit,' I said, 'holy mothering fuck.' It didn't look good. The face was a bloodied pulp, unidentifiable. Could have been any age, sex . . . I guessed by the size of the body, male. I hunkered, raised a twig and poked away at the loose covering of leaves. This was one shallow grave: whoever dumped him here wasn't giving a rat's hump who found him.

No shit . . . This is Corstorphine Hill, next to the zoo, a bloody tourist trap.

We had buildings going up all over the city; there was never a better time to pour a bit of concrete over some inconvenient stiff.

'This is fucking madness.'

I poked some more with the twig. It was the body of a man, what they call *skelky* in Scotland, or sometimes *eight stone dripping wet*. His hands were cut to ribbons on the palms. Looked like he'd fended off some fierce swipes from a sharp knife. I turned them over. The knuckles were smooth.

'You didn't put up much of a fight, mate.'

He hadn't been here long, I'd say it was a matter of hours more

6

than days. He had, however, been soundly slit from – as the saying goes – neck to nuts. Deep wounds had shredded his shirt and jacket to nothing; he was to all intents naked save his sleeves and trousers. How he'd got here, and who'd put him here, I'd no desire to find out. But old habits die hard. I lifted up the flap of his jacket with the twig. There was a wallet in the inside pocket; I pulled my shirt-sleeve over my fingertips, fished it out.

Two tenners and a twenty. A flyer for a sauna in Leith. An RBS bank card. A driving licence that read: Thomas Fulton.

The name meant nothing to me, it was too common. But the face in the photograph sparked some dim recollection; of whom, though, I'd no idea. I put the wallet back.

That I'd been rolling around in Tam Fulton's claret was something I could have done without. From my experience plod tends to take a dim view of such occurrences around a murder scene. Something like self-preservation kicked in, told me to play it by the book. A stretch for me, but the only option.

I replaced the branches, pulled out my mobi and dialled 999.

Got 'Emergency. Which service?'

'Police.'

I took a last glance down at the corpse, caught an eyeful of dark viscera and spilled entrails. Felt another heave. Figured this image was staying with me for a while.

As the operator connected me I stamped out my misgivings, my urge to run, told myself I was doing the right thing.

A firm voice: 'Police, emergency.'

'Yes, hello . . . I, eh, seem to have stumbled across a . . .' – it was clearly murder, but I chose my words carefully – 'dead body.'

A gap on the line, then, 'Are you sure the person is dead, sir? Do you require an ambulance?'

'I'm pretty sure he's dead . . . The blood's everywhere and there's a lot of stuff that should be inside him lying about on the ground.'

Another silence.

'Sir, can I take your details?'

I felt my pulse quicken. What was I getting myself into?

Said, 'My name's Gus Dury.' My address and the location on Corstorphine Hill followed.

'There are officers on their way to the locus now, Mr Dury . . . Can you keep an eye out for them?'

Trembling: 'Erm, yes.'

'The officers will take your statement when they arrive.'

'Fine, yes.'

I hung up.

As I clicked the mobi off there was a rustle in the distance. It put the shits up me. I froze. I'd definite company. Sure as shooting, I wouldn't be too charmed to meet our man's acquaintances.

Another rustle. Same spot. I felt sweat form on the back of my neck.

My head buzzed, thoughts going round faster than a mixer. None gave me a get-out.

My jaw clenched, fists followed, both on auto.

Fight or flight?

This scenario: I'd take the latter.

Since the yobs had legged it in the Corrado visibility was blacker than my thoughts. The moon had escaped the cloud, though, and the clearing caught more light now. Could I risk being spotted if I made a dash for it? What would plod have to say about that?

I felt another bucket of adrenaline tipped in my veins. I got ready to mush, then: a whimper. It came from the same spot as the rustle.

'The dog . . . Fuck, the dog.'

I can't say the wee fella was glad to see me. He cowered, back against the tree, and put his big black eyes on me.

'It's okay, boy . . . it's okay.'

He looked like a Staffie. I wasn't sure, but he ticked all the boxes: stocky, deep-chested, your average tinpot hard man's hound. I'd have expected more of a put-up, snarling. Some teeth-baring maybe. Biting. But got none of it.

'That's it, that's it . . . the good guys are here, boy.'

As I untied him from the tree he trembled. He'd been traumatised.

I lifted him and he yelped, as near to the noise a baby makes as I'd reckon a dog could manage.

'Sorry, fella, that hurts, huh?'

I tucked him under my coat and he curled into a ball, laid his chops on my shoulder. I swear he was docile. Me, I'd have been ready to kill the first bastard who came my way after what he'd been through.

'Think we'll have to get you to a vet,' I said.

I made for the clearing.

The sky's edges started to bleed blue. A violet glow began on the horizon. I could hear the sirens of the police cars bombing it up Corstorphine Road already. In no time this place would be swarming with filth.

The hack in me – or was it the bad bastard? – forced out another call: I dialled my sometime employers, hoped there was still money in the budget for a late shift.

The number rang three times.

An eager voice: 'Newsdesk.'

'If I remember what nights are like in there, I'm dragging you away from a crossword.'

'Sudoku, actually.'

Well, it *was* 2009.

'Gotcha. You'd like a tip-off for tomorrow's page-one splash, then.'

I heard the reporter's chair creak as he sat upright. 'Tell me more.'

Chapter 3

I SAT TIGHT. WISHED I could say the same for the dog. He squirmed under my coat and whined and whimpered with every movement.

'Come on now, you're not doing yourself any favours,' I told him.

He looked at me with wide eyes, his fat tongue lolling out the side of his mouth. He did not look a well beast; if I didn't get him some veterinary attention soon, he wasn't long for this world.

I felt my heart blacken at the sight of him. 'Those little fuckers.'

The police cars had stopped and a trail of searchlights made their way up the hill to the clearing.

I had, I guessed, time to make one last call. If this dog was to have any hope I needed to get moving soon.

I dialled Mac. He still owed me after all I'd done for him of late.

'Mac, it's Gus.'

'How goes it? You done with the badgers?'

Oh yeah, that was the job: stake-out on the hill, to catch badger-baiters. These days, I was big time. My late friend Col had left me his pub, but it wasn't doing too well. We had more debts than punters. I'd been picking up what extra work I could, in any line. Going back to hack work was looking like a more tempting offer than ever.

10

'Fuck the badgers, Mac.'

'Gus, what are you saying? Are you off the job?'

'I don't have time for this . . .'

'Gus, those Badger Protection boyos are paying top whack . . . Are you pissed?'

'Mac, just listen the fuck up!' Where I found the balls to speak to Mac the Knife, with all his form, like that, I'd no idea. 'Give them back their fucking deposit.'

A pause, then, 'I'm listening, Dury.'

'Good. Now get in your car and drive to the foot of Corstorphine Hill . . . Right now.'

'Gus, I've got the pub to look after.'

'Fuck the pub . . . Shut the pub.'

A moment of silence, the radgeness of the idea registered, then: 'Okay. I'm on my way.'

'And bring towels, lots of them. And some water if you can manage it.'

'What the . . . are you delivering a baby?'

'No, I've just had a fucking cow. Now shift your arse, Mac.'

I hit 'end call'. My phone smelled of Regal – made me want to spark up. As I fished in my pocket for my smokes the dog yelped.

'Sorry, boy . . . we'll get you to a vet soon. Mac's on the way.'

I just got my Marlboro lit when a torch was shone in my face. I raised my hand, said, 'You're blinding me.'

A uniform stomped over. As he approached, the dog let out a bark – bravely, I thought, given his injuries. Had we bonded already?

'What the fuck are you doing here?' said the uniform.

'I called you. I'm the one that found the body.'

He shone the torch on me again, ran the light up and down. For the first time since my fall I copped an eyeful of my new Leatherface get-up.

Uniform's jaw drooped; his eyes didn't blink. 'You're fucking covered in blood.'

'I know . . . I, eh . . .'

'You're dripping in it.'

11

'I fell and, well . . .'

He turned away, gave a groan, chucked up. I figured he hadn't been on the job long.

More uniforms arrived; I pointed them to the corpse. There was suddenly a lot of movement about the place. Radios buzzing, people running back and forth. I pointed the way, retold my story twice, three times to uniforms. Then the big guns got rolled out.

I'd seen a suit like it before, in the window of Jenners, but I never dared to check the price. Like they say, if you need to ask, you can't afford it. I remembered the make though, Hugo Boss – mob that made the SS uniforms.

Boss Suit strutted past me, shot me the kind of look I guessed he normally kept for *Big Issue* sellers on the Mile. He took some directions from uniform then followed the by now well-trodden path to the corpse. He kept his hands in his pockets, except for when he wanted to wave away his underlings, or point them in a new direction. He was big on himself, no question.

I followed to the edge of the clearing. There was yellow crime-scene tape being rolled around the trees and a white tent being unfurled, but I could see everything clearly in the breaking light.

It seemed all straightforward: Boss Suit was leaving it to the shit-kickers. Then someone handed him a plastic tray with the corpse's wallet. I was close enough to see the change of expression from cocksure to shit-scared when he registered the victim's details.

He wiped his mouth. It was only a few seconds, but telling. Immediately he dropped the wallet back in the tray, ordered the uniform away and strolled to the side of the clearing to make a call.

I tried to get closer. Caught the words 'It's fucking Moosey!' Then he turned, caught me in his gaze. He lowered the phone. 'Who the fuck are you?'

'I found the body.'

'Dury!' It seemed my reputation preceded me. 'Well, well, well . . . the mighty Gus Dury. I don't know whether to shake your hand or bow.'

I tried a smile. Nah, wasn't happening.

He walked over to me, checked me up and down. I got the impression he'd been rehearsing this bit. 'Well indeed . . . I had you down as quite different.'

'You did?'

'Oh, yes . . . I didn't have you down as a total fucking jakey.'

The dog squirmed. I did too.

'Look, I don't think I've had the pleasure.' I held out my hand. It was covered in blood. Dark, almost black blood.

Boss Suit looked down, laughed. 'I don't fucking think so . . . Though, given I wouldn't be standing here now if it wasn't for you, maybe I *should* be shaking your hand, Dury.'

I saw where this was going: my last case had made some waves with Lothian and Borders plod. 'I don't think that's true.'

'No, you're right. I was fucking fast-track; that wee shit storm you caused with the people-smugglers just sped things up. But if the force hadn't shed a dozen-plus of the top brass, who's to say I might not be poking about in the grass with those uniform retards?'

I looked away, tried to appear bored. Truth was, I'd heard it all before. I'd blown the lid on an Eastern European people-smuggling racket that was bringing young girls into the city, forcing them into prostitution. My discovery led to some big boys in the force being shown the door. The papers ran with it for weeks. I was the man pointing the finger but I sure as fuck didn't get anything out of it. This prick, though, seemed to have done all right.

I fronted him: 'Look, this is all very interesting, going over old times and all that, but if you don't mind—'

'What, the case in hand?'

'Well . . .'

He smiled. Teeth dazzled me more than the torches going about the place. 'I'm happy to take your statement . . . In fact, it would be my pleasure.'

He produced a Moleskine notebook, black with an elastic strap. He twanged the band, licked the tip of his pen. 'Go on, Dury . . .

I'm Johnstone by the way, Jonny Johnstone. You might be hearing more of me.'

'Really?'

'Oh, I'd say so . . . But to your statement.'

He had me rattled and knew it; he was enjoying winding me up. I tried to calm it, but my nerves were shot. 'I was just going down the hill after these yobs —'

A hand went up. 'Whoa, whoa, whoa . . . back up. What were you doing here?'

'I was on a case . . . badger-baiting job.'

He burst out laughing, had to wipe his eyes, near toppled over. 'Come again . . . badger what?'

I repeated.

'Fuck me, Dury . . . you're big time, eh.'

I was beginning to lose it. 'Look, d'you want to hear this or what? I could just as easily have fucked off and left you to it.'

He straightened, put a bead on me. 'Ah, but your sense of civic duty wouldn't allow that now, would it?'

I turned away. 'Fuck this.'

'Not so fast, Dury.'

I swung back. 'Look, I have a dog here that's been shot at with air pellets. I need to take it to a vet.'

Another smirk. 'Badgers, dogs . . . You'll be doing Rolf Harris out a job.'

I moved off.

'Stop. You're not going anywhere until I'm well and truly fucking finished with you, Dury . . . and I mean finished.'

I stood still. I had my back to him now. He walked slowly towards me, then around my right side until he faced me. He said, 'We have more in common than you think, Dury.'

I wasn't biting, though he had my full interest. I let it slide. He seemed almost disappointed, went back to the job in hand, said, 'So, these yobs . . . descriptions.'

'I gave your boys the descriptions.'

'And they were in a car, you say?'

'Corrado, a white one.'

'Probably not related.'

'You seem very sure.'

He raised his brow. 'I'm a proper detective, fuckface. Don't even think of questioning my judgement.'

'Are we done here, *Detective*?'

'Oh, I think we're done, don't you?'

I nodded, said, 'Good.'

As I turned he called me: 'Oh, Dury . . . don't be leaving the city any time soon.'

'You what?'

'I think you heard.'

As he walked past me he twanged the elastic on his notebook again, tucked it inside his suit. I clocked the lining: purple silk. 'We may need to talk to you again . . . so make sure we can get hold of you, nice and easy, eh.'

Chapter 4

THE DOG SQUIRMED UNDER MY coat. I didn't think he was trying to get comfortable, more like seeking a way to escape the pain of his wounds. I took a look: some of the deeper gashes would need stitching for sure. At a guess I'd say those little fuckers had been at him with some kind of lash before they got started with the airguns.

'That's a proper doing-over you've had, pal,' I whispered.

He put those eyes on me again. Heart-melters. If I'd less to worry about, I'd be looking for those yobs, tearing them new arseholes, more than they could make use of.

The sky verged on fully lit now. I saw the blood congealed on my hands. It had dried in dark streaks; under my fingernails it looked black. I tried to rub it away and then, the worst, I got a waft of that smell again.

I couldn't stop my guts heaving. I'd more in the tank, copped for a barf. It sprayed my Docs. I put my hand to my mouth, but the smell of blood caused another burst. I chucked and chucked until I was left dry-retching. The dog whined and clawed at me.

As I straightened I saw the reporter from the paper arriving. He had a snapper with him who was firing off shots of the scene. Boss Suit had a hand up, but it was all pretence – he looked delighted to have his picture taken.

16

'Fucking ponce,' I muttered.

I stepped into the path down the hill, looked to the road. I could see a set of headlights; turned out to be a Joe Baxi. I knew Mac would be on his way, but I was anxious now for the dog. His breathing had got heavier. He seemed more sluggish. I thought I might be losing him and it punched my heart.

Another set of lights, not a cab this time.

It was Mac. I sighed with relief.

'About fucking time.' As he pulled in there was no screech of tyres. He even used indicators. I grabbed the door. 'You know, you could work for Meals on *fucking* Wheels.'

'It's speed cameras all the way down the road.'

'Towels . . . where's the towels . . . and the water?'

Mac yanked on the handbrake, leaned forward. 'Holy buggery . . . What the hell's happened to you?'

'Don't ask?'

'Is that blood?'

'No. It's creosote . . . Thought I'd do a few fences while I waited.'

Mac's eyebrows lifted, then shot down. 'What's the fucking Hampden roar here, Gus?'

I patted out a towel on the front seat, got in.

'Gus?'

The dog's head popped out of my jacket.

Mac screamed, 'Fuck me! What's that?'

'You never seen a dog before?'

'Not popping out a man's chest like fucking John Hurt in *Alien* I haven't, no!'

I pushed the dog's head back under my jacket. 'Mac, you realise it's probably not got long to live.'

That registered, a wince stretching out his half-Chelsea smile. Now he gunned it. Tyre-screeching, the lot.

I smacked my brow with the heel of my hand, tried to get into gear. 'You'll have to take him to the Vet School, they do emergency cases.'

'Aye, okay. I'm on it, eh.'

The dog wouldn't take the water. His head lolled from side to side, his eyes were slits. 'Better fucking nash, Mac.'

My guts started to churn again with the motion of the car.

'Don't you be puking in my motor.'

The stench of blood in the confined space hit me. 'I feel rough.'

Mac opened the windows. 'I'll drop you at the pub . . . You're in no state to be seen out anyway.'

Like I could argue with that.

The streets were empty of traffic; we got there in no time. I placed the dog on the seat I'd vacated. He yelped, had a fit of panting then looked up at me. I placed a hand gently on his head, said, 'Good luck, fella.'

Mac didn't hang about, tore away leaving tyre marks on the street. I felt better in the open air again. My legs were rubber but I was used to that; could have done with a large one to settle me down.

A jakey was sleeping in the doorway of the Wall. I lifted his collar, told him, 'Do one.'

Grunts, bit of a grumble. Think I woke him. Asked, 'Do you need a kick in the arse as well?'

He got the message. Stumbled off, good few bottles of White Lightning rattling around inside him.

I had to get out of these clothes, get in the shower, ease the bruising and swelling I could feel coming up on my face, the raw knuckles and the rest of it.

First things first, though. I flicked the bar lights on, raised a glass. The nearest to hand was a pint mug. Filled it to nearly halfway with Johnnie Walker. The taste came to me like a recurring dream. People watch me at the scoosh and say, 'You take that like tea.' They're wrong, of course: I don't take tea. Lately, I don't touch much other than this.

I hit the optic again, swirled a shot in the bottom of the glass. Fired it like a twelve-gauge, then got moving.

I took a few bar towels and nashed through to the gents' cludgie.

The lights blasting off the white tiles stung my eyes, nearly felled me. But it was the smell of rank piss that set my guts heaving.

As I hit the nearest sink I caught sight of my hands. They looked raw as minced meat. I followed the length of my arms, took in my jacket, my shirt. Holy shit: I wore more blood than a slaughterhouse.

The thought of the corpse on the hill rose, and I wanted to get tanked up, *immediately*. That's how I do business: problem rears its head – drown it.

I got the gear off, started to fill the sink. My hands trembled. I needed another drink.

I grabbed soap, dooked the bar towels. It was cheap soap, took a while to work up a lather, but we got there. The blood went from black to red as the soap foamed. I dropped the bar in the sink, got to scrubbing. In a minute or two, the blood was merely pink streaks. I pulled the plug, ran my hands under the gushing taps.

Couldn't say I'd scrubbed up like they do on *ER*, but I was in the ballpark. I didn't want dead-guy blood on me; call me picky.

I caught a glance at myself in the mirror. From somewhere, the phrase *death warmed up* hit me. My skin looked grey, hollows in my cheeks like Peter Cushing. I could see past the fact that I needed a shave, a haircut, some serious dietary attention, but the man before me was someone I didn't recognise.

'Who or what the fuck is haunting you, Gus Dury?'

'Tits up' might describe my life. What shocked me was the way I seemed to be projecting this to the world.

I touched my face. When did my skin get so leathery? When I was a kid, Clint Eastwood had skin like this. What had happened to me? I didn't want to look, but something held my gaze where it was.

I had black rings under my eyes. When I was a hack, back in the day, my wife – scrub that, ex-wife, I recently got the papers to prove it – would say I had panda eyes when I worked too late. I wonder what she'd make of these jobs? The predominant colour was red, where it should be white, few specks of yellow creeping in.

'Quite a look, buddy,' I said into the mirror. 'You make touchline Alex Ferguson look a picture of health.'

I turned away. Just as Debs had. We'd tried to patch up our marriage recently, had made a trip to Ireland with high hopes, but my self-destruction had terrified her; she said that she couldn't watch me 'doing myself in slowly'. I knew I couldn't change, but I also knew I couldn't put Debs through any more hurt. I'd done enough of that.

I lifted my pile of clothes, took them up to my flat and dumped them in the laundry.

I showered, hot as I could take it for near on an hour. Got dressed in a pair of Levi's, frayed and faded, white T-shirt, and a black cardigan from Markies. Looked like a jazz musician, said, 'Not nice!'

My problem was footwear. My Docs were wasted, caked in blood and dirt. I was down to an old pair of Converse All Stars. There were holes at the edges. I could hear my mother say, 'They've seen better days.' I thought, Haven't we all?

I went back down to the bar, grabbed a pack of B&H off the shelf, sparked up. The blue smoke was a comfort. Since the ban, pubs don't quite have the same appeal, the same . . . atmosphere.

I took time over a pint of Guinness. Less time over the chaser; it became more of a starter.

I was verging on comfortable – there's something about a good wash and clean clothes that can make you feel like a new man – when in walked Mac. Straight away, he reminded me I inhabited a world of shit.

'You all right?' he said.

'Och, you know . . . usual.'

'Fair to fucked.'

'Sounds about right . . . The dog, how'd it go?'

'Those wee bastards,' Mac strangled the air in front of him, 'I swear, I ever get my hands on them they'll need photographs to put them back together.'

He wasn't kidding. I hit my Guinness. 'Well, is the dog gonna be okay?'

'Hard to say, doing X-rays and that. Vet said this kinda thing's all too common these days.'

I shook my head. 'When will we know?'

'Says we can call tomorrow . . . Can't do anything else, Gus.'

He was right. The night's events suddenly seemed to overwhelm me. I was glad to know the dog had survived this far, felt a surge of relief. The exhaustion hit.

Said, 'I'm gonna hit the hay, mate.'

Thought the sky was coming down.

'The fuck's this . . . Armageddon?'

It was noise to split eardrums. I jumped out of bed, checked the window. Two hardy types rolling steel barrels off the back of a brewery truck. I say rolling: there was more dropping involved. By the look of things, it was just the start too – they had a lorryful to unload.

I opened the window, yelled, 'Can you keep it the fuck down?'

The pair halted, shrugged shoulders at each other, then the bigger one puffed out his chest from under an England top, said, 'Geezer, we don't have a fahkin' off switch.' He put his hands together, scrunched his big padded gloves tight. There was a definite bead in his eye. Like I was having that.

'All right, fine, sorry to trouble you,' I said. 'As you are, lads . . . Oh, one thing: use the word "geezer" round me again, I'll install an off switch in your fucking mouth.'

I put eyes on him for a few seconds. Was enough. He turned back to his mate, who was laughing at him.

As I closed the window I heard the barrels start to roll again. Couldn't say they were any quieter. Least I'd made my point on that score.

Truth told, I was glad to be out of bed. I'd had a restless night. Kept waking, visions of Tam Fulton's corpse coming back to me. Over and over. It was going to play on me day and night.

Usually I sleep sound as a pound. Few brews, maybe a Jack Daniel's or ten, and it's sayonara, suckers. Till last night it was my one great source of escape. But drink will only take you so far when it's oblivion you're after. Blackout's the house next door, and it was a comfortable one until this shit broke. The thought of trudging on without that safe haven at the end of the trail was something that, to say the least, shook me up.

I put on some Clash. Joe Strummer's demise still taking the shine off them for me, but I was working through it. Felt more for that man's passing than my own father's. True fighter. So few of us left.

Put 'Train in Vain' on repeat play as I showered again. Still enough blood on me to turn the soap pink. Had it loud enough to drown out the brewery diddies' best work.

I had a three-day growth. On some this says style. The old designer-stubble look. Me, it yells 'Jakey'. Maybe a 'Get a job, y'bum!' thrown in. I wasn't far south of Spencer Tracy in *The Old Man and the Sea* . . . all I needed was the grey hair to kick in. Still, it was staying for a few more days. My jaw was bruised, tender. Couldn't match the shiner I had going on with my left eye, but it was running a close second.

'Real nice look, Gus,' I told myself.

I put on the old Levi's again, found a T-shirt with a picture of a Pernod bottle on it – had a stack of them from a failed promo at the pub downstairs. Covered it with a heavy-check flannel. Thought: Kurt Cobain, go spin. Had the man upstaged in the grunge stakes. Tatty All Stars kicking the look down another level. Oh yeah, I was gutter. No boho chic here.

I grabbed my Bensons and headed for the bar.

Mac stood polishing a pint glass. His last business had gone tits up thanks to my involvement with gangsters; minding the bar was helping us both out for now.

'Morning, Gus.'

'Is it?'

Sighs. Glass clanged on glass. 'Get you anything?'

'Usual.'

'No' fancy a bite to eat?'

I'd just sparked up, unplugged the tab, rose quickly. 'No thanks, usual's fine . . . Is that the paper?'

Mac leaned over to pick up the morning paper. The page-one splash made my heart jump: CORSTORPHINE HILL MURDER.

I snatched it from his hand, scanned the text. It was what I thought – the bare bones; the late reporter had got nothing from the filth.

Mac brought over my pint of Guinness, a grim nod towards the paper, said, 'They were quick.'

'I tipped them off last night.'

'You did what?'

'Called them from the hill.'

'Is that wise, Gus?'

I looked up, put on my 'since when was I wise?' look.

Mac came round from the bar and sat down beside me. 'Right, c'mon, Dury, what the fuck are you up to here?'

I took the head off my Guinness, tipped back the glass, said, 'You ever hear of a bloke called Thomas Fulton?'

Mac's gaze went up to the ceiling. 'Fulton, nah, can't say it rings a bell, why?'

'He's our corpse. I know the name, just can't place it.'

'Common name.'

'I know, I know. But that cop last night, when he saw who it was he was rattled, really rattled. He got on the blower, called someone, called this Tam bloke *Moosey* . . . You know that one?'

'I knew a bookie once called Moosey, and there was a Moosey in the Riddrie Hilton as well. Haven't heard hide nor hair of them for years.'

'Will you ask about?'

'Aye, sure . . .' He sat back, took a sharp intake of breath. 'But what's the point in all this? You've got a business to run here; you don't need this aggro.'

I chugged back my pint, rose. 'It's got my interest.'

Mac watched me as I put on my coat. He had a pained look on his face, brows pressed hard on his slit eyes. 'Interest?'

'Something's not right.'

He stood up. 'So fucking what? It's not your problem.'

Funny thing was, I agreed. 'I know. I just want to satisfy a . . . professional curiosity.'

Chapter 5

ON THE STREET I FELL into near-shock: we had sunshine. It bounced off the cobbles and brought back memories of better days. Christ, I'd be listening out for birdsong next. I walked through the close skirting the Holy Wall and onto the main drag of Easter Road. The street was packed, builders mainly. The flats round here had been late to get dragged into the property-price surge. Now they'd shot-up twenty per cent in six months; not even the news of a credit crunch had put a halt to them. Our massive immigrant influx had put such a pressure on housing we were insulated. Least that's what the estate agents were telling us.

When I was a lad, this street rang with old women in headscarves, dashing between the little grocers' and butchers' shops. Now, not a one. Where did they suddenly go? And all those headscarves – must be enough of them lying about to sail Scotland to Australia.

I caught the bus into the city's mangled, tourist-drenched heart. I made a mental note: never again. The street seethed. Unctuous, lardass businessmen from Nowhere, Arkansas with wives who share a plastic surgeon with Joan Rivers in tow. All screaming out for McDonald's and Starbucks.

Why I'm slamming Americans, I don't know. These days, they're as likely to be Russian, Chinese, French – like it matters in our tragic little globalised world.

My real interest was in what I'd stumbled across on Corstorphine Hill. And I knew who to ask about it; there was even a slight possibility of feathering my own nest at the same time. The money would be very handy; dire straits was the address next door to the Wall. I didn't want to be the man who ran Col's pub into the ground in under a year since he'd passed.

I made my way to my former employers' premises – oh yeah, once I had prospects, gym membership, the whole nine yards. The paper used to be based in one of the city's old baronial buildings. They sold it, turned it into a hotel. The office is now housed in one of Edinburgh's many chucked-up-in-five-minutes jobs. I hear if times get tough the building can be quickly converted into a shopping mall. Forget about the workers who spend all their waking lives in there; best to keep those options open. The way newspapers were going since the web came along, I could see a Portakabin on the horizon.

As I walked in the front door I looked about for Auld Davey. He'd been the doorman since Adam was a boy. Okay, it was a wee while since I'd been in the place but things had changed – Davey's desk was gone for a start. I looked about for someone. Nobody in sight. Then I spotted it: a touch screen on the wall.

What the fuck?

Davey had been carted, then.

Departments were listed on a kind of spider-graph. I tapped 'Editorial'. Faces from the newsdesk flashed up.

'Holy crap, it's like *Press Gang*!'

To a one they were twenty-somethings. Did any of them have the shoulders for this job? I scrolled up the K-ladder, found the man I was after. My esteemed former editor, Mr Bacon, or Rasher as I still called him, was clinging to his job in a world of much younger, brighter, sparklier new recruits.

I pressed his 'call' button.

'Hello,' I said, too quickly. The computer screen was still loading. Felt a bit stupid; checked over my shoulder instinctively. No one had clocked my mistake.

An electronic beep came from the box, 'connected' flashed up on the screen. 'Hello, Bacon here.'

'Bingo.'

'Excuse me?'

I tried again. 'Ah, hello . . . just so chuffed to have this screen thing working.'

A note of impatience crept into Rasher's voice. 'Who is this?'

'Well, I wasn't expecting the red carpet but perhaps a bit more of a welcome after that last scoop I handed you.' I'd delivered the results of my previous case – and attendant political sleaze – in a package with a bow for Rasher.

'Dury! By the cringe . . . I'll buzz you.'

'You what? I'm here at the front door. Don't pull the old "I'll call later" caper.'

A huff. Loud one.

'Dury, I mean the gate . . . I'll buzz the gate open. Grab the lift to the top floor, I'll get you in the newsroom.'

Felt like a dope, not for the first time. 'Right. Gotcha.'

The lift was marked 'elevator'. Made sense: Christ, we're all so mid-Atlantic now, aren't we? As I ascended I saw the place had changed more than I'd imagined. The biggest department, by a country mile, was advertising. There used to be a running joke between the sales force and the reporters that their work paid all the wages. The old joke never took into account the reason why people were buying the paper in the first place; it looked like the idea had filtered all the way up to the board-room.

The newsroom had been decimated. I remembered the days when this place hummed with activity. Now it was a sorry reflection of its former glory. The staff numbers must have been cut by fifty per cent, padded out a bit by a few kids chasing work experience. I shook my head.

Rasher was in full flow, blasting a subeditor for a headline. '"*Heartless* thieves",' he roared. '"*Heartless* thieves" . . . Is there another type?'

27

I crept up, said, 'Well, there's the thieves that took the Stone of Destiny.'

Sniggers.

Rasher turned, black-faced, ready to pounce. His mutton chop sideburns caught stray static as he creased his face. 'Dury, I might have fucking known!'

I'd got away with it. He offered a hand, said, 'Man, you're a sight for sore eyes.' He'd put on a Sean Connery accent: 'sight' came out as 'shite'. Like I could argue with that.

'You're still hanging in there, then . . . Bit thin on staff, no?'

He raised an arm, circled a finger for effect. 'You'll see more than a few changes, Gus.'

'Oh yeah, at least one or two.' I could remember when news-rooms reeked with ciggie smoke; this lot, at a guess, were green-tea drinkers.

'Would you like the tour?'

I smiled, a wry one. 'Eh, another time maybe . . . I'm, er, here on business.'

Rasher stopped still. 'Sounds ominous.'

I knew my smile had slipped. 'It is.'

He led the way through the newsroom. Not one reporter looked away from their screen. It was like a call centre, or worse, a battery farm. In my day reporters did their job on the streets. I wondered if this lot would last a day without Google.

Rasher closed the door to his office, pulled out a chair, waved sit.

'Thanks,' I said.

'Coffee?'

My lip twitched – a betrayal, what poker players call a 'tell'.

'Ah, of course,' said Rasher. He dipped into a drawer in his desk, produced a bottle of Talisker. 'A drop of this, perhaps.'

He had my number.

'So, you mentioned business . . .'

That I had for him. In spades.

'The Corstorphine Hill murder . . . what have you got on it?'

Rasher leaned forward in his chair, looked uneasy. 'You're working that?'

'Not really. I just got started.'

'How come?'

'That tip-off you got last night?'

'Bizarro – guy on the scene.'

'Yeah . . . that was me.'

He looked scoobied. 'That was you? Who found the body?'

I spilled. Told him about stumbling over the corpse; think I stumbled over a few of my words in the telling. The memory was chilling.

Rasher beamed. 'That's a page-one exclusive.'

'You what?'

'I'll give you a front-page byline for that . . . The story in your own words: "How I happened on the murder scene". Fucking magic stuff.' He was out of his chair, flashing headlines at me as he perched on the edge of his desk. 'This is top flight, Gus. Jesus, thanks for bringing this in.'

The idea of resurrecting my writing career sent my mind racing. What would my ex-wife make of that? It would be an eye-opener for Debs all right.

I played Rasher, said, 'I'm actually after information.'

'Fire away, whatever I can do to help flesh out the article.'

The word 'flesh' sent a jolt through me.

'I picked up the name of the victim. I take it plod hasn't let you know yet.'

Rasher sat down, leaned forward and put his elbows on the desk. 'I spoke to the wee arsewipe this morning . . . Didn't give me a thing, except that "waiting to notify next of kin" shite.'

'Johnstone?'

'That's him. Right cheeky wee cunt – thinks he's doing you a favour when he's really just doing a job we pay him for.'

'I met him last night. He doesn't know I have the name.'

Rasher opened his palms. 'Well, I'm all ears . . . and it stays here.'

He didn't need to add that last bit – I knew Rasher wouldn't run the name until plod had released it. I said, 'Thomas Fulton.'

Rasher leaned back, tucked his hands behind his head, 'The Moose.'

'You know this guy?'

He was up again, pacing about the room. The static from the cheap carpet tiles set his sideburns twitching once more. 'You don't remember the skinny wee runt, Gus?'

'I thought I'd heard the name.'

Rasher picked up the scoosh bottle, topped himself up then offered me a refill. I nodded.

'Moosey was the one the police had down for the Crawford kid's mauling.'

I came up blank. 'The what?'

'The kid that got attacked by a pit bull. They reckoned it was Moosey's dog . . . Never managed to pin it on him, though.'

I twisted round to face him. He'd dropped his pitch, found a reverent tone, was enough to capture my interest. 'Why not?'

Rasher sat back down. He exhaled slowly as he placed his glass down in front of him, 'Moosey was one of Rab Hart's crew.'

'Shit.' Much as I tried to keep my nose clean, stay away from the city's knuckle-breakers and pugs, there was one name everybody knew. Of a bad lot, Rab Hart was the worst.

'Aye, shit's about the strength of it.' Rasher took a deep swig on his whisky. 'Things are very lively in that outfit right now.'

'Lively?'

'Well, I say lively – chaos would be more like it. You know Rab's inside . . .'

I didn't.

'Facing a ten stretch for counterfeiting.' He paused. 'Ralph Lauren shirts. He was yanked with a warehouse full of them. There was a raid; some polis got battered.'

'So who's running Rab's firm?'

'He is, from Saughton Prison. Only, from what I hear there's been some jostling to take over in his absence.'

30

'Not folk I'd want to be jostling with – could get nasty.'

Rasher nodded. 'Aye, oh aye, especially if Rab wins his appeal
... be a few heads cracked then.'

The words made me tense in my seat – did I want my head to
be one of them?

'When's his appeal?' I said.

Rasher put down his glass, rubbed hands together. 'Any day
now.'

Chapter 6

SPENT A COUPLE OF HOURS on Rasher's article. Can't say it was my best work – was a bit ring-rusty. But still, it felt good to be back doing the do. I even allowed myself to entertain the idea that I might be resurrecting my career, and all that might entail. Had even fooled myself with a notion of justice – not for Moosey, who looked like the worst kind of criminal trash, but because I could see something wasn't right here.

The way plod had behaved was off for sure. I was convinced Jonny Johnstone was all needle; those boys have my card marked, but I didn't like the kip of him. I wanted to have all my ducks in a row if he decided to take an interest in me.

Rasher said he'd get one of his office juniors to pull some files off the system for me, old newspaper cuttings detailing the Crawford child's killing, and some stuff on Edinburgh's answer to Al Capone – Rab Hart. He saw a series of articles, with a big photo byline; I was a name again. Nearly.

I looked out of the cafe window: an endless trail of backpacks, all shapes and sizes, traipsing up and down the streets. They'd stop, stare up at buildings on the sniff for a plaque or anything that would give resonance to their visit. A close. A pend. A wynd. All endless opportunities for photographs. I swear, I've seen these people on their knees photographing the cobbles.

I was waiting for my mate Hod. Since his property business had taken off, he'd decided there was more to life than sitting behind a desk. He'd appointed managers, become an adrenaline junkie for a while. Now he was bored again, thought I was a route to some action. Truth told, I was glad of the help. He'd jumped at the chance to track down the Crawfords for me, do some snooping.

There was a CD being pumped out in the cafe, Lennon covers by contemporary artists. I caught the first one on the way in – Lenny Kravitz doing 'Cold Turkey' . . . Not for the first time, I thought. U2 had grabbed 'Instant Karma!' by the bollocks; sounded painful. Now the Black Eyed Peas were murdering 'Power to the People'.

I'd had enough. Muttered, 'Is nothing sacred any more?'

'Dream the fuck on.' It was Hod.

'What's that on your face?'

'Trying for a beard. I hear it looks distinguished.'

'Dishevelled more like.'

He took that where it was intended, on the chin; changed subject. 'I've checked out the Crawfords. They've got a place on Ann Street.'

I knew it well – on the edge of Stockbridge; the pretentious called it New Town.

'Good for them.'

'Did you know they had another kid?'

I didn't. But it interested me no end when he spilled the details before me. The Crawfords had a lad about the same age as the yobs on the hill. Hod had pictures on his camera phone. Showed me a skelf of a youth. They were poor quality.

'I can't place him. They all look alike these days,' I said.

'Yeah, fucking Bay City Rollers rejects. Look at that hair: it's in a side-sweep.'

He wasn't wrong. 'It's the fashion.'

'Y'what? The fashion's to look like Archie *fucking* Macpherson?'

'Would you prefer Arthur Montford and those jackets?'

We laughed it up.

33

Hod said, 'You don't think our boyo there could be one of those yobs off the hill.'

I looked closer. 'Well, he's in the right gear.'

'It doesn't make sense, though, y'know . . .' Hod brushed at the stubble on his chin, turned away to look out the window. 'Him coming from a good family.'

There were more tourists passing by.

'Does anything make sense, ever?'

He didn't answer me. I knew where he was coming from. This kid was up to no fucking good.

Hod spoke, got agitated, brought down his finger on the tabletop. The salt-shaker trembled. 'The guy who we're told was responsible for killing this kid's sister turns up gutted like a fish and he's maybe yards away on the night in question . . . Are you thinking what I'm thinking?'

I looked at him, shook my head. 'I'm thinking the beard's not gonna work, Hod.'

He stood up. 'Fuck off. Ready to rumble?'

I took out my mobi. 'Can you put those pictures on my phone? They might be useful.'

'Sure – I'll Bluetooth it.'

'Yeah, whatever . . . Here it is. Do your stuff.'

Hod fiddled with the settings, sent the pictures, then we got moving. At the door he turned. 'One more thing . . . Joseph Crawford, the kid's father, he was a lawyer.'

'*Was* a lawyer?'

'He's a judge now.'

'You mean we're about to doorstep a judge?'

'Thought it worth mentioning.'

They say Ann Street was the Queen Mum's favourite street in Edinburgh. When she was on her way to the Palace of Holyroodhouse, so the story goes, she would always ask her chauffeur to make a detour down Ann Street. She loved the Georgian splendour of the architecture; reminded her of a bygone era. I could do without

34

it myself. Reminded me of what had always been wrong with this city and the country in general – the haves having far too fucking much at the expense of the have-nots.

I checked out the Crawfords' place – a carefully manicured lawn and, what was that, topiary? I shuddered at the thought. Their one concession to conspicuous parading of their wealth, however, was a silver-grey 5 Series Beemer, just pulling in. A 5 Series says one thing: 'still on the up'. Not quite a 7 Series; that says 'I've arrived'. A car like this, you have a ways to go. Gave me some room to negotiate.

'That him?' I asked, pointing to the bloke getting out the driver's door.

Small, thin, a black suit and brown shoes – eccentric, or another new fashion I'd missed? Either way, I didn't like the look.

'He's our man,' said Hod.

We walked over, there's a phrase – *calm as you like*. Hod firmed his features, had his patter all planned out. 'Mr Crawford?'

'Yes?'

'Mr Joseph Crawford?'

'Yes, what is this?' He flustered real easy; the distance between his brows and his rapidly receding hairline shrank fast.

Hod worked him, took out a little notebook, opened up, tested the spine, said, 'You are the father of one Mark Crawford, an employee of the Royal Bank on Nicolson Street . . . Both of you reside here at number—'

The judge butted in, set his briefcase down on the road. 'Look, what the hell is this? I demand to know.'

I intervened, crossed the distance between Hod and the man, said, 'I don't think we want to set any curtains twitching. We should go inside.'

He looked over my shoulder, checked all the curtains were still in place, raised his briefcase. 'What? Who are you?'

'You lost a child some years ago, didn't you?' His complexion changed. I went on, 'I believe a man called Fulton was in the frame. He's been killed.'

The judge's brow glistened. 'I don't see how that concerns me.'

I had the words ready but Hod jumped in first. 'Look, your son was spotted at the murder scene.'

Subtle as fucking ever; Hod could give Alf Garnett lessons. I took over. 'I don't want to alarm you, but I think that it might be best if we go inside, Mr Crawford.'

The front door was immaculately painted in cornflower blue, the window showing a Charles Rennie Mackintosh-style scene in stained glass. The judge turned the key in the lock, prised open the door. Inside I heard loud, repetitive dance music. Christ, have kids today no ear for a tune?

The carpet covered only three-quarters of the hallway; at the edges were polished boards. There was a time when this look spelled poverty – fitted carpets were a luxury – now it reeked of trendiness and ersatz nostalgia. The judge put his briefcase on the hallstand, dropped the keys of the Beemer in a little brass tray.

'Shall we?' He motioned to a door.

In the living room our yoof sat sprawled on a green chesterfield, feet up on the arm, reading a copy of *Viz*. The judge ran in and slapped down his feet, yelled, 'Get that bloody garbage turned off!'

I recognised him at once as one of the yobs from the hill. Every fibre of me wailed 'Boot his balls into his neck'. I fought an urge to drag him from the couch and set about his head with fists. I looked at Hod, expected an acknowledgement, but he was too busy eyeing the cornicing, running calculations in his head. Old habits die hard: once a property speculator . . .

The wee prick tried to speak: 'I was listening to that—'

'Shut up,' said his father.

As the lad turned he saw myself and Hod in his home and firmed his jaw as if he was ready for a fight.

'Hello, Mark,' I said. I gave him a couple of nods in quick succession, as if to confirm the thoughts running through his head. '. . . We meet again.'

'You know these men?' said his father.

Mark Crawford was frozen to the spot, trapped by the instinct to have a pop at me and the need to stay calm in front of his father. The power of speech deserted him. Where he held on to his comic his knuckles turned white. I thought he might lose it any minute.

'Should we wait for the lady of the house?' said Hod. He returned to the notebook. '. . . That would be Mrs Katrina Crawford, née Fairbanks.'

The judge took his hands from his pockets, a white handkerchief in one. 'Look, no, we don't need my wife. What is this all about?' He mopped his large brow, returned the handkerchief to his pocket. He had no sooner completed the movement when his wife appeared through the doorway.

She was what the Scots call *thrawn*. A tall woman with pale skin and paler eyes, she haunted the room like a ghost. As she walked in, her mouth parted ever so slightly. Words, suspended on her lips, never appeared. She wore an apron, which she hastily tried to unfasten as she moved towards us. She faced me, managed some sangfroid. 'What is going on here?'

I motioned Hod to put away the notebook, walked into the centre of the room. 'Nice place you have here.'

Mrs Crawford turned to her husband. 'Joe, what is this?'

The judge looked lost. 'Look, if this is some kind of—'

'Some kind of *what*, Mr Crawford?' I said.

'Well, I don't know . . .'

I walked over to the yob, stared right into his eyes. 'What were you doing on Corstorphine Hill the other night, Mark?'

He said nothing. He had a strong gaze for his years. Most would have turned away; I raised my volume a notch. 'With the dog and the gang and the guns, Mark.'

The woman approached. Hod stepped in, raised a palm – it was enough.

I grabbed the yob's shoulders. He spun them away, drew fists. It made me smile. 'A man's dead, Mark . . . His name was Thomas Fulton.'

His mother lurched for me, grabbed my arm. 'Please, please, he's just a boy.'

I turned. Her grip was strong – I could feel her anguish. I didn't want to bring any more hurt to her but what else could I do? 'Look, I appreciate how painful this must be, but you must see how this looks.'

The judge moved towards his wife, put an arm round her shoulder, led her away from me.

Mark was still staring at me. His eyes were slits, his fists still balled up in anticipation.

The judge spoke: 'If this is about money . . .'

I was incredulous. 'How much money do you think it would take to cover up a murder?'

Mrs Crawford's eyes widened; her mouth fell open. 'What . . . *what*?'

Hod spoke: 'You heard right.'

The judge stepped in front of his wife. 'I've had just about enough of this. Get out of my house or I'm calling the police.'

I laughed out, couldn't help myself. 'Somehow, Your Honour . . . I think that's the last thing you'll be doing.'

Chapter 7

ON THE STREET I SPARKED up an Embassy, watched Hod come trailing down after me.

He said, 'Think we got to them?'

I drew deep, said, 'No chance.'

I moved off. Hod clipped at my heels, yelled, 'Why not?'

'Their lot have had centuries of practice.' As I looked up to the window I could see Katrina Crawford was watching us. I felt a stab of guilt; the woman had suffered enough with the loss of a child. My face must have conveyed my thoughts – she shook her head and turned away.

'What's up?' said Hod.

'Nothing. Let's get out of here.'

I lay in bed listening to a bit of synthpop. Oh yeah, there's still a place for Depeche Mode – if you remember 'Enjoy the Silence', you forgive them the last ten years. I had a bottle of gin to the side of the bed, an ashtray balanced on my chest and a pack of Marlboro within grabbing distance. The red tops. Proper lethal. Was the best I could do; nearest I got to therapy.

For some time I'd had a rage on. Long before this corpse-on-the-hill headache; this goes way back. I'd hit the books. Close as I got to an approximation of myself was from Virgil: 'Impotent fury rages powerless and to no purpose.' That was me. Debs, my ex-wife, put it in simpler terms: 'You take your life out on the world.'

When I took over my late friend Col's pub it came with a flat. Not the room I used to have, the one he gave me above the gents' cludgie whilst I was his doorman, but the apartment he used to share with his wife. There was a stack of books, religious mostly, but also some self-help. I don't think they were Col's, I think they belonged to his wife, Bell. She was a shy woman, quiet. One of life's strugglers. I know the type, because I struggle myself.

Some of us strugglers give in. Bell, I think, not so much lost the will as never had it in the first place. Me, I'm a rager. That's not a noble stance, it's stupid. I'm the level below Bell. Her type have the nous to know the fight's not worth it. Me, I care so little about losing that I welcome the fight with open arms. If it hastens the end, all the better.

The first time I picked up one of Bell's books, I threw it across the room. There's that anger again. It had some dumb title like *How To Be Happy* and had a headshot of the author smiling through porcelain veneers into the soft-focus lens. But if you're a reader, you read, be it cornflake packets or Jean-Paul Sartre. In a dark night of the soul, I got my introduction to this snake-oil psychology. It was full of mantras like 'Every day and in every way I am getting better and better'. Repeat ten times an hour, on the hour, for a month and the idea is you get the porcelain-veneered, soft-focus look and all's peachy.

It churned my gut. People making money out of others' misery. I felt sorry for Bell. Did she buy this? Did she think it was helping? I knew it wouldn't; it could only make her worse. I knew this because I've heard the phrase 'Get your act together' so many times. The effect of it – contrary to the intention – is to drive you closer to the abyss. It misses me, though – I'm living in the abyss.

I reached for the gin bottle. Empty.

I raised myself and went downstairs to the bar. For the first time in weeks we had a fair crowd in. Took a stool at the front, twiddled with a beer mat until Mac caught my eye.

'Want something?'

'Usual.'

He poured out a Guinness and looked down at me as I fished for the television remote control. I flicked.

Got some groans from around the room.

'Gus, there's folk watching that.'

'What?'

'*X Factor* . . .'

I scanned the place: they were all old soaks, old enough to remember proper television. I raised my voice: 'Was anyone watching that shite?'

A chorus of 'Aye. Aye. Aye.'

'You jest, surely.' I flicked back to see Simon Cowell tearing into some utterly deluded bell-end of about sixteen, a Scouser with a swagger you could power a small town on. '. . . You're encouraging this type of moron, you realise.'

'There's nothing else on,' called out one of the regulars, a stick-thin sixty-something with a crater where his nose should be.

'And there never will be if you keep watching this crap . . . Honestly, you're like gerbils in a wheel. Don't you remember when it took talent to be on television?'

The Scouser started to kick off, told Simon he was wrong, he was 'gonna be bigger than Robbeeee!'

I roared at the telly, 'Dream on! The biggest cockhead in the music industry slot's taken for now, pal. Come back in a few years, though – you look the type they're after.'

I stood up, yelled, 'Look at these strutting little twats . . . working in Sainsbury's and thinking they're the next Ricky *fucking* Martin. We've bred a generation of delusional egomaniacs and we wonder why the country's gone ape!'

I got some stares. Wide-eyed ones. I couldn't care less, I was just warming up. Said, 'C'mon, I'm right! It's a generation in for

41

massive disappointment when it wakes up. Christ, they can't even afford their own homes . . . and they think they're entitled to be idolised!'

Mac took the doofer off me, put a firm hand on my shoulder, forced me to sit.

'What's your problem?' I said.

'Gus, just fucking settle.'

'I'm perfectly settled.'

'You're perfectly pissed, and perfectly hyped . . . This hill murder has fucked with your mind.'

'Bullshit.'

Mac shook his head at me, delivered my pint. 'You're ranting at a kid on the television, Gus. What does that tell you?'

I knew exactly what it told me, but I wasn't admitting anything. 'I thought this place was bad when Col was behind the bar.'

Mac ran a towel over the countertop, changed tack: 'I took a call for you earlier . . . Debs.'

I cooled right down. My ex-wife always had that effect; still does. 'Right, what did she say?'

'Nothing much – she'll call back.'

'No emergency, then?'

'No, she just asked how you were.'

'And?'

Mac shrugged.

'Well, thanks anyway.'

He didn't respond, looked away.

Silence, then, 'I've been thinking: why don't you split, Gus?'

'*What?* Where's this came from?'

'I mean, what's to keep you here? You could go to Spain, catch some rays, maybe all this –' he leaned forward, tapped the bar – 'body on the hill malarkey will have passed over by then.'

I tasted my pint, wiped the froth from my top lip. 'Mac, I can't do that.'

'Horseshit! I'd scarper.' His brows pinched.

'You what . . . ? Why?'

'You're fucking daft, Gus. Digging into this is only going to cause you grief.'

My life was grief; why should some more bother me? 'Let's just see how it plays.'

Mac stretched the corners of his mouth, displayed his bottom row of teeth. 'I have a bad feeling about all of this: the law's involved and Rab Hart and—'

I cut him back: 'That Jonny prick's full of crap.'

He turned around. I thought he was going to the till or to grab a bag of nuts, then I felt a hand on my shoulder, saw he was passing the baton. It was Hod. He ordered up a bottle of Stella and nodded to the snug. I picked up my Guinness and followed him.

'It crossed my mind,' said Hod, 'after our last chat, you need to think about what you're getting into.'

I shook my head, said, 'Oh, y'think?'

I sparked up another tab. Like I was giving a shit about the smoke ban *now*. Right away, Hod took the cig off me, stubbed it. 'You don't need any more aggro.'

'Got *that* straight.'

'When you turned up Moosey on the hill, what did the wee pricks do?'

I kept my voice low. Even in the snug I wasn't being overheard. 'Here's the thing: when they saw him for the first time, they were scoobied. Totally stunned. It was as much a surprise to them as it was to me to find a dead fucking body lying in a patch of bushes.'

Mac came over with a tray of drinks, sat down. 'Where are we at?' he said.

'Up Shit Creek.'

I drained my Guinness, took a nip from the tray.

Mac took a sip of beer. 'I still say split. It's the best option. You've got the filth rattled, you've noised up a judge and you're forgetting Rab Hart's gonna have something to say when he sees your wee piece in the paper, Gus.'

Hod started to nod agreement, stroking the stubble on his chin to add some gravitas. 'Mac's right – in your boots, I'd nash.'

I stood up. Could have driven a Panzer through their idea, but went with: 'This is pointless. If you've no sound suggestions, I'll paddle my own canoe.'

'Mind, the water's choppy in Shit Creek,' said Mac.

Chapter 8

MY STORY APPEARED. RASHER MADE good on his promise of the front-page byline. There was a photo next to my name – I hardly recognised myself. Hoped nobody else would.

I was wrong.

Phone went: 'Hello, Mam.'

'Angus, what happened to your face?'

'My face?'

I could hear her taking breath. She said, 'I saw you in the paper. You could plant potatoes in those hollows . . . You're not eating properly.'

Not a mention of the corpse, the case. I shrugged. 'Well, y'know, I'm a busy guy, Mam.'

She didn't buy it; maybe she hadn't read the story at all. 'Haven't seen you in a while, Angus.'

'Sorry, Mam, I've been meaning to—'

'Well, you're a busy man, like you say. Can't expect you to keep up with my every move.'

I felt a wince. Flutters in my stomach. What could I say to that?

I didn't get a chance. She said, 'Are you back at the paper now, then?'

'Not exactly.'

'I can still remember the days when we'd see you in a coat and tie . . . Seems a long time ago now, since you had the job and Deborah and . . . I'm sorry, son, my mouth's running away; I just don't think.'

'Mam, it's okay.' I moved the talk along, went for enquiring after my sister and brother, said, 'And how's Catherine and Michael?'

'Well. Both well.'

'Good. Good. That's, er, good.' God, what else could I say? I felt myself involuntarily looking at the clock.

'Anyway, I'm glad to catch you, son . . . I've been meaning to ask you about something.'

'What's that?'

She paused, another deep breath, said, 'I wanted to ask you . . . how you might feel about me selling off some of your dad's trophies and medals.'

I didn't know how to feel. They were something I never looked at. But, brute that he was, I felt we'd all played a part in earning those trophies – my brother and me, sister too – with beatings and scoldings. My mother earned her share in a million and one more painful ways. I saw her face in my mind: it was a road map of lines and hurt. How could I object to anything she asked of me? I'd been little or no use to the woman, ever. And the way things looked I saw no change on that front. Certainly no good change. Maybe worse was an option, though.

I said, 'Mam, whatever you want to do is fine by me . . . whatever makes you happy.'

Her voice trembled. 'Oh, Gus, if only.'

'Come on, Mam.'

She started to cry. 'You must think I'm just a silly old fool.'

'Mam, you're nothing of the kind.'

I heard her reaching for tissues to dab her eyes. 'Well, don't you mind me, Gus.'

'Mam, there's no way I'm gonna stop minding you.'

'No, seriously. Here's me bawling away and you have your own problems to deal with . . . You're a grown man with a life to lead and I have no right putting my cares on you. I'm sorry, son. Can you ever forgive me?'

I said, 'Mam, if there's anything I can—'

She cut me off: 'I am absolutely fine, it's just ... well, just seeing you in the paper set me back and thinking about the trophies, it made me ...'

She struggled for the words.

'Mam, no need to explain. I know fine. Whatever you do, just take care.'

She said goodbye and hung up.

I put down the phone. There was a book nearby: Knut Hamsun's *Hunger*. I fingered the pages. I always carry a book; something my father never understood. His learning came from an altogether different world. Our worlds were always destined to collide. What was God thinking giving a hard man like him a bookish little nyaff like me for a son? I knew that was the question he'd asked himself all his life. On his deathbed he was still asking it, but just sounding it differently. I knew I wasn't ready to forgive my father for those years. Would I ever be?

I moved to the kitchen table, sat down and lit a Marlboro.

Rasher had sent on the cuttings from the Crawford child killing story. I'd been having difficulty reading them. Normally I have a strong stomach for this kind of thing but for some reason, lately I'd been going soft. Call it age; it certainly wasn't maturity.

Little Christine Crawford had only been a tot, three years old. There were so many pictures of her splashed over the pages it was impossible not to become attached. I was press, I knew we always chose the cutest shots. The girl they called Chrissy was a sweetheart: blonde hair, blue eyes, the apple of every parent's eye.

As I tried to read about Chrissy's death my throat froze.

She had been in the Meadows – one of Edinburgh's most popular parks – with her mother. Walking, just walking and playing on a bright spring day, when she'd run off behind a tree. Minutes, just seconds perhaps, out of her protector's sight.

Passers-by described a scream, high-pitched, the kind only a very young child makes. No one saw the moment of death. Thank God. The first on the scene, a male passer-by and the child's mother, were greeted with a sight of immense bloodletting.

Chrissy hadn't stood a chance.

The dog's owner, Thomas Fulton of Sighthill, was traced.

He'd claimed not to know that the dog, an illegal pit bull terrier, had escaped its enclosure.

I shut the folder. Kept a cutting out, one with an address in Sighthill.

My coat was hanging by the door. I knew what Mac and Hod would say about what I planned to do next, but it was something I just had to pursue.

Chapter 9

ON GORGIE ROAD THE BUS driver was forced to hit the anchors. A shower of crusties with placards had taken over the road, marching five to ten deep.

Hands went up in the cab, palms slapped on the wheel. 'Get off the road, y'bloody hippies!'

I had a laugh to myself. Driver was flat-topped, giving off more than a hint of redneck vibe. I said, 'What is it . . . ban the bomb?'

He turned, squinted at me. 'They're hippies.'

Like that was supposed to explain it all. Never ceased to amaze me, this attitude. Bit of an out-there hairstyle, to some it's worse than carrying a flaming trident. How did Shipman get away with whacking all those old ladies for so long? Short back and sides. Deffo.

As the bus driver found the high gears again, I caught a glimpse of some posters being tied to the gates, pictures of animal vivisection. Monkeys with huge metal rods stuck in their heads, great sores weeping, blood, guts. Just horrific. My stomach tightened; in the last few days I'd had more than my fair share of blood and guts. I looked away. Thought: Who *can* look at that?

The second I got off the bus in Sighthill, I was looking for syringes on the ground. In the All Stars trainers there was no way I was risking a puncture. Made a note to get the Docs cleaned up sharpish.

I followed a trail of Tesco trolleys, bashed, rusted and wrecked. Suppose a few trolleys go missing up here – who's gonna come after them without Delta Force back-up?

The scene was a *Mad Max* movie: burnt-out cars, boarded-up windows, more trash than the tip, blowing all ways.

In the city, down the East End, Leith, you see poverty, but nothing like this. This was Third World. Sure, we'd spared them the need to build their own shanty town, but only because we'd done it for them. Welcome to high-rise hell.

I grew unnerved by the lack of bodies; a place like this, it's a sign. But then I saw an old woman, struggling along with an Aldi carrier bag. She was ancient, at least eighty. Looked to be all hard years too. Wondered what she'd done to deserve being dumped out here. Christ, we look after our oldies, eh? As she approached I smiled – put the frighteners on her and she grabbed up her bag, held it to her chest.

'Good morning,' I said.

She stood still, eyes wide, trembling. I didn't know what to say. Chose the easy option: nothing. Left her be. At the end of the road she was still clutching the bag to her chest, staring.

As I turned around, an anorexic Vicky Pollard put her nose in my face. I looked her up and down, thought: When the widest part of your leg is your knee, you're in trouble.

'What you fucking after?' she spat.

'Come again?'

'You're no' from around here . . . You looking for business?' She blew a pink bubble at me, looked like the old Bazooka Joe.

'No, er, no thanks.'

'How? You no' fancy me?'

I tried to walk around her. She jumped in front of me and lifted her tight black sports vest, flashed her tits. 'How's that then?' Her ribs stuck out further than those gnat stings.

I pushed her aside. 'Put that away, I'm not interested.'

'A blow then, or a chug for a tenner?'

I didn't answer. Felt a hail of abuse showered at my back as I walked off. Was beginning to wonder if it had been a good idea coming out here without an AK-47.

I had Moosey's address from the cutting; it wasn't too hard to find. There were so many houses boarded up in the street that I could pick out the inhabited ones from a mile off – they had glass in half of their windows. There was a gate to the yard but it was lying in the middle of the lawn, poking through grass about half a foot high, flattened in part by a burst mattress that had recently been flopped down in the middle. I stepped over a car tyre with, what was that, teeth marks? It looked like it had been half chewed by Godzilla. As I banged on the door I heard the likeliest cause, barking and scratching on the other side.

'Shut it!' was yelled. A female voice, gruff.

I stepped away, looked down the street. A couple of beer guts with trackies tucked into their socks had stepped out to see what I was up to.

'Shut the fuck up, y'wee cunt!' came from the other side of the door, then there was the sound of a lash. The barking turned to a whimper in an instant.

The letter box slid open. 'Who's that?'

I knelt down. 'Eh, hello there . . . I'm looking for Vera Fulton.'

'Y'can fuck off if it's money yer after . . . I told those other cunts he left nowt!'

'No, I'm not after money. I'm here about your late husband.'

A spray of words came through the letter box: 'What about him?'

I sensed this was going to be tougher than I'd imagined. She sounded edgy. 'I'm a journalist, I'm looking into the death and . . . well, I'd like to talk to you about the way Tam passed. Mrs Fulton, I really think we should talk.'

A long pause stretched out between us. I heard whispering, then, 'I can't be blethering through the letter box. You better come round the back, this door's nailed shut.'

As I left the yard one of the beer guts stood in front of me in the path. He was a big biffer. As I sidestepped him I spotted the

Regal King Size pack tucked into the sleeve of his T-shirt. I took out my own smokes, sparked up.

Round the back was surprisingly ordered compared to the tip out front. Half of the yard was given over to a row of huge kennels with heavy criss-crossed bars holding in five or six snarling dogs, bull terriers and cross-breeds that looked ready to go. On the other side of the yard, a skinny old bloke with massive *Two Ronnies* glasses and a ponytail, had one of the dogs on a treadmill, a two-and-a-half-kilogramme weight dangled round the beast's neck. The dog put eyes on me as I appeared and the old geezer gave it a smack with a belt across its back. I didn't want to get too close, figured any objection wouldn't go down well.

'Well, what is it?' A woman in her bad forties, bloodshot eyes and a wine-stained smock greeted me at the back door.

'I'm sorry for your loss, Mrs Fulton.'

She huffed, folded her arms and looked over my shoulder. The bloke with the hardy dog approached, said, 'Who the fuck's he?'

I eyeballed him, looked him up and down. There were creases in his denims that could cut butter; thought him worth ignoring. He slunk around me, stood behind the widow. She said, 'You wrote that bit in the paper, didn't you?'

I nodded.

Her eyes looked far away. She said, 'I recognised you.'

'Do you think we might go inside? There's a few questions I'd like to ask.'

The skelky guy bridled, but Vera said, 'It's okay, Sid. Come in, son.'

Inside the house we were greeted with a hail of barking; about five or six small dogs let rip. The place was dark and stank of piss. Most of the windows and doors had been boarded up. The carpets had been torn to shreds, I was guessing dug up by dogs. I wondered how people could live like this. The joint needed hosing down, with a fucking flamethrower.

I took a chair, threw myself into it too violently and a cloud of dust was evacuated. A small terrier stuck its nose in my crotch; I pushed it away. Guessed a coffee wasn't going to be on offer.

Moosey's wife watched me look for a place to put out my cigarette, spoke: 'Just put it there.' She motioned to the floor. 'Have you any more?'

I offered round my tabs; both were takers. I felt too nauseous to join in. The place was rank.

I wasn't sure if Vera was playing the grieving widow or this was her usual state, but she seemed tranced. Sid perched beside her on the couch and watched me closely.

I said, 'I wanted to ask if Tam had any enemies, anyone who might want to harm him?'

Sid creased up. 'That's a good yin . . . Do you a fucking list?'

I was a bit lost for words. A man had just died, brutally.

'Who would be on this list?'

I looked at Vera but Sid answered. More laughs. Huge belly laughs this time. 'You're a comedian, mister,' he said. 'They were queuing in the street to kick Moosey up and doon it every day of the week!'

'And why would they be, Vera?'

She turned away. Sid answered again: 'Moosey was a right cunt, mister . . . You'll no' find much sympathy for him round here.'

This guy was pissing me off. I hit him with, 'I hear he had some friends, though . . . like Rab Hart.'

Sid's smile vanished. I watched the cocky expression melt from his face, then the streak of piss pointed a nicotine-stained finger at me. 'If you're coming round here to noise folk up, you're liable to go the same fucking way as Moosey, boy.'

I was getting somewhere. 'Was that his problem? Did Moosey noise somebody up?'

Sid rose, pointed again. 'Now, I'm fucking telling you—'

I stood up to face him. 'What, *Sid*, what are you telling me?'

I had half a foot on him. He backed down, went for the door.

Vera was still sooking on her tab, still looked out of it. I produced my mobile, brought up Hod's pictures of Mark Crawford, showed them to her. 'Have you seen this kid, Vera?'

Her moist eyes took in the image. 'He's one of the young crew . . . from the scheme.'

'Did you ever see him with Tam?'

She stared on at the picture, shook her head. 'I don't think so.'

'Do you know who he is, Vera?' I said. 'He's the brother of the little one that they say Tam's dog killed.'

Vera's gaze left the phone. She pressed it back on me. I watched her stare out the back door. Her cigarette was burnt down to the filter tip.

'Vera, did you know that he's the Crawfords' boy?'

Quieter: 'No. I didn't know that.'

As she got the words out, the beer guts from round the front came in. Sid was behind them, with the mad-looking dog on a choke chain. He shouted, 'Take a warning, y'cunt: keep your nose out our fucking business . . . or you'll get it broken.'

Chapter 10

I CAUGHT THE FIRST BUS out of Sighthill. Kept looking for the signs that read 'You are now leaving the jungle'. I was in a hurry to flee this dumping ground. It was strictly for the dispossessed. The druggies. The dangerous. The dole moles. The beyond help. I worried if I stayed there too long I'd begin to fit in. I knew that with less luck, less support, I'd be there myself. Holed up in some one-room rathole, downing Special Brew every night of the week, waiting for the next giro to arrive.

As the bus pulled out my mobi rang. Got some looks. Put on my 'like I give two fucks' face.

'Hello . . .'

'Hi, it's me.'

Most folk have a few close people in their life who can get away with that introduction. Me, I've got one. And it had been close on six months since I'd heard her voice.

'Debs, hi . . . How are you?' Sounded weird, struggling for words with my ex-wife, but there it was. No matter what kind of closeness you once shared, life has a knack of getting in the way of it.

'I'm well, y'know . . . You?'

I lied: 'Never better.'

Bit of a gap on the line.

A false start, like banging heads together.

'I was meaning to call earlier.'

'Yeah, me too,' I said.

'No you weren't. You would have let me fade to black.'

She had me taped. What was I supposed to do? Call for chats, suggest a catch-up over a bottle of Pinot Grigio now and again? Not a chance.

'Well, I'm glad you called anyway . . . It's good to hear from you, Debs.'

'You too, it's good to hear your voice, even if it is a bit croaky!'

A laugh. Some throat-clearing.

'Well, that would be cos I'm cutting back on the smokes.'

'Oh, yeah? I believe you. Look, I won't eat into your day, I just wanted to ask if you could, er, well, could we meet up?'

Mac had said she'd called. This made two calls inside a week. Something wasn't right here. Far as I knew all the solicitors' dealings were over; there was a decree absolute sitting at home to prove it.

'What's up, Debs?'

'No, it's nothing like that. Nothing's up at all. Really.' She was a bit too quick with her answer.

'Debs, you can't kid a kidder.'

Silence.

'I just thought . . . Well, first off I forgot you were so suspicious-minded, Gus.' Her voice started to tremble. 'Look, if you don't want to—'

I cut in: 'Gimme a place, Debs – I'm there already.'

The bar was empty, save for Mac and Hod. For some reason Mac was all tarted up like a carnival, Fonzie-style leather jacket and a retro Scotland shirt, Argentina '78 if I wasn't mistaken. Had seen it on Archie Gemmell.

I slunk in unnoticed, to catch them taking down one of the pictures beside the snug – my favourite one, the dogs playing snooker. It was like an episode of *Chucklevision* minus the 'To you, to me' bit. What talk there was hit high on the intellectual scale.

'See they caught that Naked Rambler guy again,' said Hod.

'You're shitting me – wasn't he just booked?'

'Oh yeah, this was after, in the meat wagon coming from the court.'

Mac stopped in his tracks. 'One minute. Let me get this straight: he's been done umpteen times, and locked up, then gets out and strips off again?'

'I dread to think how much of our taxes have been wasted on this.'

I laughed, moved towards the bar. 'Fuck, I hope they never bring *Question Time* round this way.'

Mac turned. 'It's Indiana Jones . . . How was your trip to the badlands?'

'Useful.'

I filled a glass with Jack Daniel's, then threw it back. Mac came over, took a chair at the bar while I poured out a pint of Guinness. He looked pissed off; always did when we were short of punters.

'Have you been at the Old Spice, Mac?' I said.

'It's called making an effort, for the customers.'

I laughed.

'Have you told him about the pub?' said Hod.

'About your rescue package?' Hod had cash to spare; he wanted to help put the Holy Wall back on the map. I didn't fancy the idea. I knew Hod's plans would include a glass-topped bar, Bacardi Breezer promotions and, worse, atmospheric lighting.

Mac sneered. 'Oh no . . . let's see, about our plans to stock Regal as well as B&H.'

'What's on the table then? Apart from what looks like, if I'm not mistaken, a Jack Vettriano print to replace my dogs, which, for the record, ain't happening. This is a drinking man's pub, not some poncey George Street style bar.'

Hod stepped between us. 'Gus, we're gonna have to put our heads together on this one. The pub's going down.'

This was a hurt. It was Col's pub, in memory anyway. I supped my pint. 'Later, eh. I've just escaped *Deliverance* territory and I'm mightily relieved not to have a length of hillbilly parked in my farter . . . The pub problems can wait.'

I took a stool at the bar and immediately wigged out. An almighty scuffle, then a blur of black came running across the floor to me.

'*Fucking hell*!'

Mac laughed his heart out, spacehopper guttage going up and down, as the dog I'd rescued jumped into my lap and started to lick at my face.

'Whoa! Down, boy, down, down.'

'Think he's pleased to see you,' said Mac.

I lifted the dog, put him on the ground. He jumped up again.

'Holy crap . . . let me have some peace. Can't a man get a pint?'

Mac lifted the dog away, placed him in a basket behind the bar.

'What the hell's that doing here?' I said, pointing to the new addition to the Wall.

'Where else is he gonna go? Vet said it was here or the pound.'

I shook my head. 'So we've got a dog now?'

Mac smiled. 'Aye, looks that way.' He bent down, patted the pooch on the head. It licked his hand. 'Friendly wee fella, isn't he?'

'After his last owners, guess we're an improvement.'

A bark. Loud one.

'I think he agrees.'

I wasn't sure a dog was what we needed right now; I sure as hell wasn't up for ownership. Mac could take him walkies. I'd always fancied a dog, a real mutt – man, they're loyal. But something about the current state of my life told me any more responsibility was a bad idea. I sunk my Guinness, gave the glass to Mac, said, 'Pint of the usual.'

'Usual it is.'

The dog got out of his basket and came to sit at my feet. Put those big chocolate eyes on me again. I looked away.

'What's that on his side, Mac?'

'Och, he's still some stitches to come out. They need to stay in for a week or so.'

I looked at the dog, said, 'Poor bastard.'

Mac laid my pint on the bar. Guinness spilled down the glass and onto the cardboard Tennent's mat. 'So, Sighthill . . . how did it go?'

I got started: 'You know a guy called Sid, friend of Moosey's?'

'What's he look like?'

I gave a brief description.

'Sounds like Sid the Snake . . . Sid's not his real name: he gets called that because he looks like that guy off *Little and Large*, Syd Little, has the glasses and the lot. Doesn't like the handle, though, that's why he's got the ponytail.'

Fitted perfectly.

'What's his story?'

Mac went back to the Guinness, started to fill up the rest of the pint, said, 'He's a bookie.'

Hod butted in, tapping a finger on the bar. 'I know this guy . . . I met some people at the casino, once or twice they put it my way to take a swatch at some bare-knuckle fights. I went but it wasn't my scene, too savage. Anyway, you meet people, right, and these people talk . . . This Sid keeps a book on dog fights. Fucking sure it's him.'

I was having one of my moments of clarity, said, 'Moosey's house was virtually a kennel, there's dogs fucking running about all over the place. You think Sid and Moosey were running this caper for Rab Hart?'

Mac topped off my pint, handed it over. 'Well, Sid's one of Rab's crew for sure. Has been for years.'

'Rasher says the crew's in bad shape since Rab went away, lot of tinpot hard men jostling for prominence . . . Could he have been caught in the crossfire?'

'Maybe,' Mac sneered, 'maybe you'll join him if you go there.'

I let that slide. 'And those wee pricks on the hill, what about them? Think they might be part of the scene, or hangers-on?'

'The flash, the wheels, the bling, the clobber . . . It's as obvious as a donkey's cock – they're into the dog fights too.' Mac's voice was firm. 'It's a big-money racket now.' He peered down at our own dog in his basket. 'That's what they were doing with him too – probably no use to them as a fighter.'

'So, what, they just tortured him for sport?' I said.

'Looks likely.'

I hit my pint, strolled back to the other side of the bar. Raised a shot glass to the Grouse optic. 'Hang about . . . the wee dog's soft – not exactly fighting material.'

'Practice!' snapped Hod. 'They rob dogs like that to give the fighters a bit of practice.'

I winced at the thought. Moosey had a house full of wee dogs. Were they all just there to be ripped apart to train the fight dogs?

My head dipped; I jerked it back. 'I need to talk to some of our wee dog-torturing pals.'

Chapter 11

WE HAD SUNSHINE AGAIN, SO I took a schlep through Holyrood Park, slugging on a bottle of scoosh. The place was awash with kites, cheapo tennis kits, and the worst – disposable barbecues. Knew I'd be wading through their remains for weeks to come. Although if they were going to get cleared up anywhere in the city it was within spitting distance of the queen's bedroom.

An ant-trail of tourists headed for Arthur's Seat. Once was a time, on a day like today, I might have joined them, especially with a bottle in my pocket. But the place held bad memories for me now. Col had got me into this investigating business after his son had been murdered up there. That was the city I knew, pretty fucking far from the cobbled streets and sweeping spires in the brochures.

At the traffic lights, where the tourist route takes up the streams of walkers, I spotted an act of full-on nuttery in progress. A young couple, each pushing a child's buggy, were about to attempt the hill. Okay, the buggies looked the business – mag wheels, brakes, the lot – but the path was fly-up-a-windowpane stuff. Maybe I'd missed something; it would be an exercise craze, no doubt.

I was strolling because I'd some time to kill before I had to meet Debs in the West End. I can't say I was looking forward to it. With my ex-wife there always was, and always would be, an agenda. If Debs was calling me out to sit down over coffee, you could be assured there'd be a crisis, just past, or just looming. And in one way or another yours truly would have a part to play in it all.

My ex is one of the unfulfilled. Aren't we all? But with Debs it has a realness about it you can touch. A quality of utter despair permeates her, day in, day out. Those books, the self-help jobs, they'd say there was some masochistic attraction, some denial on one or both of our parts that forced the usual 'two negatives repel' ruling to be ignored. Whatever, we were bad for each other, that was the deal. No matter how you dressed it up, no matter how much either of us had tried to make it work, it didn't. End of story. That our past was the stuff of horror stories didn't help.

I took the route through to the Grassmarket, along Holyrood Road. At the foot of St Mary's Street there are two jakey dens. On a bad day, drivers at the crossroads get the added challenge of navigating Omega cider bottles. Today, it was all clear.

A new Holiday Inn was going up, another chrome-and-glass eyesore. This time in the grounds of St Patrick's Church: let's get that history put in place, tucked away. Concrete, can't get enough of it round here.

I shuffled through the area we call the Pubic Triangle: skin bars and brassers all the way along to Lothian Road. For this neck of town, think Student Central. Have I a Paul Calf attitude to them? Have I ever. Day I see a student paying for a bag of chips with a cheque, I'll dispense a lesson he won't forget.

The walking bit wasn't for me. I jumped in a Joe Baxi. Turned out I had my times wrong anyway; I was running about half an hour late. Hoped Debs would believe my 'on the way' text message and hang fire.

Taxi driver said, 'You'll get an on-the-spot fine if you don't put on the seat belt.'

'What?'

'It's the new law – fines for not wearing the belts.'

Was I in the mood for this? Clue: no. 'City's full of radge ideas.'

I saw eyes appear in the rear-view mirror. 'Y'see, that's what I get for trying to do you a favour – nothing but abuse!'

'*Abuse?* I only said—'

'Yeah, well, don't . . . or you'll be fucking walking.'

It was a classic 'It's my ball and I'll say who's playing' statement. Got my goat. 'It's your empire, pal. You make the rules.'

A screech of the brakes.

'Do I look like I'm taking the fucking piss, boy? Always the same with you fucking winos.'

What was with this guy? He had the full-on kebab-meat complexion, about to tip me on the street for answering back. I felt my blood surge. 'You sound like you're full of shit, is what you sound like . . . Why don't you try throwing me out of your fucking cab?'

'*You what*?'

I fired a hand through the cash slot, grabbed his ear and pulled his head into the Perspex. The cab shook with the thud of it.

'Hearing better now?' I said.

He slunk back, cowered against the wheel, then grabbed up the radio.

I got out.

Had to catch the bus on the slow route. By the time I got to the caf in the West End, Debs seethed.

'I'm sorry, I ran into some transport difficulties.'

She said nothing – always a bad sign. I ignored it, asked if we should order.

The waitress came. I said, 'Two coffees.'

She asked, 'What kind of coffee?'

'Oh, Christ, this rigmarole . . . Brown ones.'

Debs crossed her legs, smiled sweetly at the waitress, said, 'Two lattes, please.'

The waitress left. There was a sign up in the shop, balloons either side of it read: HAPPY 21ST SHONA. I felt a pang of guilt for loading her with grief on her birthday. She looked a good kid. Cute. Might even have had class underneath the sunbed tan and the home-do streaks. Just knew that ten years from now she'd be living in a scheme, saddled with five kids of her own and a part-time husband who once had a Suzuki but now had nothing but convictions to his name.

Morbid? You bet. That's how it is. I had no other way to see it. What else did these girls have to look forward to? Marrying the next Wayne Rooney? Christ, those ones I felt even more sorry for.

Debs wasn't for thawing. 'That's some whisky breath you have.'

I felt sweat form on my top lip. Touched the bottle of scoosh stashed in my inside pocket. 'Debs, look, I'm really sorry for keeping you waiting, but I don't remember telling you I'd jacked the booze.'

'I just thought you might, well . . . I saw your story and I thought you might be clean again.'

Not exactly the reaction I wanted, but what did I expect? Flags? Bunting? I held schtum.

The waitress brought the coffees, laid them down gently. I tried to smile, paper things over. With Debs too. 'You look well.'

'You look like shite.'

'Thank you.'

'Does that bother you?'

'What?'

'What I think?'

'Not really. Maybe once it did.'

'Gus, there are people who do care about you.'

The coffee was too hot; I put it down. 'I know.'

'Well, why do you keep throwing their concern back at them?'

'I didn't ask for their concern.'

Debs crossed her legs the other way, stared out into the street, said, 'I'm getting married again.'

I felt my heart stop. My blood surged. '*What*?'

'I wanted you to hear it from me, not from Mac or Hod or whoever.'

My nerves shrieked; I didn't know what to think. 'They know already?'

'No, Gus . . . you're the first I've told.'

I tried my coffee again. It burnt my mouth; I didn't care. 'I'm flattered, I think.'

Debs leaned towards the table, picked up a teaspoon and started to swirl it around in the coffee. 'It's important to me that you're cool with this.'

'Cool with it. How could I be cool with it?'

'I thought—'

'Whoa, back up . . . Who is he?'

'Does that matter?'

'I think fucking so.'

Cold eyes trained on me: 'Don't get any idea about starting, Gus, don't get any idea about that.'

I sighed. Felt the life drain out of me. 'What's his name?'

'He's . . . in the force, Gus.'

'*What*?' I couldn't get my head around this at all. My ex-wife marrying filth. Had she lost it? This was call-the-madhouse time. 'You jest, right? You, Deborah, marrying a cop. You're off your fucking dial.'

A loud scrape of chair on floor. 'Right, that's it. I knew this was a mistake.'

I grabbed her arm. 'Debs, please, I'm sorry . . . Sit down.' I wiped my brow, ran my fingers through my hair. I knew I needed to batten down the anger, lock it away. 'What's his name, Debs?'

'I think you might have met recently . . . Johnstone. Jonny Johnstone.'

I couldn't believe I was hearing this. 'No fucking way!'

Debs's eyes widened. 'Gus, your face – what's the matter?'

Everything was happening in a haze of shit. 'Have you set a date?'

'July fifteenth.'

'Summer wedding – nice. We were winter, if I remember right.'

'Well, there was reasons for that.'

Those reasons were forbidden territory. Something we'd agreed not to discuss. Ever.

'I beg your pardon.'

Debs looked hurt; her lower lip trembled. 'I'm not getting any younger, Gus, and . . . what we did—'

'Stop. Stop right there. This I won't touch.'

'Gus, we should talk about it . . .'

'You agreed, we both did, not ever to discuss that again. Never. I won't.'

'Gus, it's not right to let it lie, just sweep it under the carpet . . . I was talking to Mac and—'

'You spoke to Mac about that?'

'No. No. Of course not . . . I spoke to Mac about you. He thinks you're in a bad way, getting worse, and could do with help.'

'Och, for fucksake.'

Debs started to cry. 'Gus, I am too . . . It's on my mind, all the time.'

I felt wounded, sore. I stood up, walked over to Debs and put an arm around her shoulders. She grabbed me tight. I felt my whole self healed in her arms; I wanted to cry as well. To let it all out. To stop raging at everyone and everything and admit, yes, I was wrong, we were wrong to do what we did. But that was back then, in the past. We could make it right. We had each other. Hadn't we?

I heard the cafe's doorbell sound. Footsteps. Then I felt a hand on my shoulder.

'Dury?'

I turned. The cafe was bathed in blue lights, flooding in from the street. Car tyres screeched to a halt. More lights. More police.

'Are you Angus Dury?'

I nodded, felt Debs loosen her grip on my hand. 'Yeah, that's me.'

My arms were taken, turned up my back, cuffed. 'You're coming with us.'

'*What*?' I tried to rein in my fear. Mainly for Debs. She was too shocked. I saw her hide her head behind her hand as she ran out of the place and up the road without so much as a backwards glance.

I was spun towards the meat wagon's blacked-out windows.

A twenty-something in a Hugo Boss suit got out the back door and smarmed before me, viper eyes shining as he said, 'Hello again, Dury . . . Thanks for making yourself available for further questioning!'

Chapter 12

THREE HOURS SITTING IN A cell, without so much as a knock, will get you thinking. I've tried not to think about this stuff but it has a way of coming back, time and again. You get Debs forcing it into the frame, you can't avoid it . . .

It's the words that do it for me: 'Raise yourself, Dury, and depart from the Lord's house . . . The pair of you offend the congregation with your very presence.'

I'm gobsmacked. 'You what? And how would we manage that?'

Father Eugene stoops. He seems nervous before us, his top lip twitching and sparkling with sweat. 'Now, Dury, we need have no trouble from the likes of ye in front of these good people,' he says.

The Irishman has nothing on me. I'm only here for Debs – she's the Catholic. Sure, it means a lot to her that I go through the whole church thing, but I'm not having this from anyone.

'"Good people". "Good people", is it? There's not one I would call "good" among that lot . . . Look at them. Every one of them's had the knives out for us.'

Debs touches my arm but says nothing. She's usually as fiery as me, the first to wag the finger and start shouting, but she's done with the lot of them too. She's more done than she deserves to be. I glance at her. She still looks beautiful, a knockout as they all say, but her face is hardened, no longer the image of a carefree young girl of seventeen. She's a woman, searching for courage. 'Come on, Gus,' she says, 'let's just go.'

'I will not. We have every right to be here,' I blast out.

Father Eugene straightens his back and raises his voice. 'Ye cannot seek forgiveness here, not now, not ever. Go, the pair of ye!'

Debs rises to leave and there's a flutter of tongues about the place. I glance back and see her mother and father sat at the front of the church. Her mother flinches uncomfortably where she's sat and turns towards Debs, but her ruddy-faced father lays a hand on her shoulder, jerks her round, eyes front, away from the daughter who isn't fit to be looked at.

I run to Debs. She's trembling as I place my arm around her.

'And ye can stay away,' shouts the priest at our backs, his voice emboldened. 'The Holy Mother weeps at the sight of the likes of ye in the Lord's house.'

I want to turn round, lamp him one in front of the entire church, but Debs grabs my arm. I want to shout, to show the blackness of their hearts, the falseness of their piety, but Debs leads me outside.

'What did they want, us ruined?' she says, her courage vanished now, the tears starting up. 'Me barefoot and you begging to feed us? . . . I can't take it any more, Gus, I cannot.'

My heart sears in two. I know I've done this to her. I keep waiting, hoping her family will come out of the church, pick her up, take her home and tell her that's an end to it, no more Gus Dury.

But it doesn't happen. They leave Debs to me, abandon her to her fate. All I can do is hold her and hope the tears stop soon.

Chapter 13

IT STARTED WITH A SHOW. Cell doors flung open in dramatic style. Boss Suit strutted in, touch of Pacino about him as he slapped down a folder with a flourish.

I said nowt. In the nick it's policy: keep it zipped.

There was a minute of dead air between us and then, 'You're fucked, Dury.'

I didn't know where this had come from, where he got the balls to harass me like this, but I wasn't in the mood for any of his shite after what Debs had told me.

'I've *been* fucked,' I said. 'Right now, at this moment, don't believe I *am* . . . You have a problem with your tenses, sonny.' I let the nip in the last word take hold, get a good sting in there, then . . . a smile.

He slapped palms on the table, leaned in to my face. 'I wouldn't mess with me, fuckhead.'

'Fuckhead! I like your style. You have what my mother would call "a way with words".'

He stared at me, bit thrown, a look you might expect him to use after finding he'd bought another losing Lotto ticket.

I prompted: 'Now, you see, you've missed your cue . . . You're supposed to jump in with some hilarious and witty piece of repartee about what you and my mother were up to last night . . . It's in the script. Come on now, keep up, lad.'

He laughed, full-on belly laughs, then sat down. As he dried his eyes he let out a slow trail of words: 'Dury, Dury, Dury . . . why, oh why would I waste my time joking with you about fucking your mother when in actual point of fact I am fucking your ex-wife?'

That got my attention. I took my hands out of my pockets, met his eyes across the table. I mustered all my reserves of cool to stop me lunging out of my seat.

He spoke again: 'And may I say . . . what a mighty fine fuck Debs is.'

That was it – I reached for his throat. Instantly I was grabbed from behind, dumped back in my seat. I was winded, breath taken out of me.

Boss Suit paced, sniggered.

I went with, 'She always had some bad taste: she chose me . . . Shit, there goes your advantage. Gonna have to look for some other leverage.'

'Enough badinage, Dury,' said Johnstone. He leaned over the desk, flipped open the file. 'Take a look at those.'

Inside the folder were photographs of the corpse I'd stumbled over on Corstorphine Hill. The corpse I knew to be Tam Fulton; it looked worse than I recalled. In the full flash-glare, worse even than my nightmares. Two eight-ball eyes where the blood vessels had ruptured. Lots of sliced-up flesh. The pictures showed him at the crime scene and then some had been taken at the morgue, which had yet more detail. Camera close-ups on the actual knife wounds, pink flesh spilling over bright orange fat deposits. Made me want to hurl my guts up.

I pushed the folder aside, said, 'Are you trying to gross me out?'

'Don't jerk me off, Dury.'

I pointed a finger, said, 'Jerk you off . . . ? Don't you think I've had enough sick images for one day?'

He slapped his palms on the table again – it was becoming a habit – then scooped up the pictures and started to flick through

71

them one at a time. 'Murder, Dury, is not something we like to joke about in the police force.'

He was too close to me, so close I could smell the expensive aftershave, the breath fresheners. I leaned back.

'Oh, it's unpleasant, isn't it?' said Johnstone.

'What I find unpleasant is being in the same room as some jumped-up little prick in a shiny suit, and being presented with puzzles. If you have something to say, say it . . . otherwise, let me the fuck out.'

He cooled, closed the folder, fastened the clip. 'What were you doing on Corstorphine Hill on the night of May fifteenth, Mr Dury?'

'I've already told you.'

A long slow trail around the room, hands in pockets, then, 'You'd be better to come clean with me now, Dury . . . It could all get terribly messy if you leave it too late. All those deals you see on the telly are bullshit. Real police work is a lot more . . . intense.' He illustrated the last word, raised his hands and splayed fingers out either side of his head. If this was the international symbol for 'intense' I'd missed the memo.

I wanted to give him the full intensity of my boot in his arse. I felt my mouth go dry, my teeth stick to my lips. Johnstone had nothing on me – it was all histrionics. All strutting. If he hoped I'd bottle it under the harsh lights, so he'd have a nice wee story to go back home and tell Debs, he was going to be disappointed.

I said, 'For the record – and can you make sure this is noted down? I wouldn't want you to bollocks your proper grown-up police procedures – for the record, I have no clue what in Christ's name you're on about.'

A grin. 'All right, all right.' He turned to the pug on the door. 'Constable, the case, please.'

Johnstone pulled a laptop from a black briefcase and placed it in front of me. It booted up quickly. Few clicks later, I was shown some footage. I sussed at once that it was the security reel from the twenty-four-hour BP garage at the foot of Corstorphine Hill.

Some white lettering in the corner of the screen told me the date it was taken was 15 May.

The reel started shakily, then jumped about as the cameras shifted their feeds. It was jerky, nothing you could watch without squinting eyes. And then, a figure dashed into the bottom-left corner. I knew at once who it was, I recognised the clothes: Tam Fulton. I'd say, though, given the amount of screen snow, any identification beyond male, short-ish and carrying something was a stretch.

'Not exactly *Citizen Kane*, is it?' I said.

The uniform pug pushed my head back to the feature presentation.

Johnstone spoke: 'See anything of interest to you, Mr Dury?'

'No, although . . .' I leaned in to the screen.

Johnstone came with me, scrunched up his brow. 'Yes? What?'

'This is night-time, right?'

Interested: 'Yes, it is.'

'It's night-time and we're talking late, late at night.'

Intrigued: 'Uh-huh.'

I leaned in closer, touched the screen. 'Look here, outside the garage, on the forecourt . . .'

The eager cop lurched, said, 'Where? There?'

'Yeah, right there.'

'What about it?'

'Well . . .' I said, staring at the forecourt stands, 'who do you think is likely to be buying a bunch of flowers at that hour?'

I saw a vein twitch in his forehead. He clenched his teeth. The laptop was snatched from me, the lid slammed shut.

I lolled back on my chair. The Robocop behind me pushed my shoulders and shoved me under the desk again.

Johnstone spoke through his gritted teeth: 'Laugh it up, Dury.'

I said nothing, let him say his piece.

'You might think you're smart but join the fucking dots . . .'

I shrugged. 'What's the picture? A confused-looking little twat in a Boss suit desperately trying to find someone to frame for a murder he can't solve?'

'Dury, are you as dumb as you look?' He motioned away the pug then crouched to speak in my ear. 'You and I both know what was in that package Moosey was carrying. Now, given that Rab Hart wants to know what happened to it every bit as much as I do, I'd say dealing with me was your best option.'

Now I was scoobied, but I knew there was only one thing that Rab Hart was interested in, said, 'What the fuck are you on about?'

He put away the laptop, slung the case strap over his shoulder. I thought he might have put out a smile there, but no. 'I knew that's how you were going to play it, Dury . . . That's why I have forensics going over your gaff.'

'They won't find anything.'

'You seem very sure.'

'As sure as there's a hole in your arse.'

Now the smile. 'Funny, your mate wasn't so cocky when we took him in . . . Then again, with a record like Mac the Knife's I guess he has more to think about than saving your scrawny arse, Dury.'

It was time to ruin Johnstone's party. 'If you want to pull anyone in it's Joseph Crawford's son . . . I saw him on the hill: he was one of the yobs taking potshots at the dog.'

'*Judge* Crawford? You must be off your box, Dury.'

'Give him a pull, then . . . see what he says.'

He squeezed his brows together. 'Fuck that.'

'What, you don't think it's even a little bit unusual that Moosey was accused of killing Mark's sister and then turns up in the same state?'

Johnstone blew his top. 'On whose say? Yours Dury? A washed-up hack who was half-cut when we took his statement . . . ?'

I stood up, fronted him. 'You're up to no fucking good here, mate . . . You're sweeping the facts under the carpet.'

Johnstone squared up to me. 'It's my version of the facts that counts here, Dury, and I'd say you're the one who should be worried. Tam Fulton was carrying fifty grand the night he was

74

killed and it's missing. I don't think the Crawfords are short of a few quid, but from what I hear your new pub's going tits up.'

'Oh, come on . . . that's a motive?'

Jonny Johnstone smiled. 'In my book, that's one hell of a motive.'

Chapter 14

JOHNSTONE WAS GETTING THE BOOT in. No question. But if Rab Hart was missing fifty Gs I could expect much worse. Either Moosey had ripped him off and been turned over himself, or somebody else had done a job on them both. Felt like I was limbering up to go the same way; I'd be turned into Spam.

I could see why Johnstone might want me to have something to do with this, but I couldn't see how he could make it stick without some serious fitting up. It had me worried because he didn't look like the usual lazy doughnut-muncher from Lothian and Borders plod. He was sly, what the Scots call *sleekit*. And worse, he had Debs.

The tie to my ex-wife, I was pretty sure, put an edge on things for him. It was a motivator. He'd be making comparisons between us now we'd met; it was human nature. But what worried me most was how I was going to handle the man Debs was about to marry coming for me. I'd a notion that if my short fuse got any shorter I'd go off like an Exocet missile. I needed to cool right down, go Gandhi.

They kept me in all night.

By morning I was twitching, breaking out in sweats. Ganting for a drink. Could see a bar full of Guinness lined up before me, the smell of it taunting me.

People will tell you it's an inner need, the drink. You have demons calling out to be quenched. With me it's more than that. I crave the smell and the taste almost as much as the effect. If I don't see drink I can fantasise about the head of a pint, the way it sits on the inside of the rim. The way the dark liquid swirls. The condensation droplets on the glass.

I thought about nothing else now. My stomach felt empty. I can go for days without food; that kind of emptiness I can handle. The emptiness that calls out for the burn of a whisky shot is something altogether different. It's a hunger that won't go without feeding. An angry beast inside that scratches at your innards and demands action. Immediately.

When the cell doors opened this time there was no fanfare. An old desk sergeant, ticking off the days to retirement, dawdled in and dropped a tray before me. I looked down: a plate of beans and two potato scones.

'You expect me to eat that muck?' I said.

A heavily wrinkled brow raised. 'You can take it or leave it.'

I took up the coffee – looked not long poured – said, 'You can take the rest away.'

The uniform leaned back on his hip, straightened his back, said, 'There's a fella upstairs asked me to give you something.'

'Upstairs?'

An eyebrow pointed to the ceiling. 'Aye. Says you might need this.'

He reached into his pocket and I flinched. I'd been in this station before and seen some of the upstairs mob; I wasn't too keen to take any of their offerings without closer inspection.

A quarter-bottle of Bell's came out, topped up my coffee. 'How's that look?'

I felt my pulse quicken, devoured a good lash, said, 'Beautiful.' I nodded to the bottle again. 'Couldn't leave it, could you?'

'Nae danger!' A shake of the head, then another top-up, right to the brim.

'Thanks, man . . . Can't tell you how much of a help that is.'

He screwed the cap, said, 'Your friend upstairs said you might thank me for it.'

'Oh yeah . . . and my friend, who would that be?'

A laugh; phlegm rattled in his chest. 'Walls have ears, son.'

My heart twinged to be called 'son'. It had been a long time since I felt like anybody's boy. I watched him carry off the tray, turn the key in the lock and walk out the door. As he went I dashed up to the slot, yanked it open, asked, 'This friend – I was wondering, would it be an old friend or a new friend?'

'How the hell would I know? . . . I'm just the messenger.'

I let him saunter off up the hall to the desk. He seemed an all right sort of bloke. I could do with a few more of those about the place. I had a fair idea who my friend might be. I'd already decided to make a visit to him, if I ever got out of the nick. But the whole issue raised an interesting question – the prospect that Johnstone wasn't as popular as he liked to make out was something I could play about with.

They let me stew some more. Hours passed.

I was gonna start banging on the cell door, ask what the hold-without-charge limit was, when I got my second visitor of the morning.

Jonny Johnstone had changed his suit, a nice new one, grey this time and smartly pressed. His white shirt was so bright I almost had to turn away.

'What's this, the Daz doorstep challenge?' I said.

'Droll, Dury.' He strutted. 'If I were you I wouldn't be laughing it up.'

'And if I were you, I'd tone down the flash . . . Folk might start to wonder how you can afford so many designer suits on your salary.'

That struck just the note I'd wanted. The strut halted mid-step. 'Don't even try to shine me, Dury.'

'Ha, like I could compete with the suit. Fuck off, Johnstone, I've had enough lame plays. You have nothing on me.'

He didn't even blink. 'Well, let's see about that, eh?'

I was thrown by a wide grin. 'What?' I said.

'Let's see how you do in the line-up I've arranged.'

'Line-up? What the fuck are you on about?'

'See if our witness can pick you out ... Course, I wouldn't dream of leading our witness in your direction, Dury. That would just be wrong.'

He laughed as he left the cell.

I had another hour to myself before I was called. Sixty minutes of trembling and despair – set the mood for what followed.

I'd like to know where they'd picked this crew from. If they had another in the group even close to my height and build I was a Dutchman. Three had beards for a kick-off. None of this made sense to me: who was the witness, and what were they a witness to? Moosey's murder?

A uniform roared, 'Right, form an orderly queue.'

The group of us marched up to the end of the room and got in line.

'You, down here.' I followed the order.

I had what looked like a Canadian trapper to my left and Rod Hull – *sans* Emu – to my right.

As the cop left the room the lights went up.

My heart pounded. I wanted to yell that there had been a mistake; I was the one who had called the police. Only the few slurps of Bell's I'd had kept me upright.

I looked down the row of people and, from nowhere, a voice boomed, 'Eyes front.'

It felt like Big Brother was watching. Replayed Orwell's quote: 'If you want a picture of the future, imagine a boot stamping on a human face – for ever.' From where I stood, that looked about right.

The mirrored window before us let on nothing. I knew, behind it, Johnstone was walking the floor. He'd be prodding his witness, directing whoever it was to point me out for something I hadn't done. I knew it. I could sense it. My mind ran riot with what went on beyond that window.

79

'Everyone turn to the right.'

I felt my knees weaken as I moved. The back of Rod Hull's head looked to be crawling with something. Like maggots on a corpse. I had to turn away; my stomach flinched.

'Keep still, arms to your side.'

I shut my eyes and tried to imagine myself elsewhere. Then the pictures came back. The corpse in the bushes, the blood. The photographs of the cadaver, lying on the mortuary slab. Was I seriously in the frame for this? Was I really here? It was a dream, surely.

'Everyone turn to the left.'

I opened my eyes and stood in the lee of the Canadian trapper. His back was as broad as a shithouse door. I couldn't believe it had come to this. Where the fuck did it all go wrong? I had a life once . . . career, job, no kids, but whose fault was that?

'Everyone turn back to the front.'

I faced the window again. I didn't try to imagine what was behind it now. It was what was in front of it that grabbed my attention. There I was. Me. Gus Dury. Rough as all guts. Face still bruised and battered. A hint of a shiner. And those bags under the eyes. God, Gus, where did it all go wrong? Where? Where did it all go so motherfuckingly wrong?

'Could everyone exit by the door to the rear, please.'

I shook myself from my daze. '*Everyone*?'

I schlepped out with the rest of them. At the door I looked for Johnstone, cuffs at the ready. He was nowhere to be seen. Then a kerfuffle up the corridor, a flash of Boss tailoring and some swing doors being pounded.

'Mr Dury, could you come this way, please?' said the desk sergeant.

'Where are we going?'

'Get you booked out.'

'What? Come again?'

'You're free to go.'

'So the line-up . . . all a fucking farce.'

The sergeant leaned into my collar, spoke softly: 'Him – he was picked out.' He pointed to Rod Hull.

I smiled, let out a sigh of relief, said, 'He just doesn't look right without that Emu under his arm, does he?'

'You what?'

'No matter.'

Chapter 15

IT TOOK FOR EVER TO check me out of the station. A mob of teenagers, wankered on cheap cider and alcopops, were being booked in. They were all trussed up with cable ties. The girls among them were crying their eyes out, black mascara running down their cheeks. The boys were silent enough, save for the times when they started hacking their guts up. It was a scene I knew was being repeated up and down the country on an almost nightly basis. It had been this way for as long as I'd known. Scots and drink . . . O'er a' the ills o' life victorious.

Said, 'It'll be the good weather, brings out the party spirit.'

'Bollocks,' said the desk sergeant, 'it's like this the year through.'

I resisted another comment – like I could judge.

I was handed my belt and laces and two plastic bags, one containing my wallet and some loose change, the other with my mobile phone, tabs and matches.

'That you?' said the sergeant.

I nodded. 'We're good.' It could have been two bags of air; I wouldn't have complained if it meant getting free of the place.

'I'm so dead,' said one of the teenage girls. 'My dad's gonna kill me.' She burst into tears, set off her friend. I couldn't stand any more. Strangely, the scene made me even more desperate for a drink.

Outside the nick I breathed deep, though not so easy.

A kid on Heelys sped past me, nearly put me in the gutter – as if I needed help. There was a throbbing in my head, an ache in my chest. Both called for attention, the type that comes in quarter-bottles. I looked about, tried to catch my bearings, and then a horn sounded.

A Smart car across the street looked nearest; driver crouched up looked like an Easter Island statue behind the wheel. I didn't recognise him. The horn blasted again and this time I caught where it came from: black E-class Merc parked further away. I recognised this face.

As I walked over, Fitz the Crime drummed his fingers on the steering wheel. More filth was the last thing I needed, but this one might be some use. The fact remained: he owed me. Big time. Fitz and I went way back. We'd both been known to help each other out from time to time. By the kip of him he'd done very well out of the last favour I put his way – blowing the lid on that Eastern European people-smuggling racket. Fitz had taken all the collars, whilst some of his colleagues had taken their jotters.

'Could ye make any more of a feckin' show of it, Dury?' said Fitz as I reached the door of his new motor.

'You what?'

'Feck me, 'tis yerself in the frame for murder and you walk the road like a brass . . . Get in, would ye!'

I opened the door, tried to make myself invisible as I sat down. Fitz gunned the engine, burnt up the road.

We drove in silence for a few minutes then I asked, 'Any smokes?'

Pack of Lambert & Butler tossed in my direction. Sparked up.

'There's a heart-warmer in the glovebox,' said Fitz.

I dived in. It was Dalwhinnie; seriously expensive malt. 'My, Fitz, you're moving up in the world.'

He fingered his collar. 'Well, the work's its own reward.'

I gave a loud tut.

'And that would be supposed to mean something, I suppose.'

I unscrewed the bottle, quaffed more than I should, felt a heavy burn, said, 'Is anything?'

'Oh, the feckin' riddles already, is it? Always the riddles with ye, Dury.'

He asked for it, so I let him have it. Both barrels. 'What is it now? Detective sergeant? Chief fucking super? You were padding Leith Walk in uniform before I handed you that . . . white arrest.'

A screech of tyres. The car halted and a hail of angry horns belted out behind us.

Fitz jumped from the car. I watched him walk over to the multi-storey. He flashed his badge at the attendant and up went the barrier. A row of traffic immediately cleared as he headed back.

'*Noblesse oblige,*' I muttered.

'What?'

'Rank has its privileges, I see.'

He laid a glass eye on me as he put the Merc in gear again, screeched off. The multi-storey was dark; it took headlights to get around the bays. When he parked, Fitz killed the engine.

We were in almost total darkness, silence too. Was this the effect he was going for? He turned, uneasy, with his vast gut pressing on the wheel.

As Fitz spoke he spat through his tiny teeth: 'Now I want feckin' answers, Dury. No bullshit. No riddles. And nothing else that'll put me closer to cracking yer feckin' head this minute . . . You got me?'

I nodded. What was I going to do – walk home?

Fitz grabbed the bottle, unscrewed the cap and tanked it.

He said, 'This Moosey fella, did ye kill him?'

I grabbed the whisky back, roared, 'Are you fucking serious?'

Fitz put his bulb-nose in my face, spat at me. There was madness on him. 'I will do for ye, Dury, I swear it! Feckin' tell me. Is it you?'

'No! For Chrissake, no . . . Of course it's not me.'

'Well, it could look that way.'

'If you're following the fantasy of that dumb fuck you have on the case, maybe.'

It felt like waiting for traffic lights to change hanging on Fitz's response.

'Johnstone's that . . . I'll grant ye.'

'You're not one of his fans, then?'

'He's fast-track, been blazing a trail through the ranks. Nobody likes a big shot . . . I'm no different, but there's nothing personal in it, I just think the cocky wee prick needs taking down a peg or two.'

I ran my hand over the walnut dash of the Merc. 'Frightened he's got an eye on your new car, Fitz?'

'Feck off! I'm rock. After the people-smuggling bust I'm . . . well, I'm solid, that's all.'

The Eastern European gang I handed to Fitz a while back held precisely zero weight here. We both knew this. However, were it to become public knowledge that a murder suspect had, in any way, been linked to a senior member of the force – that gave Fitz something to think about.

I trod carefully. This was filth we were dealing with, I wouldn't have put it past him to be on a fishing expedition for Johnstone. I said, 'You know who to thank for that.'

'Dury, don't play that tune with me. Don't feckin' even try it.'

'I'm not playing any tune, all I'm saying is, there is a tune . . . and if it gets played, you'll be paying the piper.'

Fitz's face changed colour; his skin took on the texture of corned beef. He pulled at his shirt cuff, mopped his brow. As he carefully wiped the sweat on the white cotton his voice dropped: 'We have a garden now, Gus . . . Missus is overjoyed to have it, spends all the hours God sends picking out the weeds and tending the little flowerbeds. I've never seen her so happy . . . She never had a garden before, never in her life, y'know, not even in the old country.'

I drew on my tab, kept schtum.

'If you want my help, Dury, you better be cleaner than a cat's arse.'

'I am.'

'More than that, boyo, you better be onto the real murderer, because laughing boy has no hope other than to hang it on you . . . and he's a boner for ye.'

I threw my dowp out the window, said, 'And for my ex-wife.'

Fitz wiped his lips. 'You what? He's balling your ex?'

'I think the term's "cohabiting".'

'The mad bastard . . .'

'Come on, Fitz, she's not a bad-looking bird.'

'Dury, I'm not on about that. He's only throwing due process out the window. How's that going to look to the courts if he gets you to trial?'

My pulse jumped a notch. 'Can you get him hauled off?'

'No. No. No. These chickens need to roost.'

'Now it's you with the riddles.'

Fitz held out a hand for the bottle, took it, slugged slow, said, 'Getting him hauled off the case, sure, that's only showing our hand.'

'Fitz, we have no hand.'

'Neither has he. Didn't the line-up come down on your side? Now, he gets booted off the job, we're in a much better position . . . unless anything else turns up.'

I didn't like his reasoning, sounded dodgy, said, 'This is all making me more than a bit uneasy, Fitz.'

He turned over the engine, made to pull out. 'Leave it with me, Dury . . . Sure, your wee revelation might just prove to be for the best. Keep your hopes up our wide boy likes playing it close to the knuckle. That ambition of his might be his undoing.'

I watched Fitz settle into the heated leather seat and drive smoothly. One of his little crises might be over but I knew my major one wasn't. I mean, what did it matter to me who took the case at the end of the day? I was still being put in the frame for murder.

'Fitz, if Jonny gets his arse canned, that's got to be bad.'

'No, it's good.'

'For who?'

Fitz frowned, reached for a tab and pushed in the cigarette lighter button. 'Me and you, sure.'

'How does it help me to know the man who wants to bust my

balls, for a murder I didn't commit, is rousted off the case? It's only gonna make him madder.'

Fitz held the fag in his mush, pursed his lips, made little kisses on the filter as he got it going. 'Dury, chill the feck out . . . You're not seeing the bigger picture.'

'Then fill me in, Fitz . . . what is the bigger picture?'

'Way I see it, Jonny gets canned, you get more time to find Fulton's killer. Harsh, but them's the facts.'

'That's your considered opinion?'

'Yes . . . call it my professional assessment of all the, er, known factors.'

'I know what I'd call it.'

'*What*?'

'A ticket to jam with Bubba in the showers.'

Chapter 16

FITZ DROPPED ME IN THE New Town, middle of Queen Street. An African drum quartet, kitted out in lion manes and warpaint, competed with a lone piper. Tourists shunned the home-grown gig and he upped the volume. I thought I wouldn't like to see this scene get messy: lions are one thing, but the Scots know how to fight dirty. The city had been making it tough for our national musicians, banning them from the main thoroughfare, the Royal Mile. In their wisdom, the city fathers had even decided to dish out antisocial-behaviour contracts to those pipers who flouted the new regulations. Antisocial behaviour? What the hell was that? In my day antisocial meant staying in to watch the footy on *Scotsport* instead of going down the drinker. They were mangling the language to mangle with our heads . . . as if mine needed any more of that.

I lolled along in a daze. Don't know how many times I got asked for directions to Rosslyn Chapel. Fucking *Da Vinci Code*. Had ceased to be an amusement long ago; man, was this ever letting up? One of these days, someone is going to end up wearing that book like a butt-plug.

I knew I was moping. My feet slid along the pavement. Could hear the words 'You've a face like a constipated greyhound' coming my way soon. I didn't care. Like I could feel worse.

Gutted

At the junction with St Andrew Street, the Portrait Gallery halted me. Always does. The red sandstone's a show-stopper among the grey squares, circuses, parks and terraces of this aristocratic ghetto. Add Italian Gothic architecture to the mix, you're in serious eye-catcher territory. None of that does it for me, though: they have my father's portrait in there.

CANNIS DURY, WORLD CUP SQUAD, SPAIN '82 it says on the brass plaque beneath. Must stand about six feet high. He never stood that tall in real life. He never needed to. A finer example of the wee man complex would be hard to find. With this type the mantra is fight for the respect your size denies you.

And he did. Not just on the park either. My mother, God bless her battered heart and soul, bore the brunt of it. Just the thought reminded me how much I'd neglected her since my father's funeral. I knew I must call her soon; what was stopping me?

The sight of the gallery, every time, reminds me that my father's in there. Larger than life. Living on. As if I ever needed a reminder. On his deathbed he begged my forgiveness, but it made no difference.

An old woman caught me staring at the spires and turrets. 'Are you going in?'

'Excuse me?'

'I think it's a disgrace!' She shook her head. A baby-blue bobble on her tam-o'-shanter rolled from side to side. 'An absolute disgrace.'

I had no idea what she was on about, said, 'You're right . . . disgraceful.'

'When I think of the paintings they have in there . . . kings and queens, done by masters, too.'

I tried to get an inkling of where she was going with this, spotted a banner, a sculpted six-pack and a tranche of female thigh on it. The current exhibition was on naked celebrities.

'This is just typical,' I said. 'We're celebrity obsessed . . . It's like *Hello!* magazine in oils.'

The oldie smiled. 'You're a man of some sense.'

'Some would say . . . a cynic.'

A heart-stopping smile. 'They'd be wrong, so they would.'

I took the compliment, smiled back. 'Well, I don't know about the price of everything but I do know the value of nothing.'

And did I ever. Nothing was my current score in the game of life.

I traipsed on, passed the Sherlock Holmes statue outside Arthur Conan Doyle's birthplace, crossed over to Greenside Place and onto London Road, then schlepped down all the way to the Holy Wall.

I realised I'd forgotten my key.

Rapped on the door.

Nothing.

Another rap, louder.

Heard movement, bit of shuffling, then a 'Shit' and a 'Fucksake'.

When the lock turned in the door I saw one bleary eye pushed into the gap. 'Who is it?'

'Me, the one with his name above the door.'

'Gus . . . bloody hellfire, get in!'

Mac opened up. He stood in the daylight wearing a pair of budgie-smugglers, bright yellow ones. A 'Makin' Bacon' T-shirt maintained his modesty from the waist up.

I shielded my eyes. 'Get some clothes on. Your skanky arse is the last thing I want to see.'

He slapped his butt cheeks, called out, 'What you on about? I'm a fine figure of a man.'

'Aye, if the figure's zero . . . a big round one.'

'Och, get yerself hunted.'

As he shut the door I saw plod had been at work. The pub had been turned over, drawers lying out, cupboard doors open, smashed glass everywhere. I was surprised they hadn't had the floorboards up.

'Holy shit,' I blurted, 'we've had company, then . . .'

Mac frowned, pulled a checked dressing gown over himself, said, 'You could say that. Not any company I'd like to see, though . . .

Bastards left the place in some kip, haven't they? It's like Steptoe's yard now.'

As we moved into the bar area I stopped in my tracks. Loud barking greeted us. It lasted all of a few seconds until the dog came running through from the next room, started to jump at me, clawing and pawing.

Mac said, 'Better give him a hello, Gus.'

I walked around the love-fest. 'What, and encourage him? Uh-uh.'

'But he doesn't carry on like that with anyone else. Fair puts the shits up the punters, let me tell you.'

'Are you going soft, Mac? Why's he still here?'

'Can't just chuck him on the scrapheap, Gus ... Where's your heart?'

I knew exactly where it was. 'Pretty fucking well buried.'

Mac knelt, started to ruffle the dog's ears, clapped his back. 'Bollocks! I know you, you'll come round to this wee one. Be bezzie mates, so you will.'

I saw the dog had kept his bandage on. 'When did you say his stitches come out?'

'At least a week. Vet said it's a deep wound. Might take longer.'

'Well, in the meantime, who do you have to kill to get a drink around here?'

'*Och* ... bad word choice, pal. No' the subject for humour right now.'

I let that slide. Stating the obvious wasn't my thing.

As I sat at the bar, the dog settled at my feet.

'What can I get you?'

'Usual.'

The dog looked up, put his chops on my foot.

Mac spoke: 'So, the nick ... what happened?'

'Can I get a pint down me first?'

Mac thinned his eyes. It was enough. 'Better we get it sorted right off, Gus. You know they had me in as well.'

I shuffled on my bar stool. The dog jumped up as I lurched

across to grab a fresh pack of Bensons. Said, 'Yeah, they mentioned it.'

'Aye, yon Jonny ponce has your card marked . . . Fuck knows what he thought he was gonna get out of me.'

'There's fifty Gs missing of Rab Hart's and he thinks I took it.'

'Shitballs.' Mac laid down a pint of Guinness. It looked just like I'd imagined it in the cell, moist jewels glistening on the glass. I picked it up, quaffed through to the halfway line in a oner.

I nodded, said, 'Man, that tastes good.'

'Gus.' He didn't need to say any more than that. It was a prompt: his tone told me there was a pressing need to crack on and solve this case, to get my knackers out the vice.

'I know. Believe me, Mac, I'm on to it . . . soon as I get this down me.'

I took the wrapping off my smokes, sparked up. Said, 'What about you? When they hoicked you in.'

He laid an ashtray in front of me, said, 'Was a heavy session.'

'And?'

'And what?' His tone changed. 'What you asking me?'

I flicked ash off my cigarette, said, 'Did they ask about my state of mind? I know that's been a big concern of yours lately.'

'If you think I would shit on you with the filth then we can't be the friends I thought we were.'

'Mac,' I shut him down, 'I'm not saying that. Get that straight. Okay?'

A nod. Shoulders pulled back. Hard man on the defensive. 'It just sounded like, y'know . . .'

'Cool the beans . . . I just need to know what they asked you.'

He turned, hit the optics for a hefty tequila, put a glaze of water on it, said, 'I told them . . . well, er, I did mention we were in some financial strife here at the pub.'

Great.

'Did they put a threat on you?'

He screwed up his face. 'Gus, this is the filth . . . Of course they dug up some dirt, threatened this, that.'

I crushed the cellophane from the fag packet in my hand, said, 'Y'know, they have nothing . . . but they're gonna go digging for more dirt.'

Another shrug. 'So what?'

'This Jonny fucker's all over me like a cheap suit . . . That suggestion you gave me earlier about splitting, might be a wise move for yourself now if you know what I mean.'

He grabbed the cellophane from me, binned it. Mac put his hands on my shoulders. 'Gus, pal . . . I'm going nowhere! You understand? I'm sticking with you on this. You'll beat this.'

I removed his hands, stood up. 'I know what you think you're doing but what you have to understand is this: myself, I couldn't give two fucks about; dragging you down with me is a whole other ball game.'

Mac lit a tab, cupped it in his hand prison-yard style and blew on the tip. We'd been through some scrapes, but none like this. He moved across the floor, went to sit at a table. 'Can't expect them to be pleased with you down the nick after that last caper.'

I sighed. 'You think this was how Col imagined it would play out?'

'What you mean?'

'The bar . . .'

'He left the bar to you, Gus. He wanted you to have it.'

'Mac, he left the bar to his wife.'

'He couldn't have seen she'd cark it inside a month.'

'It's playing on my mind.'

Mac leaned forward, balanced on one arse cheek as he reached into his back pocket, took out his wallet. 'I'm gonna give you something.' He ferreted about for a card, pulled it out and laid it on the table.

'What's that?' I said.

His eyes drooped; he seemed ashamed. 'I, eh, when I got out the jail they put me on this course to get my shit together.'

I looked at the card. 'Mac, this is a head-shrinker.'

'No. Therapist – different.'

I tapped the name. 'Mac, let me get this straight: you want me to get my head tested?' Something simmered in me – anger.

'She can help you. She helped me. There's no shame in it.'

'Mac, there's no anything in it . . . It's all psychobabble!'

He put a glower on me. 'Gus, you've took me all wrong here.'

I tipped back a chair, jerked it out. Legs scratched across the bar floor as I sat down.

Mac went on: 'You've been through a lot lately with the divorce, the death of your old fella . . . I was talking to Hod and we're both concerned.'

'Concerned my arse! The pair of you have been jangling, that's all this is. What is it? I'm not doing my bit in the bar? Or am I drinking too much of the profits? Fuck me, Mac, since when did you and Hod go all bleeding-heart and Oprah on me?'

I was in a rage, out of control. Wrecking-ball mad. Off the dial.

I stood up again, knocked over the chair. I had the card in my hand and shoved it in Mac's top pocket. He didn't so much as flinch as I waved the back of my hand at him.

I took up my pint of Guinness, drained it.

There was one hell of an atmosphere in the room. There's a phrase – *cut the air with a knife.*

I kept my gaze on him, waited for a response. None came. You get to my age, live the life I have, you think you've seen every reaction in the book. This I had not. Mac stood up, took the deepest breath, held it, and walked away from me. As the door swung behind him I was alone with my troubles.

I felt confused. Had I shocked him so much? Surely not. This was Mac the Knife we were talking about, hardy Glasgow chib merchant. Was my take on life, the situation, so off-whack?

As I watched the door shut itself, I suddenly sussed the look: it was despair. Utter despair was what Mac felt for me now. Something twisted inside me, a pang. It wasn't physical, but emotional.

I felt my gaze fall. My head drooped.

Where my eyes rested I saw two others staring back at me. Slowly, the dog came closer, crouched at my feet and stretched out two paws.

I said, 'We're having a time of it, boy.'

His tail wagged. It didn't seem like the right response.

'It gets worse . . .' I turned to see Mac back standing in the doorway. 'I was going to leave this till the morning, but I thought I better not.'

'What is it?'

'You had a visit . . . Rab Hart wants you to go and see him in Saughton.'

Chapter 17

IT WAS A RESTLESS NIGHT. Tossed and turned for hours before I found sleep. Then I woke bolt upright in the darkness, my heart banging harder than a marching band. I'd seen the gutted corpse of Tam Fulton flash before my eyes again. I was beginning to wonder if I'd ever shake the image. Didn't seem like it.

I got up and paced the flat; had every light blazing. I tanned a few cans, smoked nearly a full pack of Superkings. The only thing that got me back into bed was the prospect of having to navigate the dark stairs to the bar to restock. I wasn't risking the sight of another corpse coming out the blackness.

Had managed to catch some kip, but not enough, when Hod appeared. 'You're cracked, y'know that!' He fiddled with my books, got bored too easy, turned to the CDs.

'Well, you know cracks . . . must have brown-nosed enough of them to get so set up.'

A CD frisbeed at me. I yelled, 'Jesus, that better not be Lennon!' I knelt down, picked up the disc. It was Franz Ferdinand. 'You're lucky it's one of yours. Have it back – shite anyway.'

Hod ducked as the CD went his way. It missed, hit the dresser. 'I mean it, Gus, now you've rattled the filth it's time to shoot the crow.'

'I couldn't if I wanted to.' I climbed over a pile of old clothes, dumped on the floor by Lothian's finest in their recent investigation of my property. 'They've taken my passport.'

'Seized it?'

'Seized, lost, does it matter? Like I'd get far anyway. Have you seen the new street furniture?'

'Come again?'

I pointed to the window. Hod dipped his head through the curtains, said, 'What am I looking for?'

'Red Golf . . . It's plod.'

'How can you tell?'

'You want a bag of doughnuts for proof? Trust me, I know.'

'How long's he been out there?'

'Since I got out.'

'So it's official – you're a suspect?'

'Och, I'd say they were taking a serious interest in me.'

Hod released the curtain, paced, tugged at his wispy chin. He said, 'And under surveillance. This is bad shit.'

I collected a roll-on deodorant from the dresser, looked about for a comb, razor. 'No kidding.'

'You're remarkably chilled for a man who's being investigated for murder.'

'What would you like me to do, piss myself? Whine, maybe? Not my style.'

I made Hod's choice of CD for him. Morrissey wailed out 'Heaven Knows I'm Miserable Now'.

'Gus, man.'

'*What*?'

'Do you have to?'

'Do I have to what?'

'Play that . . . It's depressing.'

I put a hand on Hod's shoulder, squeezed hard. 'Believe me, mate, in my world, this is pretty fucking far shy of depressing.'

Eyes rolled again. A blank look, then a hand brought up to his chin again. 'Gus, I was wondering, y'know the therapist that Mac suggested—'

The word put my stomach on spin cycle. 'Hod, don't get on that.'

He stopped rubbing his chin – was too Freud a look even for him – clasped both hands together. 'Sure. Sure. It's your call totally, but if you're feeling any pressure, on the purse strings, I could sort out the fees.'

I swung him by the shoulders towards the door. 'Out!'

'What? I'm only trying to help. You've been so zoned lately, Gus, it might help.'

I shot him a glower as I grabbed for the door handle, watched his arse bump against the corridor wall. 'Next word I hear about a therapist, I'm up for two murders. Got it?'

A nod. Eyebrows drooped towards the nascent beard.

'And tell Mac if he starts again, he'll see a side of me he won't like either.'

I slammed the door. Bounded back to Morrissey, turned up the volume. Thought: The cheeky bastards.

I knew the therapist was a ruse to get me off the sauce. I'd been drinking the bar dry. Since Mac took over the running of it he'd been watching how much I put away. He didn't understand the quantity was nothing special. I'd been drinking from morning till night for years. Was I going to change without a reason? Was I buggery.

I set the shower running, collected up my things, took a last glance onto the street. Plod was reading the *Daily Star*. Copping an eyeful of Candy, 22, from Essex on page three. I thought: You sad fuck. Mouthed, *Don't let me catch you having a tug down there*.

The shower was hot. Near boiled the skin off me. Imperial Leather label peeled off the soap, I'd such a lather going. For some reason I was scrubbing at myself like I'd been interned in Bar-L. I wondered if subconsciously I expected to be.

There seemed no end of shit piling up on my doorstep. Of most concern was a visit from one of Rab Hart's goons. Mac and Hod leaning on me was only making things worse, though.

As I got out of the shower I saw I had Morrissey jammed on

repeat. Further along the track, he wailed about giving his valuable time to people who didn't care if he lived or died. Got my vote. Nodded to the CD player.

I picked up some clothes from the ground: crisp white oxford, newish pair of dark-blue Diesel and a black lambswool cardigan. A few years ago, you wore a cardy, you were borderline care-in-the-community. Now, it was *the* look. I checked myself in the mirror: *the* look worked. Seemed to fit my mood.

I grabbed my mobi.

There was a heap of calls I needed to make, but only one pressed. Only one I knew might help my case.

Dialled.

Girl on the switchboard said, 'Lothian and Borders Police. How may I help you?'

'Eh, Fitzsimmons, please?'

'Would that be Detective Sergeant Fitzsimmons?'

'That's him.'

'Connecting you to his line. Thank you.'

I waited, got the feeling I'd missed him, then, 'Yes?'

Gruff, to say the least.

'Good morning to you too.'

Bit of edge creeping in now. 'Who the hell is this?'

'Oh, I think you know. Shall we say . . . a friend in need?'

Full-on badass mode hit fast: 'Are you out your feckin' mind?'

'I'd like to meet you.'

'I don't believe my feckin' ears . . . I have no idea who this is calling and I want to point out wasting police time is a criminal offence. Good day to you, sir.'

The fucker hung up.

I stared at my phone in disbelief. It began to ring. Showed a mobile number.

'Hello . . .'

'Dury, ye have pulled some feckin' stunts but calling me at my own desk is the limit . . . Is it the sack you're after for me?'

I sighed. 'Yeah, that's it, I'm that mad.'

'Dury, get a feckin' grip, and fast.'

'Easier said than done in the current state of play. There's a pair of your little helpers sitting outside my house.'

'What did you expect – tickets to the Bahamas?'

'I didn't expect . . . Look, it doesn't matter what I expected, what I need is some information.'

'Am I feckin' hearing this?'

'*What*?'

'Are ye on the tap for police intelligence?'

'That's an oxymoron, Fitz.'

Gap on the line. Silence.

I continued: 'What I want, and what you want, are one and the same here, so before you go all righteous on me just remember your wife's new-found interest in her lovely garden.'

'Dury, don't push it.'

'See sense, Fitz. I'll meet you by the National Monument. Off the track enough?'

'Is this entirely necessary?'

'Shall we say midday?'

I did the hanging up this time.

Chapter 18

HOD SAT AT THE BAR, moving dust about with his finger. Mac looked bored. There were no punters in.

'Why are you still here, Hod?' I said.

A spin on the stool, eyes flared. 'I'm, er, at a loose end.'

I spotted Mac. He scratched his palm nervously.

'This better not be what I think it is.'

Mac let out a sigh, fiddled with the little stud earring in his left ear, said, 'And what would that be?'

'Minding . . . I don't need looking after!' I pointed to the pump beside Mac's elbow. 'Usual.'

The dog came running up to meet me, put claws up. I swear that dog smiled. I looked down at him. He barked. Turned his head to one side, then the other. An ear sat up.

'Gimme a Grouse whilst you're there.'

Mac poured the whisky, placed it down. I fired it, said, 'Another like it.'

Looks passed between the pair of them.

'*Yes*?'

In unison: 'Nothing. Nothing.'

'Make it a double. Fuck it, treble.' I smiled. '. . . As well hung for a sheep as a lamb.' I sparked up a smoke, inhaled deep, said, 'So spill.'

Hod bridled, tweaked the hair on the back of his knuckles. 'I'm at a loose end.'

'Horseshit.'

'I am, straight up . . . I wouldn't shit you about that. Why? Why would I?'

'Cos you're a born horseshitter.'

He rose. Walked over to me and stole a smoke from the pack that sat on top of the bar. I waited for him to speak. What he did was cough on the first drag, then make a sharp exhalation.

'What are you doing?'

'I'm bored, Gus . . . I told you.'

'What about the burgeoning Hod empire . . . Bedsitland-by-the-Sea division must be keeping you busy with the kip of the students I see about the streets.'

'I've got staff to do that now. There's nothing left for me, Gus, business runs itself. I need something else – I'm as flat as a plate of piss.'

At once, I saw where this was going. Put the nail in that one. 'Get a hobby.'

Hod puffed his chest at me, got bolshie. 'I've done every hobby going: diving, archery – all wank.'

I wasn't playing along. I knew the pair of them had cooked this up. The idea was to make Hod my sidekick; he could keep an eye on me. If there was one thing I didn't need it was Hod Arnie-ing through this case, shooting all to buggery any chance I had of getting out of Dodge. I'd seen him in action before. Hod's action I could do without.

Mac placed my pint on the bar. I raised it, slugged. Took the break in proceedings to change tack, shove Hod off balance.

'What have you got for me this morning, Mac?'

He flung the towel over his shoulder. 'By way of business, you mean? Well, there's the bill from the brewery and the rates are due . . . Some damp in the cludgie I'd say needs looking at smartish. Apart from that, diddly.'

'Mac, you're giving me chatter. This is avoidance.'

He looked at Hod. The pair put eyes on me.

I turned to the wall, checked the calendar – had a Scots piper on it in a field of bluebells. Mac seemed to get the hint. He put his hands on the bar, leaned forward. 'There's still a hole in the books. There was another letter from the bank.'

'Get it over.'

Mac leaned under the bar, took out the petty cash box. He ferreted in his pocket for a bunch of keys, found the one, opened up. I snatched the envelope. It was taped along the seal. Same Manila deal as usual, same threats from the manager. 'This looks great,' I said.

'We need about thirty grand to keep afloat, and that's before any refit to get new punters in. We can't remortgage either,' said Mac.

I put the letter back inside the envelope, tucked it in my pocket, said, 'Did plod see this?'

Mac nodded.

'Great.' If Jonny Johnstone was looking for a motive, he had one in black and white.

In the last twenty-four hours I'd been planted firmly in the shit. The funny thing was, though I was fucked, all I could think about was letting Col down. I'd run his pub into the ground. I could feel his eyes on me where I stood, admonishing me, telling me I was better than I gave myself credit for, that I could pull this back. 'Quality ye are, boyo,' he'd said. God, hadn't I proved him wrong, though. Col was the only man who had ever let me make mistakes without judging. He was the only man I knew who had ever felt genuinely proud of any minor achievement I'd made in my life, had shown faith in me, trusted that I wasn't washed up, when all evidence pointed the other way. He was nothing like my own father.

Hod smoothed down the hair at the sides of his mouth. 'Look, I can help out, but what you need is a buyer . . . If I put that to the firm, they'll think I'm running a charity. If I take over the Wall, you'll be left with nothing, Gus.'

I didn't want to contemplate that. It sounded far too much like what I deserved.

I went to the window, stared out. A dog barked on the street and the one at my feet let off with a round of its own.

'*Usual . . . Usual*, down, boy!' roared Mac.

I was taken out of my gloom at the sight of the dog scurrying off to his basket, tail between legs. What that beast had been through put things into perspective. Thank Christ he was still in one piece.

'What did you call him?' I said.

Mac grinned. 'Usual.'

'*What*?'

The pair laughed. Hod butted in: 'He thinks it's his name . . . Fits, don't you think?'

I turned to my pint, said, 'Jesus H. Christ . . . I don't know what to think any more.'

Chapter 19

'NOW, YOU KNOW WHAT TO DO?' I said.

Hod put up his collar, locked his jaw. 'Course I do.'

'No. You don't, obviously.' I turned down the collar, playfully slapped his chops, said, 'Lose the roughhouse demeanour.'

He slouched, nearly dropped the tray of sandwiches, pies and coffee. 'I just don't do this nice thing too well, Gus.'

'Look, you want to help out, right?'

'I do, yeah.'

'Well, this is test number one – you get this right, well, we'll see.'

Mac appeared at my back. His face was set hard as granite. He had a donkey jacket on that wouldn't have looked out of place on an Irish navvy of the seventies.

'Dressing down?'

'We're going to Sighthill, Gus.' He spat the words like bullets. As he stood before me he was transformed into the chib-man of old. Mac was ready for a pagger, I could see it in his eyes.

'Now, you'll behave yourself, won't you?'

He didn't answer; brushed past me and made for the door. He was a fearsome sight with the threat of violence upon him.

I caught Hod checking himself out in the Younger's Tartan Special mirror that hung in the hallway. He seemed to be psyching himself up, but looked more like a learner driver waiting for the test examiner.

'You cool with this?' I asked.

'Sure, aye . . . *Aye*.' He straightened his back, showed teeth.

I nodded approval. 'That's the face you show them!'

'*Gotcha*.'

'Then let's do this.'

First out the door was Mac. He schlepped over to the red Golf. I saw plod following his every move. They never saw Hod approach and put a knock on the driver's window.

'Morning, chaps. How goes it today?' he said.

The window was wound down; a head popped out.

'I saw you sitting out here and I was thinking to myself, Poor buggers – bet they never even get a break for a bit of breckie.'

Hod passed in the tray. Hands went up. Heads went down. They checked out what the go was with all the smiling and the free scran. They never saw Mac creeping behind to pack the exhaust flange with a damp bar towel.

'So, you'll be the early shift?' Hod said, his mock-bonhomie at full blast. 'Beats the graveyard shift, eh?'

Plod took over the tray, seemed a bit conflicted. He said, 'I can't discuss that kind of thing . . . Look, who the hell are you?'

I started to hear whistling: if I wasn't wrong, *The Great Escape*. Mac sauntered round to the front of the car. As he passed Hod he gave a little tap on his back. In no time at all, he was behind the wheel of the van, starting up. He had the side door open for me to dive in before plod rumbled.

We pulled out.

The red Golf revved high. Then cut out. Revved again. Cut out.

There was some serious burn from within the engine. Lots of smoke. Suddenly the Golf's wheels screeched into the street, all of five yards, then the car stalled.

Hod smiled as I checked him in the rear-view. I said to Mac, 'Nice work, fella.'

His short arms wrestled with the big steering wheel, wide turning circle playing havoc with the needle tickling sixty. 'Turned out quite well, I thought.'

I grinned. 'Tell me, the towel ... where did you get that idea?'

'Flash of genius, wasn't it? Truth told, I snaffled it.'

'From who?'

'Eddie Murphy.'

I turned in my seat. Mac scrunched the gears, pulled out into traffic, said, '*Beverly Hills Cop* ... He used bananas, though. We were out of them, but the bar towel did the trick.'

I had to laugh. Put the Eddie Murphy *eeh-eeh-eeh* in there, said, 'Get the fuck outta here!'

We snaked through traffic for a few minutes, working the bus lanes to get as far away from the Wall – and plod – as quickly as possible. We did well – Mac might have made a wheelman in another incarnation. I knew the bus route to Sighthill, but Mac was taking me – there's a phrase – *all around the houses*.

'You're sure about this?' he said.

'Am I sure? Of course I'm sure.' I wondered why Mac the Knife was asking me this. Had he changed his mind about what we were about to do? 'Are *you* sure?'

He took his eyes off the road, turned to me. 'Fucking right.' He pointed me to a carrier bag at my feet. 'Check that.' Inside was a length of rope, tied at one end in a hangman's noose.

Of all the people I knew, Mac was the last one to go bottling it on me. I said, 'This wee prick's got something to hide; I can feel it in my bones.'

He crunched the gears, upped the speed as we took a steep hill with a curve to the left. 'Well, if the Sid you saw is Sid the Snake, you can bet on that.'

'I'm sure that Vera Fulton's got more to give us as well, but this Sid fella was rattled, seriously rattled, when I went round there the last time.'

'Well, we'll give him a tug and see what's what.'

107

I held on to the handle above the door as Mac tanked it into Sighthill.

'What's the Jackanory with him and Rab Hart?' I said.

'That's a tricky one. We definitely don't want to be pissing Rab off.'

'Think they're thick?'

Mac eyed me again. 'Rab and Sid? . . . I'd fucking doubt it. Sid's a bottom feeder. He'll have been running some small-time racket for Rab. My guess, since Sid's a bookie, it'll be a book on the dog fighting . . . but hey, you can ask Rab yourself when you get up to the big hoose.'

'You think that's likely?'

'Gus, you better get in and see him. He'll only send someone for you if you don't.'

'No thanks.'

'Gus, the pug he sent round wasn't messing about . . . Rab wants to see you like fucking yesterday.'

As we arrived, the jungle bus was pulling in just ahead of us, dislodging a grim cargo of trackie-wearing neds and defeated old folk too afraid to lift their heads from the streets.

'Look at the state of this,' said Mac.

'Tell me. It's grim as death.'

An old man, so bloated he could hardly walk, was struggling with two Lidl carrier bags at the side of the road. As he waited for a gap in the traffic, two young yobs sneaked up behind him and pulled down his joggers. The bloke was exposed to the world, but too scared to put down his bags for fear they'd be stolen. He struggled to get both bags in one hand before struggling again to hitch up his joggers.

'The wee bastards,' said Mac.

The yobs stood at the side of the street laughing it up. Between them they were an advertisement for fluoridation of the water supply – hardly a good tooth in either head.

'This place is a fucking nightmare.'

'Think yourself lucky you're not living here.'

It was on my mind to say 'Maybe soon', or perhaps 'I could be facing worse', but I let the thought pass without giving voice to it.

We pitched up outside Moosey's home. The street was deserted, save a few half-starved mongrels that trotted about in packs, sniffing at bin bags and the litter and scraps that blew everywhere.

'You think those dogs belong to anyone?' I asked.

'Aye,' said Mac, 'fucking everyone.'

'What – they're a feral pack?'

'What else would you call them? They're not looked after, that's for sure . . .' He sat upright behind the wheel. 'Oh, hang on: show time.'

Voices came from Moosey's house. A couple of young yobs emerged, spraffin' away together and passing a bottle of Woodpecker between them.

'Thought they'd be on the White Lightning,' I said.

'Did you check the clobber?'

'Can hardly miss Tommy Hilfiger lettering a mile high.'

'They're wedged up, those wee bastards.'

'No question.'

As the young crew schlepped down the street, Mac said, 'Recognise any?'

'Nah, not them. They're about fifteen, sixteen . . . The pricks on the hill were older, eighteen at least. I'd clock them straight off too.'

In a minute, another figure appeared. Shuffling and hunched, leaning over a tab as if it was a life-support machine.

I clocked him straight away. It was Sid, though looking a little less sure of himself than on our last meeting.

'That the Sid you know?'

Mac squinted over the steering wheel, peered down to the gate where Sid emerged onto the street. 'That's the Snake all right. No missing the slimy wee bastard.'

'Let's give him a tug.'

Mac took the keys out the ignition. 'C'mon and boost.'

I climbed out the door, caught sight of Mac putting on a pair of black leather gloves. 'What's this? Anticipating bruised knuckles?'

A grunt: 'Worse than that . . . much fucking worse.'

Chapter 20

SID LOOKED SHIFTY. AS HE walked down the street he kept turning left to right as if he expected someone to emerge from one of the half-derelict hovels and lay about him. Mac and I watched the Snake with suspicion.

'What the fuck's he up to?'

'Dunno. All very sus,' I said.

At the end of Moosey's row, Sid turned left and continued down past the high-rises to another street of mainly boarded-up and deteriorating homes. The pack of dogs had migrated to this end of the scheme and were running about, barking and savaging each other and anything else they could get their jaws around. Sid shuffled through them, let out a few shouts to disperse the pack as he reached the gate at the bourne of his own run-down heap.

Mac prodded me. 'Round the back.'

I nodded.

In the alley skirting the street, two teenage girls were buzzing lighter fluid. They didn't look up as we passed, even as I kicked at the canisters around their heels. They were too far gone to register it. I tapped Mac on the arm, shook my head, but he didn't so much as blink.

The back gardens lined up against the street consisted mainly of grass that had grown out of control, a couple of feet high, and the usual schemie detritus – burst couches, wrecked children's toys, rusting engine parts and the occasional burnt-out car. Sid's garden was more orderly. For a kick-off it was secured like Fort Knox – a six-foot fence and razor wire over the top of it.

'What the fuck's with the wire?' I said. As we got closer a volley of deep, vicious barking started to rumble from the garden.

Mac didn't answer. He had a hand-jemmy at the padlock and was already through the gate before I needed to know any more.

The yard was fitted out with some of the same gear as there had been in Moosey's – treadmills, weights and car tyres with teeth-marks in them. There was a kid of about thirteen standing with a six-foot-long flirt-pole, what looked like a dog's tail on the end of it, taunting an angry bull terrier that had been tied to a stake.

Mac grabbed the pole, smacked the kid on the side of the head. 'Beat it, fannybaws.'

The kid shot a hand up to his head, took a look at Mac's face and ran for the gate. I took the flirt-pole from him, looked at the end of it. The dog snarled and strained as I took the tail into my hands. 'That's off a fucking Labrador or something . . . Check it.'

Mac looked uninterested. He'd already located Sid – who was walking towards us. The dog pulled on his rope when he saw his master, his own tail going into motion. Sid carried a racing pigeon in his hands. He saw us in his yard but played it cool: 'Wee bastard, ain't he?'

'The dog?' said Mac. 'He's that.'

'No' a patch on the pit bull, though. Yon forty-two-teeth American's a bastard and a half.' Sid held up the pigeon. 'I do the burds as well . . . but they piss me off. This cunt should have been back two days ago. Fucking no good to me!' He snapped the pigeon's wing in his hand, dropped the bird to the ground and laughed as it flailed about helplessly. 'Fucking no good to me!' He watched the bird complete a few desperate circles, creasing up his hollow cheeks – it was a deep pleasure to him – then he kicked the creature towards the snarling bull terrier.

The dog lunged on the pigeon and caught it in his jaws. He threw it in the air and then pounced on it again before shaking it violently. The dog was still shaking the bird as I looked back at Sid to see him laughing so much he had to take off his big glasses and wipe his eyes.

'You are one sick fuck,' said Mac.

'It's just some fucking fun; a wee bit of sport.'

'You what?'

'Come here.' Sid motioned us over to the wire mesh cages he kept his dogs in. 'Look at that.' He became excited, animated, as he pointed to a fox that was pacing one of the far enclosures. 'Caught that wee bastard under the pigeon hoose the other night . . . Going to make some pagger, that, eh!' He was smiling and laughing, rubbing his hands at the thought.

Mac lost it, 'This guy's a fucking roach . . . You want me to do him?'

I saw Sid reach for the handle of the enclosure that held the dogs. He was too slow. Mac was close enough to throw a wind-mill right, decked Sid. As he lay pegged out on the ground I told Mac to pick him up.

'You better watch yourself, Sid . . . Mac the Knife's got form for this lark.'

I saw the name registered with him. He spluttered, gripped at his collar with his fingernails and yelled, 'What the fucking hell do you want with me?'

'Oh, I think you know . . . You were very reluctant to let me speak to Vera Fulton.'

Mac pressed his forearm hard against Sid's neck. 'You poking her? That what the game is here? You were poking Moosey's wife and decided to do away with him, that it?'

I wanted to congratulate Mac. He was doing a great job of putting the shits up Sid, said, 'All the more attractive a proposition, given Moosey was holding fifty grand of Rab's, eh, Sid?'

'I don't know what you're fucking talking about . . . I don't.'

I glanced at Mac. It was enough. He put a wrecking-ball right into Sid's gut. The gimp bent in two and fell to the ground, clutching at his stomach as though his insides were about to become outsides. Over the chaos the caged dogs went mad, barking and clawing at the wire. I could see a dash of red as the fox tried to leap out. It had no chance.

I bent down, leaned over Sid. His glasses had come off. I picked them up, snapped them in two between the lenses. 'Shame – they're broken . . . Might need a wee bit of Elastoplast for them now.'

Sid wheezed, tried for words. Found none.

'Where did Moosey get the fifty grand?'

Sid struggled to speak, 'It was the takings . . . Rab's takings from the pagger.'

'Dog fights?'

'Aye, aye . . . the whole fifty fucking grand.'

'What was he doing with it?'

'Holding it for Rab. We do the books – we did together – but when Rab went inside, the money was just sitting about.'

'So you and Moosey thought you'd have it?'

'Naw, it wasn't like that . . . We wanted to get it to Rab.'

Mac sighed, said, 'Aye, right . . . and I button up the back.'

He leaned over and grabbed Sid by the collar. Sid kicked out, tried to push him away. 'Call him off. Call him fucking off!'

I nodded to Mac. He dropped him on the flags. Sid collapsed again, panting.

'Speak,' said Mac. 'I can easy fucking pound you into those slabs.'

Sid spoke, 'Moosey was angling for a bigger cut of the game . . . The dog fights have gone mental. The take's pure crazy compared to the auld days.'

'And so Moosey decided to cut you pair in for more?'

'There was no "us pair", I just helped oot. Moosey was Rab's main man. He was talking about getting a bigger cut after Rab got put doon . . . but it was just talk, we didn't . . . he didn't do anything about it.'

I was pretty sure that if Moosey had decided to cut himself in for more, Rab would have put him in the ground. 'Rab found out about this?' I said.

'No chance. No fucking danger. Rab's looking for his money, and he's not fucking happy . . .'

If Rab had done Moosey, he'd have the money. Much as I despised this little arsecrack, he was speaking sense.

Mac pushed in. 'Sid, you are a lying wee cunt. You and Moosey were running Rab's rackets together. Do you expect us to believe you weren't in on it with Moosey?'

'I wasn't. I wasn't. I was just doing the numbers, I never touched the cash – that was all Moosey. Who'd trust me with that kinda wonga? Think I'd still be walking about if Rab thought I had his cash?'

He was a smart talker, I'd give him that. 'So who took the money off Moosey?'

'I don't know. Could be anybody . . . everything's gone mental since Rab got put away. The young crew are knifing each other in the back all the time.'

'Gimme some names.'

'I dunno . . . fucking anybody . . . It's like World War Three oot there, I'm not shitting you.'

The dogs' barking lost its edge, decreased in pitch. I think Sid could sense the danger was over, too. I nodded to Mac to raise him.

'What about the young crew?' I said. 'Is Mark Crawford running with the young mob?'

'Who?'

I showed him the picture on my phone, the one Vera Fulton had already recognised.

'I've seen him about. He's just a laddie; he's no' one of the top men.'

'Did you ever see him with Moosey?'

'No, I didn't.'

'Who's in this young crew, Sid? I want names and addresses.'

'I don't know any of them, I just did the books . . .'

Sid's ponytail had fallen out. His long greasy grey hair fell over his thin face. I grabbed a bunch. 'You better fucking find out. Because the way I see it, Sid, you're up to your nuts in this and if I drop the hint to Rab, you'll be lucky to keep those fucking nuts, you get me?'

He didn't say a word. I released his hair and walked over to the end of the dog enclosure. He watched me standing before the end kennel where the fox was still pacing. 'Mac, gimme that jemmy.'

I turned the jemmy in the padlock and the door swung open. The fox shot past me as if it had been scalded. I watched Sid's mouth droop at the sight of the fox jinxing round the edges of the path, down the yard, and out the gate to some kind of freedom.

Chapter 21

I PLAYED OVER WHAT SID had told us. It almost made sense. Maybe it made too much sense. If Mark Crawford was smart enough to hype up the young crew to do his dirty work – on the promise of a sizeable pay-off – then maybe he never needed to get his own hands dirty.

Mac spoke: 'You're sure the Crawford kid's our best bet?'

'What do you mean? He's got the motive, we have him in the right place at the right time.'

'Aye, right enough . . .'

'No, come on, you don't agree?'

'I'm just not sure . . . I mean why would a kid in that situation – so set-up, from a good background and everything – go and off Moosey?'

'They say Moosey killed his sister.'

'That was years ago.'

'You think it doesn't fester?'

Mac ran fingers through his hair. 'I just think we're missing something . . . Something's not right.'

I knew exactly what he meant. There was much more going on than I'd been able to uncover; there was something sinister beneath the surface. 'Sid's covering up for someone,' I said.

'Himself, probably.'

'You think he's got the balls to off Moosey and take fifty Gs off Rab?'

Mac found the low gears as we got back into the city centre, pulled onto North Bridge. 'He's a sleekit wee bastard. If the opportunity was there, I wouldn't put anything past him.'

'We need to keep an eye on him. He's rattled, so his next move might be interesting.'

'Hod's your man for that. You need to go burst a few heads with the young crew because time's running out.'

I agreed with him, I couldn't rely on Sid to bring us any names. I had a plan for that, though.

'Pull over here.'

We were outside the old Royal High. One of the most impressive buildings in the city, it had been cited as the home of the Scottish Parliament, but we'd opted instead for a half-billion-pound version of a Spanish airport, so now the place was empty, falling into dereliction. I could empathise with that.

'What you up to?'

'Off to see a man about a dog.' I jumped out the van and waved Mac off with a slap on the door.

I followed Regent Road round to the steps of Calton Hill. A bus party of Japanese tourists made the schlep heavy work; I slowed down to a crawl behind them as they pointed to the dome of the Observatory. It had been stripped of its copper for the second time in six months – all that was showing was the wooden support underneath. Thought: What a place.

Up here you can see the whole city. Just about. It's not big by any means. Do a three-sixty and you can take it all in. But from here I always feel part of the history of the place: the grey buildings, the grey skyline – makes me forget we're in a new millennium. The National Monument just adds to it. Reminds me how Scotland's reach has always exceeded its grasp. Think of the Parthenon: that's what they were going for, but ran out of cash. What the city got left with was twelve stone pillars, looking decidedly out of place on a hilltop. Fitting tribute to those who died in the Napoleonic Wars I *don't* think. Fitting tribute to flawed ambition? You bet.

That's us Scots all over. We have ambition in spades; what we don't have is confidence. The ambition only takes us so far, then we fold. Cosy up to our larger, stronger neighbour. Our history is littered with sell-outs.

When I was younger I used to come up here to get wasted. It's a national obsession: get blootered drunk on Buckfast, or some cheapo lager, start bumping your gums about how shit the place we live in is.

When I got older, I came up here with a proper carry-out. Scotland had one decent beer of its own then – Gillespie's. What did we do with it? We dropped it. Stopped making it for no apparent reason. It could wipe the floor with Guinness, and Murphy's too. And we dumped it.

The thing with Scotland, the root of it all, is that we're a defeated nation. The Scots are the Australian Aborigines of Europe. We're the Native American Indians of round here.

I used to wish we could be more like the Irish. They did okay. Never got into bed with the English. Never caved. It's said the difference between the Scots and the Irish is that we moan about all this kind of crap: about having the worst health record of any civilised country in the world, the worst rates of alcoholism, suicide; about being the only country to discover oil and get poorer . . . Whereas the Irish, on the other hand, take action. And fair fucks to them. I mean, at least they've still got the knackers to fight for their country. We just handed ours over. Gave it away.

I looked out to the crags and the castle. We gave this away. We just gave all this away . . . for nothing.

Sometimes, when I come up here now, I'm amazed by the beauty of the city. It's as though my memory of how the place looks gets sealed off and I'm seeing it for the first time again. It holds me. All those old turrets and spires, the hotchpotch of the Old Town, buildings leaning into each other: it seems like another city entirely.

'God, that would be nice,' I whispered.

Debs and I had honeymooned in Paris. I winced to remember. Back then we hadn't two ha'pennies to rub together but after the wedding farce we needed to get away. Carded it. Good old Visatabulous. We really couldn't care how long it took us to pay it off. It was an escape.

I caught sunlight hitting off the Observatory building, shifted focus. More and more now, I knew, I was living in the past. I knew why that was. Anniversaries will do it every time. I didn't want to think about this anniversary. When you have one dark moment from the past that haunts, even when your past is as dark as mine, you lock it away. Hide from it.

I'd been reading a lot of Fitzgerald lately. Wasn't a fan of his prose style, but I could identify with his *Crack-up*. Perhaps more than I wanted to admit. I'd read this: 'In a real dark night of the soul it is always three o'clock in the morning, day after day.' I checked my watch: it was approaching midday, but I knew, like Fitzgerald, it was always going to be three o'clock in the morning for me.

I pulled out my mobi. Debs's number was on the top of my contacts list. I felt I'd put this off long enough. Pressed the call key.

Ringing.

'Hello . . .'

Knew at once she'd not checked her caller ID; or worse, she'd deleted my number.

Softly, I said, 'Hello, Debs.'

Silence.

She didn't hang up, probably thought about it though, tried, 'I need to talk to you.'

Her voice had a familiar timbre. It was the tone a mother uses to talk to a child who's disappointed her time and time again. 'Gus . . . that's not a good idea.'

She caught me blindsided. I felt a flicker in my eyelids, said, 'Hang on – I thought that's what you wanted. You said in the cafe you wanted to talk about, y'know, stuff.'

Her voice raised: 'That was before you were carted away by the police.'

A skirl of bagpipes started on the street below. A cloud passed over the sun and a shadow covered the ground where I sat. 'But you sounded eager to talk. I thought you had something to get off your chest.'

Silence once more.

The gap on the line stretched out. I wondered if I should speak up.

Then, 'Gus, that was before I had to watch you being thrown in the back of a police van . . . again.'

My nostrils flared, I don't know why. Likewise, a spasm shook my head quickly. I knew my anger was ramping up. It was the injustice; it's always the same. It's what fires me. I could do nothing about any of what had happened and here was Debs persecuting me for it.

I felt trapped, said, 'Not my fault, I'm—'

'Innocent,' she cut in, 'yeah, I know.'

Was she being sarky? Down the line I heard a kettle whistle. Movement, cups being rattled on a kitchen surface. I didn't think I had her full attention. I felt like I was talking into an empty phone, or to a call centre maybe, a foreign one where the people on the other end of the line sound as if they're reading a script in a language they don't understand a word of.

'Debs, this isn't a joke.'

'Gus, I know.' Her voice raised on the last word, then, with almost a hint of laughter creeping in, 'Jonny told me.'

I felt like I'd been punched in the guts, a sucker punch I didn't see coming. Said, 'I suppose you think your *new man* is quite a catch . . . Don't be fooled, Debs.'

'Gus, he's not the one facing a murder charge.'

'*Trumped-up* murder charge – that's the phrase you missed out.' I felt my pulse quicken, gone in sixty seconds, that's the hold I have on my temper these days. 'You don't seriously believe I could have killed a man, do you?'

A sigh. Loud enough to get that extra inflection in there, one that says 'Are you for real?' or, worse, 'I don't give a shit'.

'Gus, I have to go.' She was curt.

I snapped, 'Debs, answer the fucking question.'

Another pause.

A deep breath.

She was forcing herself to concentrate on her words, but she was distracted. I wanted to ask if Jonny Come Lately was there with her.

She said, 'Gus, I don't know anything any more.'

'You seriously believe what he's feeding you . . . ? Fuck me!' I'd lost the plot. Gone postal. 'Deborah, I thought you were better than that. Can't you see he's an utter cockhead? . . . He's a cheesy little shiny-arsed bastard with his nose sniffing the K-ladder to the top office . . .' I vented. Full on. Way out of control. 'Fucking hell, Deborah, I thought you had more sense . . . falling for such an utter wanker.'

Finished, I waited for a response.

None came.

I looked at the phone. The time and date flashed beside the battery charge level. She'd hung up.

Said, 'Och, shit.'

I knew I'd blown it. The situation with Debs was worse than I'd thought. I felt panic. If Jonny Johnstone could work such a number on someone like Debs, someone with her head screwed on, someone who actually knew me, someone who shared history with me, then I was seriously up to my neck in the brown stuff.

I put the phone in my pocket. Tipped back my head. The cloud covering the sun had been joined by more. Great black jobs. A wind began to blow. Cold one. The sky was turning purplish at its edges. Threatened rain.

Chapter 22

I KNEW I SHOULD CALL Debs back, say sorry, but I couldn't. I scrolled my phone's contacts and hovered over the green call key again and again but it just wouldn't happen. Couldn't happen. It seemed beyond senseless after all we'd been through together. But so much of that was getting to me now. Kept flooding back . . .

The priest started it, but now everyone's at it. Seems the whole city knows. Wherever we go people stop, stare, shake heads.

'What's your problem?' I say, but Debs wants none of it. My blood's curdling, but she looks the other way. Even when the fag dowps are thrown at us in the street and the name-calling starts.

'Leave it, Gus, just leave it . . . It'll be over soon.'

'No way, Deborah, I'm not having it. What right have they got? We've done nothing wrong . . . we've broken no law.'

I wonder, how long will this last? How long will it be before I am locked up for banjoing someone, or worse? But Debs sails high, holds her head up. I've never admired another soul more. She floats above all the scorn and hate.

Only one thing, the sight of young children pulled to their mothers, gets to her. Brings tears when she remembers, at night, when we're alone.

The bigger kids calling out names she handles, even lets me kick the arse of any who are old enough to know better. But then it all gets too much, even for her, when the word DAMNED is scrawled on our doorstep.

'It's too much, Gus. It's all too much,' she says.

'It's just kids messing,' I say, but she's buying none of it.

'No, it's what they think of us now. We're nothing; we don't exist.' She goes out, gets on her knees. The whole street can see. It's what they want. She rubs and rubs at the step with her coat sleeve.

'Stop, Debs. Come away in.' A crowd forms to watch as her tears fall on the step and get smeared into the jagged letters. 'Debs, you're only putting on a show,' I say.

'Is that what you think I am now?' she says. 'A show?'

'No, Debs.' She's better than all of them; she's borne the taunts with dignity until now. It's scalding my heart to see her brought to her knees before them. What have they done to her? She was once so full of life, more full of it than anyone. It strikes me deep to see her this way, but I think no less of her for it, only more. She is worth more than I deserve.

'You're ashamed of me as well, aren't you?' she says.

'No. No . . . Now stop!' I grab her arm. 'This is what they want – to see you broken.'

She pulls away. 'Well, let them look.' Debs keeps rubbing. Her coat sleeve wears to a hole, her palm bleeds on the step as she forces it back and forth, back and forth. 'Let them see me broken if that's what they want. Are they happy?' She turns to them, yells, 'Are you happy now?'

I put my arms under her and lift her back indoors. She screams out, 'No! No!'

'Debs, it'll be over soon, like you say.'

'No. Gus, no . . . it will never be over,' she wails. Tears roll over her face and then she buries her head in her bloodied and blackened hands. Her sobbing is silent, like all the noise is located deep inside her, wrapped up in her pain, unable to get out. When she removes her hands and tips back her head I look at her face, smeared in blood and dirt, and wonder what to do. Her mouth's open, she's trying to wail but is unable. Her screams stay trapped in her. She seems hollow, like there's nothing left but the deepest misery inside. And I know it will never leave her.

Chapter 23

I CLOSED MY EYES.

Tried to think.

Wasn't happening.

Then I heard, 'Dury.'

The last thing you want to see when you're lying with your head tipped over the back of a park bench is a man with a scarf covering his face. Mirror shades and shoulders wide enough to block out the sky.

I'd trouble adjusting to the picture, he was upside down from my perspective. I spun round, sat upright to front the source of the voice.

'What in the wide world of—'

The scarf moved as he spoke. 'Did you expect me to meet you out in the open, in the full glare of the world?'

'With you, Fitz, I never know what to expect.'

He was dressed head to toe in black. With the shades he looked like Roy Orbison, said, 'Don't tell me . . . you drove all night?'

'What?'

'To get to me?'

'You're bollix mad, Dury!'

Like I'd give him any argument.

Fitz removed his scarf, sat. He took out some smokes, Lambert &

Butler. As he sparked up, he looked out at the city. 'I'd no idea you got such a view from up here.'

'You're not telling me this is your first time on Calton Hill?'

'Och no, been up here once or twice of a night, mainly chasing off junkies shooting up, or some young heller with a bottle of Mad Dog in him who's decided to have a go at the school hog-beast . . . Always turns nasty, that one.'

I was shocked Fitz had only been up the hill on police business. This was the spot on all the postcards, for Chrissake, said, 'You never did the tourist bit when you first got here?'

He put his pale eyes on me, turned down the corners of his mouth. 'Gus, I was an economic migrant back then. I had no feckin' time or money for fannying about on tour buses and the like. Jeez, would ye ever get real there.'

I took the blast as it was intended. Moved on. 'So, what have you got for me, Fitz?'

He turned sideways on the bench, an arm curled around my back. 'Lesser men, in your boots, would get a good fong in the arse.'

'That sounds uncomfortable – ' I made a show of removing his arm – 'and very definitely not my kinda thing.'

'Feck off, Dury, don't be trying to paint me as a spunk-farter, even in jest.'

I got the impression I was noising Fitz up here, so eased off, took out one of my own tabs. I was back on the Mayfair, sound expensive, but the cheapest tabs on the shelf.

Fitz lit me up.

I said, 'Look, I don't expect the file of anything, I'm just—'

A laugh, 'I'm feckin' well glad to hear it because ye have more chance of me joining yon Naked Rambler for a tour round the old country, with a feckin' fridge 'n'all!'

'But I do need some help here, Fitz.' I put just enough edge in my tone to let him know I wasn't going to be fucked over.

He lunged at me, pointed his cigarette like a dart. 'You have no idea how things are stacking up in that station.' He turned, shook his head violently. 'No idea!'

For the second time I eased off. 'Then tell me.'

Fitz jumped to his feet. I was surprised he could move so quickly for a big fella. He was animated now, flicked the barely lit cig onto the ground and leaned over me like some mad puppeteer. 'For a kick-off, Dury, let's just say Jonny Johnstone is well ahead of the game.'

I didn't want to hear this. I told him as much, 'What do you mean?'

Head shake.

'J.J., smart little fecker that he is, has relinquished the case.'

'You what?'

'Right after your little chat. Said he only *unearthed* your relationship with his fiancée during the interview.'

I was relieved, but intrigued, said, 'And this puts me where?'

Fitz laid a foot on the bench, crossed his hands. 'Deeper in the shit.'

This was definitely not what I wanted to hear.

He explained Jonny's aim was a quick confession, that he probably thought he could use the leverage he had with Debs to put pressure on me, force me to crack. It seems my reputation as a hothead went before me. The plan, however, hadn't so much backfired as, well, not gone off at all.

Fitz said, 'It was a risky strategy, Gus, but that's him – a risk taker, a high-wire operator.'

'I don't see how it's worse for me to have Jonny off my back, though.'

'Because, Dury . . .' Fitz stepped away, put out his arms, spread-eagle, 'now McAvoy's on the job.'

The name meant nothing. I ran it through my mind again. Nah, only McAvoy I got was the bloke who tried to buy Celtic with Bono and Jim Kerr about ten years ago. Sure as hell wasn't him.

I said, 'Who the fuck's McAvoy?'

Fitz had been waiting for me to ask, still leaning over me like a praying mantis. He got his bite, said, 'McAvoy's silk. He's the kind of cop Jonny Boy would like to be, but can only dream of.

128

With him leading the case, you're dealing with one hard, smart bastard.'

My guts twisted involuntarily. The thought of Jonny Johnstone on my case was suddenly not such a bad deal.

I said, 'Shit.'

'You're dealing with the best now, Dury.'

I'd never seen Fitz so impressed with anyone. I felt tempted to ask what this guy had done to float his boat, but I knew I needed all the friends I could muster, said, 'Well, at least it can't get any worse now.'

Uproarious laughter, 'Ha! You think?'

'Och, fuck me . . . what now?'

Fitz clapped his hands together. 'McAvoy taught young J.J. all he knows. He's like his . . . prodigy.'

'Protégé.'

'Yeah, whatever . . . Thing is, my worry is Jonny Boy's still gonna be feeding in to the case, unofficially of course, but feeding in nonetheless. He can likely be more of a menace off the case than on it.'

I had nothing to say to this. It was the kind of cruel blow I'd come to expect from life, but it stung like a bastard all the same. I brought out a quarter-bottle of Glenlivet, took a good hit on it.

'Ah, the very stuff,' said Fitz. He wet his lips as I passed over the bottle, took a swig. 'Oh, yes . . . 'tis a fine drop ye have there, Dury. Fine indeed. Not sparing any expense.'

I grabbed it back, belted it. Fitz watched, waiting for another slug, but I put it to my mouth and drained it.

'Man, that's a thirst for ye . . . Have ye always pelted it like yon?'

I stood up, walked the bottle over to the bin, said, 'You're a long time dead.' This phrase is one hundred per cent proof Scots. Only a race like ours could come up with it. Its meaning is interchangeable with 'Fuck it'.

I lolled back over to the bench. Sat down. Fitz joined me. His little piece of street theatre over, he calmed, said, 'So what's your plan, Dury?'

I knew exactly what I needed to do. I needed to get myself off the hook. Finding a cast-iron alibi for my movements on the night of 15 May, *understood*, was next door to impossible. More than ever, I needed to find Moosey's real killer. It wasn't about righting a wrong or restarting my stalled career any more; it was about avoiding being ass-fucked by Jonny Boy and this McAvoy character. I was beginning to wonder why I hadn't followed Mac and Hod's advice to split sooner.

'Well . . . what's it to be?' Fitz pressed.

'First off, tell me all they've got.'

'A wino.'

'Y'what?'

Fitz reached in his pocket, pulled out a little black notebook, read out, 'Male, of indeterminate age, possibly late seventies, goes by the name of Tupac.'

Was he shitting me? 'Tupac?'

He let me hang for a moment, till he was sure he had my full attention. 'He's a fucking tramp. He carries a pack on his back and one on his front, it's what they call him.'

'A paraffin lamp, with two packs . . . Brilliant.'

Fitz tucked away his notebook. 'I can tell you this: yer Tupac fella there saved your bacon on the line-up. He as good as lives on Corstorphine Hill and he's the man that spotted someone with Moosey on the night.'

'Did he now.'

'I'll tell ye, he's nobody's fool either . . . J.J. plied the old soak with Buckfast all night before that line-up and he still never did as he was told.'

I liked the sound of this Tupac already. 'A true gentleman of the road.'

Fitz tied his scarf round his neck, said, 'More likely angling for a feckin' barrel of the stuff. His type are always after something for feckin' nowt.' He stood up. 'Right, I'm offski.'

I was still digesting this information, planning my next move. I almost forgot I had one more task for Fitz. I put up a hand. 'Before you go, can you check something for me?'

A glower. Bite of lower lip. The saggy jowls started to tremble as Fitz stoked himself for another display of dramatics. 'Dury, yer pushing yer feckin' luck.'

I raised myself from the bench. 'Can you run a search for a white Corrado, address likely as not in Sighthill?'

There was a bit of a nod. He didn't look too fazed by the suggestion. I pressed my luck further. 'If there's a file on the owner, it'd be good to get a look at it too.'

'Are ye off yer feckin' head, Dury?' His face coloured round the edges; his mouth slit into a crease. 'I can't go putting yer every hunch through the system without good reason.'

I moved forwards, faced him, said, 'Here's one, then – your wife's lovely garden.'

He went white. 'I'll feckin' do for ye one of these days, boyo. I swear, I swear . . .'

I put my hands in my pockets, spoke softly: 'Fitz, pull your head in. You're in your heart-attack years – don't give yourself a coronary.'

He waved a fist at me. His knuckles were white now as well. 'Dury, what I will do is give ye some good advice, for free, mind: watch yer feckin' back!'

I smiled, said, 'I do that anyway.'

'I mean close to home . . . Your ex is on the other side now. Remember that.'

Chapter 24

I AWOKE IN UTTER BLACKNESS. Beyond dark. Felt like Gregor Samsa from Kafka's 'Metamorphosis'. Remember the one? Gregor opens his eyes one morning to find he's been transformed into an insect. His family outside are banging on the door telling him to get up, get out, get to work. Gregor, however, is too busy struggling with his numerous legs and new, hard, armour-plated bulk. When I remember this story, the part that strikes hardest is that Gregor's room, his surroundings, the world he knows, remain unchanged. It's him alone that's been altered, fucked up. The world is indifferent.

As I lay staring into the darkness, I knew I was in a world of shit. And it was mine alone. A personal hell I'd devised for myself. I was trapped in my very own insect body. I couldn't move. I felt swaying beneath me, all around, but I was paralysed.

Was it fear?

Was it panic?

Anger turned in?

Worse – it was all of the above. I felt trapped.

I'd read Kafka endlessly as a teenager. Right into my twenties and thirties I'd always picked up the latest biographies. He was a man who knew suffering. Not like mine, not self-inflicted. But suffering is suffering and I understood Kafka right from an early age.

I'd once read he had asked to have his stomach pumped, purely because he 'had a feeling disgusting things would come out'.

I empathised with that kind of self-loathing.

I'd memorised these words of Kafka's: 'God knows how I can possibly feel any more pain, since in my sheer urgency to inflict it upon myself I never get round to perceiving it.' I must have read that passage a thousand times. Always with a sense of sorrow and, dangerously, identification. I identified with Kafka's pain. He knew he had an illness and it would kill him. I did too.

Lately I'd seen my thoughts go way beyond their usual angry depression. I was nudging despair. The kind that has only one conclusion. Like Kafka I thought, God knows how I can possibly feel any more pain . . .

I lay for an hour until light started to stream through the small windows of Hod's boat. I'd made the decision to move out of the Holy Wall whilst plod had a tail on me. I figured the boat would be the best bet. Hod had warned me about people having difficulties sleeping in the swaying berth. I'd set him straight on that score: when you're an alcoholic, the swaying bed is something you get used to pretty early on. It's when the bed doesn't sway that you have difficulties.

I rose and showered in the small cabin. The water was tepid. Scrub that, the water was cold. The all-over shivers came afterwards, but again these were something I could live with. Another by-product of my particular disease that I was well and truly used to.

I dressed in a grey marl T-shirt, one of Gap's finest. It had the little pocket on the breast just perfect for a pack of smokes. I finished the look with a pair of navy Dockers and my Docs, which I'd scrubbed clean of Tam Fulton's blood. There was a bit of a nip in the air so I borrowed a Berghaus windcheater from the back of the cabin door whilst I heated up the stove and got some coffee going. It was instant but better than I was used to. It tasted like the three-pound-a-cup jobs from up the road. In this part of the city, by the marina on the shore, it was millionaire central.

When I was a lad, kicking about in Leith, my brother and I

thought a millionaire was someone you read about in books. The thought of my actually meeting a millionaire back then was on a par with meeting a Tyrannosaurus rex. To look around now at the number of yachts and Porsches in our small city numbed my mind better than a bottle and a half of Wild Turkey. Some people were doing very well out of the gang rape Thatcher, Major, Blair and Brown had inflicted on this country. The flip side, of course, was some were headed exactly the opposite way.

I knew I was close to home and I felt a pressing need to check on my mother. She was older now, and looking frail the last time we had met. I didn't think she was handling my father's death well; she should have been relieved, singing from the rooftops. I knew *I* was. But my mother was a very different person to me: she could forgive.

I made a phone call.

Ringing.

A young male voice: 'Aye-aye.'

'Who's this?' I demanded.

'Barry. How, who the fuck are you?'

It was my nephew. I recognised the name but it had been more than a few years since I'd seen hide or hair of my sister's boys. They had always been spoilt; it didn't sound like the years had improved this one any.

'Gus. What are you doing using language like that on your grand-mother's phone?'

He slammed the receiver down on the table. I heard him banging on a door and hollering at my mother. I was beyond enraged. 'Hello ... *hello* ...'

It took several minutes for my mother to come to the telephone.

'Hello,' she said. Her voice was strained, bereft of emotion, energy.

'Mam, you sound terrible.'

A cough. I heard her reaching for her asthma inhaler. 'I'm fine.'

'Clearly you're not ... Are you back on the inhaler?' She hadn't used it for years; I knew she was stressed.

'I just had a wee turn there and—'

I did not want to hear this. Pelted her with questions: 'Mam, are you okay now? Should I come round?'

She was quick to respond. 'No, no . . . I'm fine, Angus.'

'Is Catherine with you?'

'Och, no . . . just the boys, I'm looking after the boys.'

The boys were old enough to look after themselves. Christ alone knew what they were doing there. 'Catherine's lads must be sixteen now, Mam.'

Silence.

I worried about that.

'Mam, I'm staying nearby . . . I'll pay you a wee visit soon.'

'No, Angus.' She sounded fearful. 'Don't do that.'

I heard her reach for the inhaler again. I didn't want to upset her any more. 'Okay, okay. Just look after yourself, Mam.'

She calmed. 'I will. I will.'

'Okay, Mam. Be well.'

I cried off, feeling nothing but deep misgivings about the call. I needed to pay my mother a visit soon. Whether she wanted me to or not.

I was rattled, checked about the boat for a stowaway bottle of scoosh to top up my coffee. I found some empties, but nothing I could put to use.

I had a habit to feed; my nerves were jangling. I tanned the coffee and hit the street.

The scaffies were out, hosing down the pavement. I liked the aura of early morning – it felt like the end of the world, which suited my mood. Orange streetlights still fizzed away overhead; occasionally a whole street of lights would go out and jolt my senses. Though the roads were empty, every now and again white van man came rattling over the cobbles as he went to drop off the morning papers. In days gone by you might have seen a postman . . . how things have changed.

I knew a pub off Constitution Street that opened at six in the a.m. It was a tradition for the dockers to come off the night shift, get a pint on the way home. Now it was full to bursting with jakeys and addicts. Boys just off the boat looking for a bit of Dutch courage before assessing their first move in a new city.

I put in an order: 'Pint, chaser – double it.'

The pint was poured in quick time, no standing period, slung before me by a heavyset barman who had all the sympathy of a contestant on *Runaround*.

I put the double to bed smartish, let the pint go down slower. When it hit the halfway mark I downed it and left the bar. I could have stayed till closing but I had a different mission today – to find Tupac.

If there were buses going down this end of town at this time, I didn't see any. Blame the trams. Edinburgh had signed up for a £700 million new tram system, the installation of which entailed the ripping-up of Leith Walk. Traders were going out of business every day of the week. But they were sole traders. As if the powers that be gave a fuck about anyone that wasn't one of their *players*.

I schlepped through the town. I needed the air anyway, but could have done without the exercise. Sure, I needed that too. However, whether I could handle it was another question. I got as far as the west end of Princes Street when I decided enough was enough, flagged a Joe Baxi and took the road out past the zoo to Corstorphine Hill. I had Fitz's description of Tupac to go on, that and the fact that he 'lived on the hill' would make him easy to find. Surely.

I schlepped all over, through dub and mire. It felt unsettling to be back near the scene of Moosey's murder. The place I once knew as a beauty spot had changed; more and more this city was revealing its true nature to me. In the most brutal ways imaginable. Try as they might to paint the place as a capital of culture, as 'genteel' Edinburgh, I knew the real deal. They could stick their tartan troosers, their tea towels with the castle on, and the Scott Monument shortbread tins, I knew what this joint was made of, and it was rotten through.

I thought of the absurdity of my situation. Corrupt police were putting me in the frame for a man's murder – a man who was widely believed to have been responsible for a toddler's brutal killing that the courts couldn't make stick. And now, here I was, in city parkland, chasing down a septuagenarian witness who was living rough in one of the richest countries in Europe. If we'd had a Scottish Enlightenment in Edinburgh I missed that meeting. The state of the city made me want to spit bullets.

I marched on but by midday I was ready to jack it, then I found what in my boyhood would have been called a den. A rough shelter under a tree, an old bit of carpet laid down and a few sheets of chipboard to keep out the elements. I pulled a pile of newspapers down and made myself an approximation of a chair. I settled into a David Goodis novel that I was carrying, *The Moon in the Gutter*, and waited for Tupac to return.

I was rereading the last page of the book, skipping back and looking for the bit where the story gets wrapped up in a neat little bow and delighted to find it wasn't there, when a figure loomed out of the distance. It was an old man, bent over with a heavy rucksack on his back and a smaller, though equally well stuffed, one on his front.

I stood up, crossed the ground to meet him and gave a wave. 'You'd be Tupac, then.'

Chapter 25

HE WAS AN OLD SOAK with a nose you could open bottles with and he must have been seventy-five if he was a day. His face was girded with burst veins, red patches and the kind of battered features you associate with a life on the road. Tupac ran a gnarled hand over his forehead, fingers yellow with nicotine, nails yellower yet, said, 'Christ, I've never been so popular.'

I offered him my hand to shake. 'I'm Gus . . . Gus Dury.'

He smiled, so wide his one tooth in the side of his gob got an airing. It looked like a tombstone dangling over his jaw. 'The fella from the papers!'

I felt a warmth suffuse my cheeks. 'Aye, that's me.'

'I saw your story, the murder thing.' He waved his hand over the hill, like he was signifying his own estate, then removed his heavy packs and hid them behind the den, covering them with the chipboard and some branches. 'I've followed a few of your stories over the years, but it's been a while since I mind seeing you.'

Why I felt surprised to hear a tramp had been reading the papers, when his shelter was stacked with them, I'd no idea, said, 'Yeah, well, sometimes it's a long time between drinks.'

Tupac smacked his lips; I'd caught his attention. He spoke: 'Sometimes it is that.'

I played up to him. 'I was wondering if I could get you a pint

. . . It's a chat I'm after really, but if you've got the time for a quick jar . . .'

He yelled, excited as a five-year-old, 'I'll take ye up on the offer, Gus Dury!'

The barmaid looked about eighteen, an age group I'd been paying a lot of attention to these days. Not perving, far from it. On top of the dog-abusing little bastards I had my eye out for, and the anniversary that Debs had reminded me was on the way – as if I needed reminding – there was also the lingering feeling of my own mortality creeping up on me.

In the last few years I had aged terribly. I'd managed to skip the whole bloated, pot-bellied, middle-age-spread deal and go straight to gaga decrepitude. I woke in agonies of aches running the length of my body. My back alone took an hour or so each morning to become usable. In the last few weeks I'd also started to suffer terrible blackouts. I'd had those before on the drink but my memory had always remained patchy throughout them. Now each blackout brought . . . nothingness.

Still, I liked to fool myself it was all a matter of signing off the sauce for a few weeks. A bit of healthy eating, taking up my five portions, maybe, dare I say it, exercise. If I could grab some rays while I was at it, surely that would be all I needed to fire myself back to the level of health I'd previously enjoyed.

Surely it would.

Like fuck it would.

I knew I'd played Russian roulette with my body and my mental well-being for so long that I was beyond saving. I was a washed-up wreck and no amount of denial was going to paper over those cracks.

I played a line from Blake: 'The road of excess leads to the palace of wisdom.' Nice try, son.

I knew the real facts of the matter – the road of excess leads to the road of excess.

'That'll be six-fifty,' said the barmaid.

I stared at my new buddy. He didn't look like he'd eaten. I said, 'You could do with some meat on those bones.'

'No, no. I'm fine on the pint.'

I sensed he was being polite. I pushed the issue, 'A bowl of soup?'

The barmaid backed me up, 'It's Scotch broth . . . and it comes with soda bread.'

Tupac put his face close to my own. His breath could turn milk, 'Maybe a bowl of broth would be just the trick.'

I could tell this was all very embarrassing for him, but he had such an air of humanity that the barmaid didn't even acknowledge his battered appearance, the rank smell coming from him. Truth told, she probably thought we were just another pair of jakes making the most of giro day.

She left us with a smile. Flash of bright blue eyes. She was a heartbreaker; I wanted to look out for her. God, you're getting on when you look at eighteen-year-old girls and feel protective of them. I wondered about myself again.

'This is really very good of you, sir,' said Tupac.

'Holy shit, don't call me that!'

'Och sorry. It'll make you feel like your father, eh?'

If he'd done that, he'd have a sore face right now. There was little on this earth likely ever to make me feel like the late Cannis Dury.

I said, 'Call me Gus – it's my name.'

'Are you a Fergus or an Angus?'

I rolled that one over, said, 'Well, officially I'm an Angus . . . but only one person calls me that.'

'That would be your mother.'

'Spot on.'

'Mothers are precious things. Mind her well.'

I knew what he meant; it put shards of ice in my veins. I'd been far from mindful of my mother since my father had passed. Sure, I never saw eye to eye with the man – he was a tyrant, the ogre of my boyhood – but my mother had given her life to him and now that he was gone, well, it didn't bear thinking about.

140

Tupac's eyes moistened. 'I remember my own dear mother . . . sweet, sweet lady she was.'

'We all have an affection for our mothers, us lads.'

The jakey crossed his fingers together, uncrossed them. Started to fiddle with an old watch strap on his arm. There was no watch to be seen. 'My mother was an equestrian.'

The word shocked me, seemed to be too eloquent for him. 'She was?'

He glowed as he remembered his mother. 'She won prizes, rosettes.' He smiled. 'We had a room of the house full to the rafters with them, all colours they were – red, blue, yellow, green.'

His image stung me. My own father had medals and trophies galore. And what a price we'd all paid for them. My mam especially. She'd been hurting when I last spoke to her; I knew I'd neglected her since my father died. The thoughts mashed about my insides, forced black hurts into my mind. Jesus, Gus, what a terrible son you have been to her. A terrible son and husband both. I thanked the heavens I had never been a father as well.

The waitress brought the soup, laid it down on the table. A plate of bread, pan loaf, was sat beside it. The bread had been spread with margarine, nice and thick. 'I'm so sorry, we've finished the soda bread,' said the girl.

The old boy smiled, said, 'Nae worries at all. Thank you from the bottom of my heart, love!' As the girl blushed and retreated, Tupac rose from the table and blew her a kiss. 'You bring a rare presence to a room, my dear,' he announced.

She dropped her head, but her eyelids shot up.

'Take it as a compliment,' I said.

'That's how it's meant, lass,' said the old jakey, 'that's how it's meant . . . It's a blessed talent to move an old man's heart by just being there.'

I though this fella was some character. He had a warmness and sociability that's rare these days. I thought to pry, ask his name, his story. I knew it would only depress the shit out of me, though. He'd have some yarn about how he was once this or that and then

141

there'd be a dreadful incident, a fall from grace. I'd heard it all before. It was too depressing to hear again. In this city, there are thousands of stories just like it.

He fired into the broth, tipping up the bowl. His thumb touched the rim, dipped in the soup.

'Now, Angus, won't you join me in a bowl of this fine broth?'

I shook my head, said, 'No thanks.'

'But you have the look of a man who has missed a few meals of late.'

Here we go, story of my life. People wanting to fatten me up. It would never happen. I have what they call a fast metabolism. The jeans I wore were thirty-twos . . . and loose. 'I'm fine, really. I've got very little appetite.'

'Your appetites are elsewhere.'

Now he had my number.

'Look, eat the soup. Enjoy it. You have appetite enough for the two of us,' I said.

That seemed to do the job. He slurped away, finished the lot, mopped it up with the bread.

'A fine repast, my good son.'

When he called me 'son', my heart kicked in me. My own father never referred to me that way. When he used the word it appeared in the phrase *no son of mine.*

'Are you still hungry?'

'No, no. I am sated . . . but you, I believe, sir, are not.'

I couldn't deny it. 'You know why I wanted to talk to you, Tupac?'

His narrow shoulders seemed to creep closer together as he pushed the plate away. He sat facing me like a gargoyle. 'I have a fair assumption it's about the murder.'

'They had you down the station.'

'Them bastards have had me down there more than once,' he sparked up, rose from his seat again and hollered to the room, 'the bastards! Bastards to a fucking man!'

I flagged him sit. He apologised.

'Not a paid-up member of the constabulary's fan club, then?'

'They wanted me to perjure myself. I may have no respect for the bastards that enforce the law of the land, but I've a damn sight more respect for the law of this land.'

He scratched his palm, looked at his fingernails. They were black to a one. The Scots have a habit in this situation of blurting, *You could grow potatoes in there*. I resisted the training, said, 'What did they ask you to do?'

He twisted in his chair. 'They wanted me to finger you.'

I took up my pint, drained the last of it. I had a wee goldie waiting, I hit that too. 'Did they now?'

'I'd sooner cut my own fucking throat . . . I played them, though, by God I played them for a power of grog.'

I smiled, it was forced. His revelations weren't exactly heart-warming. 'Good on you.' I gathered myself. 'But you must have saw me there that night.'

'That I did, but you showed long after the chaos.'

'Chaos?'

His face lit up like a gas lamp, the one tooth sticking out over his lower lip. 'I see things on that hill, y'know.'

'Like what?'

He grew indignant. His jawline showed through the thick thatch of matted beard. 'The fella what got killed . . . he'd been up the hill before, many times, digging out fucking badgers. They pit them against dogs, y'know.'

I'd been up there to catch them in the act myself, but it didn't stop my insides churning at the thought.

'Fucking flushed the poor creatures out with terriers, that bastard did. He hit them with a bastarding spade and caged them.'

I was sickened. But my voice trembled for other reasons; I couldn't get away from the fact that the filth had tried to fit me up. My words didn't come out smoothly, 'Our victim, he wasn't alone the times you saw him, was he, Tupac?'

Head shaking, vigorous. 'No. He never was. Always had a gang of little shits with him.'

'What about the night of the murder? Did you see him then?'

He lurched in his seat, slapped a palm on the table. 'That I did!'

I felt my adrenaline spike. 'Did you tell the police?'

Again, 'That I did!'

Another spike, 'What did you tell them?'

He seemed pleased with himself. 'That I saw him up there with the gang of boys. They were all coming and going all the night in the car . . . what a commotion it was.'

I couldn't take in what I was hearing, said, 'Look, did you see the actual . . .'

His ardour dimmed, his mouth twisted. 'No. I did not. I've seen so much carrying-on up there that I tire of it. I left them to their own devices.'

I'd been going for broke, but what he'd given me was enough. I'd established that I wasn't the only witness to place the yobs on the hill. What I needed was Tupac to get me off the hook and there was still some hope he could do just that.

I pulled out my mobi, located the picture of Mark Crawford. 'Did you see him on the night?'

Tupac squinted, held the phone in his hands like it was a delicate treasure. 'I saw him. I saw him with the gang of little shits the night that fella was killed. I'm sure as eggs he was there; I'd know them wee bastards anywhere.'

As I put away the phone, Tupac spoke up again, 'You know I told the police that I saw you come along later on. The commotion had long passed and I heard the car come back and then when I was out I saw you coming down the side of the hill like a great fucking stone falling.'

'You told them all this?'

'I told them you were the one that fell on the dead fella . . . that he was long gone when you came on the scene.'

I didn't know whether to feel relieved or gutted. Tupac was my alibi, but the filth didn't want to know.

I rose, handed him over a tenner, said, 'Here, get yourself a pint.'

His eyes widened. 'Thank you very much, Angus.'

144

I peeled off another tenner, then another, handed him a bunch of them. 'And feed yourself up, get yourself a slot at the hostel for a few days. You might be better out of sight for a wee while.'

His eyes burned like candle wicks.

'I . . . I . . . don't know what to say.'

'Say nothing – it's all owed to you. Tupac, I want you to lay low for a few days, stay off the hill, and when you get yourself settled give me a call on this number.' I scribbled down my mobi on a beer mat, handed it to him.

He looked at the piece of card, open-mouthed.

'When you're settled give me a call.' My heart was pumping. I could see this all being exposed in a lengthy article for Rasher at some point down the track. 'I'll come and pick you up as soon as I get things sorted and we'll go and make this statement to a lawyer . . . Okay?'

He nodded, stood up. As he walked out of the bar I saw the elbows poking from the sleeves of his jacket.

'Hey, c'mere . . .'

He trudged back in a dream.

'Take this.'

I gave him Hod's Berghaus windcheater; like he'd miss it. I justified it to myself as wealth redistribution.

'No, I can't, I can't take any more.'

I thrust it on him, said, 'Of course you can.'

'But . . .'

'No buts. No arguing.'

He put it on, stuck his hands in the pockets. Pulled out a pack of Marlboro, red top.

'Ah, my smokes.'

I took them from his hand. He watched me.

I said, 'You smoke?'

A nod.

I handed back the pack.

Silence.

He turned for the door in a daze.

145

I called out, 'Hey, what's your real name, Tupac?'

A complete halt, stalled in the bar by the door, said, 'It's Kenneth.'

'Just like the old king of Scotland!'

He smiled, weakly. 'Do you mean MacAlpin . . . or Dalglish?'

It was my turn to smile, said, 'Take your pick.'

He seemed to brighten. Then went through the door and back to the street.

Chapter 26

I SETTLED IN MY CHAIR and tipped the last of the goldie down my neck. As the whisky burn hit my stomach I sensed another strange glow, something I hadn't felt since my last visit to the nick . . . it was the return of the feeling that I might crack this case. I could see Jonny Johnstone being cuffed and stuffed in the back of a van – quite an eye-opener that would be for him. But the shiny-arsed little ponce had it coming. I knew now this was more than just a matter of stiffing me to better ingratiate himself with Debs, or, for that matter, to boost his self-worth to make him feel better than his future wife's ex-husband. Jonny was up to his neck in some serious trouble. I didn't know where any of this was leading but I felt charged with fire to find out. Whoever Jonny was protecting knew exactly who had murdered Moosey, and why. I'd make it my life's mission to discover who that person was, and just what the fuck they had over Jonny Johnstone.

As I stood up, the girl behind the bar screamed.

It was an ear-splitting scream, the kind of noise that cuts straight to some deep-rooted primeval instinct.

I ran to her. 'Jesus, girl, what's the matter?'

She was trembling, staring straight out the window at the front of the bar. 'They just drove off . . .'

I lifted the bar top and walked round beside her. Some people had come from the kitchen now. 'What is it?' I said.

'The car, the car . . .' She pointed to the window.

As I looked out my own life seemed to flash before my eyes. Tupac was lying in a heap in the middle of the road. I left the girl shaking, ran out of the pub.

Two American tourists were standing by the side of the road. A tall man stood over Tupac, trying to loosen off his collar. By the time I reached the road the man had removed his jacket and placed it under Tupac's head.

'Tupac . . . Tupac, can you hear me?' I put my hand on his face, he was cold. He didn't seem to be breathing.

'Someone should call an ambulance,' said the tall man.

One of the Americans appeared at my back. It was the woman. 'Oh my God . . . Oh my God!' She kept repeating the words over and over.

'Would you shut the fuck up, woman!' I yelled. The other American came and led her away.

'What happened?' I said.

'A car just knocked him into the air . . . It was parked over there.' The tall guy pointed to the car park. 'You should have seen the reek off the tyres – he must have been waiting for him . . . Knocked him right into the air he did.'

I looked at Tupac, he was turning blue. I tried to encourage him round by gently tapping at his cheeks, but he didn't respond. There was blood seeping from his mouth and a pool behind his head.

'Where's the fucking ambulance?' I yelled.

I stood up, I couldn't bear to look at him any more. I walked to the edge of the road and back again. A crowd formed around the dirty, unwashed heap in the road that was Tupac. I approached the tall man, pulled him aside. 'Did you see the car?'

'Yes, yes, I saw it all . . .'

'What kind of car was it?'

'Oh, I don't know, a small one . . . white. Quite an age I think but well looked after.'

'Was it a Corrado?'

'I couldn't say, yes, maybe . . . oh, I don't know.'

I started to get frustrated with him. 'What do you mean, you don't fucking know? . . . You know what a Corrado looks like, surely.'

He backed away from me. He had a look in his eye that said he felt I was deranged. 'I really couldn't say.'

I caught his arm, pulled him back. 'What about the driver?'

'I didn't see the driver.' He was edging away again, stepping backwards.

'Just tell me if it was a male or a female driver.'

'I couldn't say . . . I really couldn't say.'

I was frantic now, burst it: 'You really are a lot of fucking use, you lanky streak of piss.'

The man took one more look at me and just about sprinted off to the car park. I started to grab people at random. 'Did you see the driver? . . . What about you? . . . Did anyone see the driver?'

The American woman called out, 'It was a young man, a young man was driving the car. He had a hood on but I could see his face clearly . . . It was a young man driving the car and he drove over that poor guy with a grin on his face.' She started to cry, was comforted by the guy with her. 'I'll never forget the way he looked for the rest of my life.'

I wanted to scream out. To punch someone, to kill.

The ambulance came belting down Corstorphine Road, blue lights blazing, siren blaring. I pushed through the crowd. Tupac's face was almost black now. A middle-aged woman was holding his hand. I crouched down beside him, whispered, 'Tupac, mate, here's the cavalry . . . You're going to make it. You're going to make it.'

As I said the words the woman put down Tupac's hand, placed it over his chest and stood up. 'Son, he's already gone.'

I stayed there on the ground.

'Son,' the woman said, 'the old man's gone . . .' She rested her hand on my shoulder and spoke in the kindest of tones. 'Come away, lad . . . There's nothing you could have done.'

149

As I stood up two paramedics ran from the ambulance. One held a red medical case and the other a folded-up stretcher. I watched for a few moments as they worked around Tupac on the road. It didn't take them long before they started to shake their heads.

I felt like sand had been poured in my limbs. I was rigid, unmoving.

A red blanket was placed over Tupac's head. The paramedics placed him on the stretcher and lifted him up. He looked a surprisingly light load . . . not much to him under all those layers of clothes.

'Stop,' I said as the stretcher was carried away. I reached under and touched Tupac's small hand. It was cold as stone. I'd only known him a few hours but that was long enough for him to have touched my soul.

My Adam's apple rose and fell involuntarily. Everything had happened so fast, I just couldn't take it in. 'Tupac, I'm so sorry,' I said. 'I'm so sorry.'

Chapter 27

I SPENT FOUR DAYS NEAR-COMATOSE with drink.

Whisky was bought by the crate.

But nothing dimmed the memory of Tupac's death. I just couldn't shake the sight of him lying there in the road, a heap of nothing more than dirty old clothes and shattered bones in a pool of blood.

I was responsible for the death of an innocent man. A man who had been bruised and battered by this life, in more ways than even I could imagine, had met his end as a result of me. And how he had gone. God, he didn't deserve that.

'Please, God, say it was all a dream and take me instead,' I had ranted.

Even now, semi-sober, I'd have swapped places with Tupac. Not to rid me of the guilt – I'd gladly keep that, I deserved it – but just to restore some sense of right to this fucked-up world that knows nothing but wrong.

I settled into my bunk on the boat. Usual had been left behind with me when I'd refused company and become too aggressive to deal with, even for Mac. The dog kept smacking a squeaky hotdog toy off my leg. It was endearing for the first couple of seconds, then it got annoying. He sat with the toy, eyes on me, salivating down either side of the hot dog then, in a fit of activity, pounced and slapped me with it, saliva spraying all ways.

151

'Christ, dog, can't you give me peace?'

Those eyes again.

Guilt.

'Okay, okay . . . c'mere.'

I grabbed the toy, held it for a moment whilst Usual growled and clung on for dear life, I raised him off the ground but he still hung on by his chops to the toy.

'You're mad, animal . . . do you know that?'

Our playtime was interrupted by my mobi ringing.

'Hello.'

'Gus, is that you?'

I recognised the voice. 'Mr Bacon.'

'Hello, Gus.'

Rasher did not make social telephone calls to me. A good job, because I was in no mood for small chat.

'We need to talk,' he said.

After feeding him the scoop of the year I had, admittedly, gone a bit quiet. 'Look, I'm not really in a position to write up what I've got yet . . . Soon as I get some publishable conclusions, though, you'll be the first to know.'

'I'm glad to hear it, but we really need to talk, Gus.'

I was intrigued. 'We do?'

'Definitely.'

I played along. 'All right, say when.' Usual raised himself on his hinds, slapped the wet hotdog on my leg. It squeaked.

'Well, what about later this evening? We have a function room booked for some training shite at the Salisbury – do you know it?'

The Salisbury used to be called the Meteor back in its spit-and-sawdust day. Hod's firm had been called in to tart it up, help them cut a slice of the city's booming conference trade. 'Yeah, I know the place.'

'Great, can you make it about eight for eight-thirty?'

'No problem.'

I took Usual out for a walk around the docks. Caught sight of a few Ministry of Defence frigates but it was a sad scene all round.

A far cry from the bustling days of old. Still, the dog seemed delighted. He wouldn't be so delighted tomorrow, the time had come for him to go back to the vet and have those stitches removed.

Back on the boat, I cracked the seal on a bottle of Grouse. The low-flying birdie hit the spot.

I let the whisky dim my world view for a few hours until the clock on the wall told me it was time to go back out among the living. I perished the thought.

I put out some dinner for Usual, made him sit, then dashed for the door while he was preoccupied.

It was still light out but the warmth of the day had evaporated, replaced by a northern wind that set the hairs on the back of my hands twitching. The first cab I flagged wasn't for stopping. The second was a bit keener.

At the Salisbury I clocked Rasher's old Daimler out front. I had my suspicions about this meeting, but I figured more than anything there might be some kind of information that would be of use. I'd been licking my wounds for long enough. There'd been two murders already – was I going to just let the tally go up?

One of my suspicions was more of a fantasy, I admit it. The idea that Rasher was about to offer me my job back on the strength of one article was a fallacy, but I soaked it up anyway. What else did I have? The thought of being wanted was a feeling I hadn't known for a while. One thing was for sure, I was gonna ride it to the end of the line.

At the front desk, I asked where the newspaper's function suite was. The receptionist scanned me with contempt. Her make-up was trowelled on worse than Amy Winehouse's; she annoyed me just as much too. She opened the big book in front of her and huffed, 'There is no function.'

'Excuse me?'

'You said *function* . . . from the newspaper.'

'Aye, Mr Bacon's the editor. I saw his car out front.'

Looks askance: 'No. Nothing at all.' Then the killer, eyes up and down, 'And who might you be?'

I was on the verge of walking, but somewhere in my mind the delusion of myself and Debs, happily connected, settled, me working back at the paper and my shit together, flashed before my eyes. I said, 'Dury . . . Gus Dury.'

A flicker behind those contemptuous beads. 'Ah, I see. It's you.'

'I'm sorry?'

A smirk. 'Through the restaurant, first door on the left.'

'Thank you.'

There were some diners who looked up when I passed their tables, but mostly they kept to themselves. The older lot seemed to be the clientele the place was going for. Felt like wading through waves of grey.

At the door, I decided against knocking, walked in.

I couldn't believe my eyes.

First to spot me was my mother, looking more frail than I'd seen her in years. I almost had to do a double-take. She shuffled over and held me by my arm. 'Hello, Angus.'

'Mam, what the hell is this?'

Everyone was there: Hod, Mac, Debs, Rasher, my sister Catherine and my brother Michael; even some people I hadn't seen for years, old friends of the family I could hardly put names to.

'Mam, is everything okay? I was worried. I meant to visit you . . .'

She hushed me, motioned to a chair that had been laid out in the middle of the room, a row of others emanating back from it. I was told to sit in the hot seat. The others followed. To a one they looked stern.

I sat.

Felt my pulse quicken.

Rasher was the first to speak. Everyone sat watching, except for Mac, who told Rasher to stand.

'Gus,' Rasher said, 'do you know why you're here?'

I shook my head, said, 'Well, unless Michael Aspel's about to appear with a big red book, I have to confess, I'm scoobied.'

Rasher went on, 'Gus, your friends and family have staged this little event as a wake-up call to try and—'

Mac interrupted, 'Gus, this is an intervention!'

'A what?' Had I heard right?

Rasher waved Mac down. 'Yes, well, that's one way of putting it . . . We're here to make you aware of our concern for you, Gus.'

Hang on – was I hearing this? Mr Bacon, concerned about me? I wasn't buying it.

'Whoa! Back up. Can you cut to the chase here? I'm not overly familiar with this concern you're talking about.'

Mac rose. 'Gus, this is an alcoholic's intervention . . . We're here to shock you into taking some steps.'

Now I got the picture. Alcoholic's intervention. I'd heard nothing like it. The image I had stored in my head of Rasher presenting me with a contract, his fat hand poised, pen gripped over it as he asked me to sign, suddenly vanished. There would be no job offer, no new life. It was all dreams.

I looked to Debs. She stared at the floor. I knew she'd been dragged along for this, I felt nothing but sympathy for her. How could anyone ask her to do this, after what I'd put her through? I felt massive rage – I wanted to fire it at someone.

I stood up quickly, the chair went flying at my back.

I heard my mother gasp. 'Angus, please hear the man out.'

'No, Mam, this is stupid.'

'Now, Gus, I appreciate it must be a shock,' said Rasher.

'Shock! I'll give you shock, you deceitful bastard.'

Hod rose. 'Gus, c'mon, man, give it a chance.'

Mac followed him, put his oar in. 'People have come a long way here, Gus. You have to give them their say.'

I pointed a finger at him, but words failed me. I turned for the door.

As I stormed through the restaurant I heard Debs's voice call me, 'Gus, Gus, wait up.'

I didn't stop.

Grey heads bobbed up all over the place this time.

In the car park Debs finally caught me, grabbed my jacket and spun me round. 'I told them it was a daft idea.'

'Oh, they listened to you.'

She turned down the corners of her mouth. 'I'm sorry.'

It seemed strange hearing her say that; normally that was my line. I turned away, kept walking.

'Gus, where are you going?'

'Away from here.'

She followed. 'Then I'm coming too.'

I turned, said, 'Do you think that's a good idea?'

'I don't care.'

'I could stop you.'

'You could try.' She smiled at me, stuck out her tongue. We laughed together.

'And what use would that be?'

We walked around for about an hour, settled down on an embankment like two teenagers, a bottle of Cherry Coke between us.

'I didn't think they still made this,' I said.

'They brought it back. Wispas too.'

'Wispas were away?'

'Och yeah, for years, Gus.'

Where had I been? I'd wanted to talk to Debs for so long, about so many things, but none of it seemed to matter now. I was happier than I could ever remember being, just talking about utter nonsense.

'Look, a star,' said Debs.

'I think it's a satellite.'

'You sure?'

'No.' Christ, was I sure about anything? 'It doesn't look like a star, though.'

She passed over the bottle. 'Do you remember when we used to do this down at the chute?'

I laughed, wheezed. 'Oh yeah. How could I forget that Merrydown? It was foul.'

'Think kids today still hang about parks and drink Merrydown?'

'I don't think they make it any more.'

'Maybe they'll bring it back.'

We laughed again, huge laughs. I fell back and lay on the grass. Debs joined me.

'It's getting dark,' she said.

'Late in the day, Debs.'

She raised herself on an elbow. 'You always manage to make an unrelated statement seem related to what we're talking about.'

'No I don't.'

'And you always deny it.' She tweaked my nose.

'Yeah, you're right. I'm a wise-ass . . . but it takes one to know one.' As I stared at Debs I knew no one would ever know me as well as she did. She just understood me, inside out. No matter who I was with, nobody could match Debs for insight. It was just her, and her alone, who got me.

'Look, now that's a star,' I said.

'Wow, it's bright.'

'First of the night, too . . . Make a wish.'

She closed her eyes. 'Will I tell you what I wished for?'

'No, don't – it might not happen then.'

She was silent for a moment, then lay back down on the grass. 'Gus – I wished something for you.'

'Did you?'

'Yes.'

I sighed. 'Thank you.'

The darkness came fast now. A wind struck up, blew right along the embankment.

'Och, that's a cold breeze,' said Debs.

I sat up. 'We should get inside.'

'No, stay.' She pulled me back down, moved closer, brought her hands up under her chin and sheltered beside me. 'I like it here.'

'Okay.'

The moonlight shone on her hair. I wanted to put my arm around her, hold her close to me, but somehow I was held rigid. I was fifteen again and under the chute, and Debs hadn't changed a bit. I knew inside neither of us ever would.

157

Chapter 28

A SOPPY OLD LABRADOR WAS ready to trade teeth with a dachshund, right in the front room of the vet's.

'Harvey's quite harmless really,' said the owner, Morningside lady in twinset, tweed skirt, wellington boots. Could have done with some help restraining Harvey, I thought.

I smiled, said, 'Nerves, probably. Don't like these visits myself.'

The Lab growled, a deep noise from the pit of its chest.

'He doesn't like the vet . . . always sets him off,' said Morningside. 'I'll maybe take him outside till he calms down a bit. Will you tell them to give me a shout?'

I nodded, said, 'Will do.'

Harvey strained on the lead as he went, snarled. I gave him a little wave. The dachshund looked victorious.

'Do you have an appointment?' asked the receptionist.

'Well, no. I didn't know I needed one.' Was all too close to the real world for me. Appointments, dealing with professionals. I was more at home in less respectable establishments.

'Well, we don't normally take people without an appointment.'

'Och, it's just to take out the dog's stitches . . . He was attacked, you see.'

'Attacked!' She lifted her gaze from the counter. 'Oh, the poor love! We're seeing so much of that kind of thing now.'

I played up to her. 'Like I say, there was an attack and they had to patch him up, poor little tyke.'

'He seems okay; hasn't done him any real harm. Some of the dogs we see that have been brutalised just go in on themselves.'

I knew the territory. 'He's happy enough.'

'If it's just the stitches to come out, bring him through.'

'Okay.'

'I think we can fit him in with Mr Andrews. Can you wait and I'll see when he's got a free mo?'

Seemed Mr Andrews wasn't busy. Managed to find a slot for us right away. I got up to follow him through. Usual was none too keen to see the vet, using his front paws as brakes as he was led into the surgery. First time I'd seen any form of disobedience in him.

'C'mon, lad . . .' I said. He thawed a bit. But still determined he was going nowhere. 'I don't know what's got into him.'

'It's the animal instinct,' said the vet. 'You'll never see a beast happy to traipse through to the surgery.'

I lifted Usual up. Bit of a struggle.

On the vet's table I held the dog's head, let the man do the business. The stitches came out without any drama. Usual seemed as relieved as me.

'Is he a rescue dog?' The vet didn't seem to know the story.

'Well, yeah, kind of. I caught some little bastards— *sorry*, teenagers – using him as target practice.'

He seemed unfazed, said, 'All too common these days.' A few wipes of antiseptic and Usual was good to go. 'Right, that's us. Don't let him lick that off.'

I nodded, said, 'You hear that, boy? No licking off the medicine!'

The vet filled out some details on the computer, punched a few keys. I got ready for the fright of the bill, then, 'If that's all then, Mr Crawford.'

He'd lost me. 'I'm sorry, no – Dury.'

The vet took off his glasses, looked at the screen, then back to me, said, 'Dury's not the name we have here.'

159

'I'm not following you. Who would give you another name?'

'On the chip – this dog's microchipped.'

I walked round to the side of the screen. The dog struggled, didn't want me to leave him. I put a hand on his head. 'Just a minute, boy.'

The vet pointed, said, 'Look, Mark Crawford . . . That's the name registered on the chip.'

I scanned the details. There was an address too: Ann Street.

The vet put his glasses back on, looked at me with squinted eyes.

I bluffed. 'Well, that's fantastic. Means I can reunite the pair of them. Isn't it brilliant? This has been a visit well worth making . . . Thank you so much. Can I settle up now?'

At the reception desk I collected a pack of Bonios and the biggest dog chew they had on offer, added them to the bill.

'You look relieved to be out of there,' said the receptionist.

'Yes, I think he is.'

'I was talking about you.' She didn't know how right she was.

In the street I knelt down, grabbed Usual and ruffled his ears. 'Who's a good boy, then? . . . Eh, eh? Who's a bloody good boy then?'

I fed him a Bonio. He munched away blissfully.

'Christ, boy, you might just have saved my bacon.'

I took out my mobile.

Ringing.

'Yeah, Mac here . . .'

'Who's the man?'

A huff.

Sigh.

'Mac, what were you saying about this case being a bogey . . .?'

'Yeah, what about it?'

'Well, my son, I think I just got our first break.'

I could hear shuffling. 'You're in line for another one as well.'

'Come again?'

'Rab's heavies were round again. If we thought they were unfriendly the last time, this time they left no doubt.'

I did not want to hear this. 'You okay?'

'Well, I've got a nice piece of steak on my eye that would have been better punted out with a plate of chips for a tenner . . . a tenner we could well do with now.'

'The bar?'

'Bit more smashed up than when plod left.'

I felt a twinge in my chest that was either the onset of a coronary or my last vestige of hope dying. 'What did you tell them?'

'I told them you were at the boat.'

'Good.'

'I thought, y'know, it was better you went to see him . . . Next time he might not ask any questions. We don't want you offed for bloody-mindedness, Gus.'

I couldn't fault Mac's reasoning, he knew how these people worked. 'Okay, I'll get back to the boat right away. Get this fucking thing over with.'

I was about to hang up when Mac said, 'Mind and be careful, and especially, watch that fucking mouth of yours.'

Chapter 29

THEY WERE WAITING AT THE quayside. Two burly pugs in schemie uniform: trackies, bling, and barnets seen to with the number one. Put them beside John Goodman and people would be asking if he'd been on a diet. The biggest of the two wore a white vest that revealed not an inch of his arms hadn't been tattooed. As they saw me coming they waddled over, heads tipped back as if they were waiting to avoid a swipe. Like I'd be so stupid.

'Afternoon, gentlemen,' I said. God, they looked scoobied, could almost hear the gerbils on the little wheels inside their heads going faster to try and work that out. I fired out a joke: 'Church of Latter-Day Saints, is it?'

Nothing.

A scrunch of brows.

'No, och well, it's either that or you're selling steroids.'

The tats geezer started to stride towards me. Usual strained on the lead, let out a hail of barking. He looked fierce – I felt protected. The pug stopped in his tracks.

'Don't worry, his bark's worse than his bite. Let me put him on the boat and then I'll accompany you to Saughton ... I take it you're from Rab.'

Tats Man was first to speak, 'Aye, and we won't be hanging about.'

The other one added, 'It'll be him that's fucking hanging about if he tries anything.'

They laughed that up. Clapping, the lot.

I put some fresh water and food out for the dog. He settled down in his basket and seemed quite content to be back home. I tapped his head, said, 'See you soon, fella . . . No licking that medicine.'

Outside the pugs tried some roughhouse on me. Grabbed me by the scruff of the neck, pushed me in the back, said, 'Get in that fucking car now.'

I turned, said, 'Look, I'm coming quietly. Last thing I want is you telling Rab I was any bother. Okay? Good, now lose the fucking tone.'

The backhander came from nowhere, opened up my nose instantly, poured blood down my mouth and chin.

The pugs laughed themselves stupid. If that was possible.

I climbed in the car, put my hand to my nose, pinched, and tipped back my head.

They played the Backstreet Boys, turned up high, all the way to the prison. Their bald heads nodded to the beat, fingers tapped on the open windowsills. I'd always wondered who listened to this shite, thought it was only little girls at the school; now I knew different. Something told me today was going to be full of eye-openers.

In the car park at Saughton Prison the pugs dragged me from the vehicle and marched me to the front door. The smaller of the two – a look of the Joe Bugner about him – fished a visiting card from the zip pocket in his trackie top and shoved it at me.

'Now, go and see Mr Hart and be a good boy. We might be waiting when you get out so don't be fucking lippy would be my advice or Barney there will be fitting your head to a railway sleeper.'

'I get the message. Lovely visual image – quite a way with words you have.'

I braced myself for another swipe. None came.

'Thank you very much,' he said. As he stonked away he looked genuinely delighted.

The prison smelled like a hospital that had gone bad. Lots of disinfectant, but something told me there wasn't enough disinfectant in the world to mask the true smell of the place. The guards looked as if they were working security at B&Q – couldn't have given a toss. I thought: If Rab decides he's tearing my head off, who's going to stop him?

I took a seat in the visitors' area. It was a large room with lots of tabletops and chairs set out. I hadn't seen old chairs like these since my schooldays, metal tubing with wooden seats. There were names carved in the tables just to complete the retro look. Everywhere tearful women, battered by life, took up the seats and waited for the prisoners to come in. I felt sorry for them, to a one they had been sold a pup.

As the prisoners arrived I felt my nose start to twitch. A thin trickle of blood made its way down the inside of my left nostril and pooled on my top lip. I wiped it away with my finger, squeezed my nostrils together and began the head-tipping again.

'You've been a bastard to get hold ay!' I looked up and saw a squat forty-something with broad shoulders. 'Sit the fuck up. I've no' got all day to be fucking aboot with you, Dury.'

I turned to face him. Rab had his black hair cut short on top and at the sides but had a Billy Ray Cyrus mullet at the back. He had a star tattoo on his left earlobe and more to match on his neck going into a baggy grey T-shirt. When he spoke his dark eyes shot from left to right, making sure he wasn't missing anything going on in the room. 'I see my boys gave you a wee reminder of who you're fucking dealing with ... Good – saves me the fucking bother.'

I tried to speak.

'Shut it!' He pointed a finger at me. Rab's hands were like something out of a Peter Howson painting. Long fat fingers, heavily veined and continually being drawn into fists. His knuckles were scratched and reddened and had obviously been put to some use during his jolt.

'Right, Dury, here's how it's gonna be.' He was pointing again.

'You work for me. I've seen this fucking thing – ' he pulled the paper with my article from his back pocket and slammed it on the table – 'and that's all by the fucking by. You're my man now and you'll do what I fucking tell you.'

I had a few questions but kept my trap shut. I hoped, at some point, Rab might calm down and I'd get a few words in.

He folded the paper away, seemed even more agitated, eyes darting again. 'I don't give a fuck who killed Moosey—'

'So it wasn't you, then?' I'd said it before I realised the gravity of my words.

Rab smiled; he actually opened his mouth, showed teeth. 'If I'd killed the cunt, I wouldnae be fifty grand out of pocket. And you wouldnae be sitting here, Dury.' He took a deep breath. I could see he was trying to get himself back on track, something approaching composure. I imagined Rab Hart was far more used to roaring orders at people to get what he wanted done. He wasn't happy having to explain what was on his mind. 'Like I say, I don't give two fucks who killed Moosey, but you're gonna find out, Dury, because whoever did it, likely as not, has my fucking money. And I'm not very happy about that.'

'I'm doing that anyway.'

Rab drew fists again. 'Difference is, Dury, now you're working for me. When you go out that door you tell folk Rab Hart wants to know, you got me?'

I nodded. Was now the time to tell him his tinpot empire was in disarray? I didn't think there would ever be a good time for that. 'You know there's some manoeuvring going on . . . I hate to break it to you but your name doesn't carry the same weight from in here.'

Rab's hand came down on the table. The thud set the four legs jumping into the air. He was on his feet, pointing that finger at me again. 'Rab Hart's no' a fucking spent force, no' by a fucking long stroke!' Two of the guards came over. They had their hands on little holsters clipped to their belts. It was enough: Rab settled, returned to his seat. The guards walked away.

Rab started to smooth down his hair with the palm of his hand. His lower lip was jutting. 'Listen tae me, Dury, if folk think I'm played oot then they're fucking wrong, and I'm gonna prove them wrong. This appeal's in the bag. I'm telling you, it's taken care of.' He looked up at me to emphasise the point with his eyes. 'Now, Dury, I want you to tell folk Rab's getting oot and he wants his money back . . . Have you got that?'

A buzzer signalled the end of visiting time. The guards started to usher people out the door.

I stood up. 'I've got it.'

Rab faced me. 'Remember, you're working for me now, Dury . . . Anyone gives you any grief, I want to fucking know. They'll no' give you it a fucking second time, I'll make sure of that.'

I turned away. Could feel my nose starting to twitch again.

'And Dury . . . that money – if you don't find it, it's coming out your fucking arse.' He started to laugh, a strangled, arrogant sound. 'Fucking sure it is, Dury. Mind of that when you're on the job.'

Chapter 30

COULD THINGS GET ANY WORSE? I doubted it.

As I left the prison and headed into the car park I noticed Rab's boys had left. I took this as a good sign: only one person would have called them off. The short burst of elation was drowned out, however, by the fact that I was now being followed. And it was definitely plod. The Markies overcoats, collars turned up, gave it away. It was like suddenly catching a waft of bacon cooking. They'd been tipped off to my visit, that was a given; made me wonder about Rab some more.

I took a slower schlep than I would normally, did the old shop window reflection thing. Yep, they clocked me and stopped in their tracks, fiddled with their collars, coughed into fists. How do they train these numpties? Old *Sweeney* videos? All that was lacking was the Cortina hugging the kerb.

I was coming to the end of the road with them, in every way; decided I'd had enough. I wasn't having my every move monitored for some knuckle-dragger to take back to the nick and give yet more ammunition to Jonny Boy. My feeling was he didn't need any help on that front and I sure wasn't going to offer myself up for him.

Things had definitely taken on a more serious tint of late. I knew I'd be lucky to get ahead of the game any time soon, but I still held one or two aces. I'd like to see what Hod had turned up after following Sid the Snake's movements over the last few days – something told me Sid was going to be key to cracking this. More than ever, though, I wanted to up the heat on Mark Crawford. The fact that I had his name from Usual's microchip was something I was ready to shove in his face. Now that would be a reaction worth watching.

There was a nice-looking little drinker over the road, gas lamps hanging alongside the Younger's Tartan Special gadgie. I did the old left-to-right bit at the pavement and crossed over, went inside. The exterior had fooled me, it was about as far from traditional as you could get, even had miniature plastic furniture and colouring-in books out for the kids.

'Fucksake,' I said to the barman, 'why don't you put a seesaw in and be done with it?'

'Excuse me?'

'Gimme a pint.' I pointed to some piss-weak-looking Belgian brand on the pump. It took him all of thirty seconds to deliver me a dayglo yellow glass of the fizziest-looking beer I'd ever seen.

'Anything else?' He stepped back, waved a hand to the optics, like I didn't know where they kept these things in bars.

'Go for broke, let's see you mess up a low-flying birdie.'

He poured out a Grouse, said, 'Coke or something with it?'

I involuntarily shuddered at the thought. 'What do you think? Here's a clue – fuck no.'

The guy took my money, stood behind a young lass at the till. I could see him tapping the side of his head and pointing down the bar to me as he rang up. I looked around at the yuppies and day-trippers and got the impression this joint was a bit short of real customers, real people. No wonder I got this geezer's goat.

I took my change and fired into my wee goldie. I could see plod emerging through the door, ordering up two orange juices in long glasses. At close quarters I realised I'd never seen plod looking so young. Christ, had I hit that age already? I let them settle themselves at a table by the puggie. There was a pair of teenagers in skinny jeans, at least seventy per cent of their arses hanging out over the top, standing next to them, firing change into the slot machine. I could tell plod was pissed at having to watch these muppets' cracks at such close quarters; still, gave me a giggle.

I took as much of the pint as I could manage without gagging – it tasted like a bad alcopop, Hooch or something – and then I summoned back the barman of the year.

Raised my voice: 'Where do you keep your cludgie?'

He pointed to the stairs, said, 'Up there, first door on the right.'

I kept the volume up: 'Do you have a newspaper I can take?' Yeah, was the long haul – got that point in loud and clear.

He brought me a copy of the *Daily Ranger*. I thanked him, rolled it up and tucked it under my arm. I ignored plod on my way up, but could feel them watching me, hot little pig eyes burning into me on every step.

There was a bloke in the cludgie with a toddler of about three or four. Christ, I thought, pubs are no places for children. We need to reclaim the streets.

I let the place empty then dragged the wastepaper basket to the door, wedged it between the sink and the handle; figured it might hold for a few minutes.

There was a small frosted-glass opening window. In my more agile days I might have got through it; these days, forget it. I don't do agile. I rolled up my coat and thumped out the larger of the other glass panes. It cracked on the corner; a second thud and it shattered. I knocked out the jagged shards and peered into the street below. I'd disturbed some gulls that were picking at scraps around a massive wheelie bin – what I believe they call a dumpster in the States – directly below. Could I lower myself onto it? If I could reach it then the wall skirting the yard was within easy reach and I'd be home free.

As I folded my coat over the ledge, I heard banging on the cludgie door. I'd been rumbled. I looked back and saw a mass of blue paper towels spilling from the wire basket. The sink was coming away from the wall.

I hoisted myself onto the window ledge. As the palms of my hands took my weight a few stray shards of glass spiked into me. I winced at the pain but dragged myself over the edge. I made the dumpster. The gulls screeched at me. I had just enough height to reach up and pull down my coat. I grabbed it and stepped onto the wall. The dumpster was almost empty and had wheels. I got myself between the wall and the edge of the bin and started to push it away. As I did so, plod appeared at the window.

I clocked him face-on as his buddy reached his side. 'Nice day for it, chaps,' I said.

'Stay where you are, Dury.'

I pushed again at the dumpster. It wobbled.

Plod was climbing through the window. 'I'm warning you, stay right there.'

My palms were bleeding heavily now, little grains of broken glass pressed into the skin as I leveraged myself between the wall and the bin. I gave one last thump on the dumpster and its wheels screeched louder than the gulls hovering above. The bin overturned just as plod stuck his arse out the window. His legs kicked at the side of the building, the toes of his shoes scraping on the brickwork as he searched for the top of the dumpster.

His partner leaned out, grabbed at his buddy's coat, yelled, 'Dury, stay where you fucking are!'

'Not likely.' I was laughing my arse off at plod scrabbling up the wall. The gulls were getting fired into a selection of tomato tops and cold chips.

'Dury, you fucker, I'll swing for you.'

'Jesus, you're a fine swinger, I'll give you that.' He was yawing from side to side; it was a certain leg break on the cobbles below.

After plod was dragged back through the window I heard the pair of them running for the door. I knew I had a couple of minutes on them tops. And that was if my heart held out. I tightrope-walked across the ledge of the wall and jumped into the back alley.

Chapter 31

THE TIMES I'VE CURSED EDINBURGH buses for clogging the roads and spewing out fumes, but Christ, I was grateful for this one. As I caught the doors they were closing. Driver said, 'I should put you on the street!'

'Do me a favour – I'm just about there as it is.'

He took the fare from me and crunched the gears, grunting and moaning as though I'd jumped his bus with the sole intent of pissing him off.

I planted myself at the front and copped looks from the folk who'd avoided the seats reserved for the elderly and disabled. I was tempted to say, *Look, I'll move if anyone wants it* . . . but kept it to myself. I was still panting after the run and needed to conserve my energy for the next stop on my journey to the bottom of the heap.

I wanted to see what Mark Crawford would have to say for himself when I hit him with the fact that I knew the dog that he was using for target practice on the hill the night Moosey died was registered in his name. The vet's little revelation put a whole new perspective on things; well, did for me anyway. His legal-minded father, I'm sure, would have some way of wriggling out of it. Things had gone from weird to weirder on this one; I just didn't get the boy from Ann Street straying so far from the straight and

171

narrow. For sure, he'd lost a sister, he had the motive, but something wasn't stacking up.

I left the bus and took a slow schlep through the better end of town. I sparked up a Bensons and had a quick check that there was no filth on me. I seemed to have dropped them – at least, I couldn't spot any obvious contenders for the role in the street behind me.

Ann Street's front gardens are what can only be described as elegant. Whenever I see this kind of finery in the city I always think of Stevenson, the creator of *Dr. Jekyll and Mr. Hyde*. He grew up round this way and managed to weave a story that summed up Edinburgh's dichotomy nicely: beautiful on the outside, rotten on the inside.

I felt a twitch begin on my shoulder blades as I took the gate of the Crawfords' home. The working-class programming told me I should be doffing cap and trudging to the rear of the property. The twitch migrated, set itself up in my chest as my heart rate increased.

I pushed the buzzer, chucked my tab into the rose bushes.

No one answered. I pressed again.

Movement.

Slow footsteps towards the window. I could see a white shape flit behind the glass, then the door was opened an inch or two.

'Hello, Mark,' I said.

'You can fuck off.'

'Nice words . . . Bet the neighbours adore you.'

He widened the gap a little, spat at me. I watched him step back and try to slam the wood in my face but I was ahead of him, had my shoulder in place to take the weight and propelled myself forward. The door slipped from Mark's hands, slammed into the wall.

'Butterfingers,' I said.

He watched me for a moment then backed up the hall, balling fists.

I stepped inside. Closed the door behind me, sang at him, 'I think we're alone now . . .'

He lunged. I saw the swing of his heavy right hook and stepped

172

in to block it with my forearm. I had my own right at the ready, sledged him in the gut. He dropped to the floor, gasping. The young yob curled up, taking a fair share of Persian rug with him. I grabbed him by the collar, raised him.

'Get in there, y'daft wee cunt.'

He found it impossible to straighten. He walked like Groucho Marx into the living room, wheezing and spluttering. I put the sole of my boot on his arse and forced him onto the couch. He curled up again, still gasping for air.

'What the fuck are you playing at, laddie?' I said. 'That was the most pathetic put-up I've ever seen . . .'

'Fuck off.' He could only manage a whisper.

'I mean, running with the Sighthill massive and that's the best you can do? I'm ashamed for you.' I took out another Bensons, sparked up. As I walked about the place Mark kept his eyes on me. 'I mean, what did you think you were up to there, Mark? Playing the hard man, eh? Running with the young crew to get closer to Moosey, and maybe, just maybe, the chance to pay him back for what he did to . . . Christine?'

The mention of his sister forced him to sit upright, spew words: 'You don't know a thing, nothing. You're just a washed-up fucking alkie who's got nothing better to do with his days than go about noising other folk up.'

I laughed. 'Been doing your homework on me, Mark . . . Wise. I've been doing mine on you too. It turns out that dog on the hill, one I rescued, it's registered to you.'

He said nothing.

I pressed him. 'Is that an official "no comment"? Doesn't look very good, Mark. How do you think the police would take that news?'

He rose, shook his fist. 'The police think you're the one.'

I drew on my tab. 'Now what would give them that idea? Your father, perhaps?' I let that suggestion sting, watched him for a reaction. There was none. He stood before me, trembling.

'What were you doing up there, Mark? The night Moosey was

173

killed. The man who they say killed Christine, little Chrissy, your sister . . .'

He ran at me with his hands out. I stepped aside and booted him in the knees. He clattered into the fireguard, brought down an ornamental poker. He curled on the floor again, clutching his legs.

'Mark, I'm not fucking messing with you . . . Two men are dead, there's money missing, and some serious people are unhappy about the whole fucking situation. Now, believe me, I might just be the best friend you have. Come clean and tell me what you know or you're gonna be going the same way as Moosey and Tupac.'

He gritted his teeth. They were among the whitest teeth I'd ever seen – made me realise just how young this lad was. I knelt down, put a hand on his shoulder. 'Mark, I mean it . . . tell me what you were doing up there. Did you lead those lads on? Did you tell them about the money Moosey was carrying, was that it?'

He writhed on the floor, teeth still gritted. 'You don't know a fucking thing – you're just a dumb fucking alkie.'

'Mark, I know about the fifty grand. I know Moosey was carrying it that night and I know what the kind of crew you were running with will do for fifty grand.'

'You don't know fuck all.'

He started to get up. I rose with him, supported his elbow; he snatched it away. 'Moosey got what he fucking deserved, he killed my sister.' He bawled at me, 'He killed my fucking sister!'

His nose was inches from my face. I could see the tears spilling from his eyes as he roared, 'That man killed my fucking sister!'

I grabbed him by the shoulders, shook him. 'Mark, tell me what happened on the hill. Who killed Moosey that night?'

I was shaking him hard as the door to the living room was flung open and Katrina Crawford walked in. She was holding two heavily laden carrier bags in each hand, swung them before her and dumped them on the couch. She crossed the distance between us and forcibly snatched her son from my clutches.

'Leave him be,' she yelled, 'he's just a boy.'

I felt my brow roll up to the ceiling; I flung up my hands. 'I have this *boy* of yours on the murder scene . . . He was so stupid he registered his bloody dog!' I grabbed him by the collar, spun him to face me. He was still gritting his teeth. 'Tell her, tell her about the dog . . . Tell her how you didn't even have the marbles to register it under a false address. Makes me think you're just not cut out for the life of crime, Mark.'

His mother manhandled him out of the room, led him upstairs. I followed. When she got halfway up the wide staircase, Katrina Crawford turned. 'I bought that dog for him . . . and I want it back.'

I laughed, 'You bought it . . .'

Mark looked at his mother, wondering where this was all going. She spoke: 'I bought the dog, it's my property. Are you going to give it back?'

I smiled. 'Not a fucking chance.' I turned for the door, said, 'Tell the police. Maybe they'll haul us both in for a chat, Mrs Crawford.'

She turned her head slightly, removed a hand from her son's shoulder and tucked a stray curl of hair behind her ear. I thought she might say something but she merely opened her mouth, almost imperceptibly, then closed it again.

'Och, you don't like that idea,' I said. 'Wonder why.'

Chapter 32

MY DOCS WERE POUNDING OFF the pavement. I lit out before I was being cable-tied by plod in the Crawfords' front yard. I could see it coming, this lot were playing for keeps. It was looking as if I was up against more than a connected family. No one acts that arrogantly in the face of damning evidence unless they've got some serious protection.

At the end of Ann Street I ran into the jolly-hockey-sticks brigade. A crowd of students, chinless Home Counties types, Oxbridge rejects up here to drink our bars dry of gin at mummy and daddy's expense. They were acting up, playing slapsie and yaw-yawing at each swipe as it landed. As I waded through them I caught sight of a bloke tending his garden. He was in his element, lapping up their antics. It was the kind of metaphor for what Scotland had become that I didn't want to see. I thought: This life I could not get used to. There might be comfort in reward, but what you had to sell to reach this level I wasn't putting on the market. Ever.

A north wind T-boned me at the junction. Fastened my coat just as a Volvo estate pulled up. It was Katrina Crawford.

'I didn't mean to make you agitated,' she said.

I almost laughed – when was I never? Said, 'Oh no?'

She scanned the junction. A Tesco home delivery driver was

drumming his fingers on the steering wheel as he waited for her to pull out. 'I'd really like to talk to you if that's okay, Mr Dury.'

'What about?'

The driver sounded his horn. The judge's wife turned down the corner of her mouth, waved him away impatiently. 'Would you like to get in?'

I didn't answer that one; walked round the front of the car and opened the passenger's door. I slumped in the seat and eyed her cautiously.

'Thank you,' she said.

We drove through the city, avoiding the main thoroughfares; it was a big car but she handled it effortlessly. Small chat was all I got from her, nonsense about the state of the roads since the trams work had gone ahead. I wanted to pull on the handbrake, say *Cut the shit*, but I sat back and observed her. Katrina Crawford wasn't the type to show nerves. Likely she'd had too much practice at her New Town dinner parties to be fazed by a near-jakey like me.

She pulled the Volvo up outside the Parliament, took a slot in the car bays in Holyrood Park. 'It seems nice out. Shall we go and sit by the swan pond?'

'Okay.'

I played it cool, as cool as I could be. I wanted to grab her paisley-swirl pashmina, tighten it till she told me what the fuck was going on with her son and the murder of Tam Fulton, why I was being put in the frame for it and just what kind of a mug did she take me for?

As we walked through the park she yabbered; more small chat. 'It's so lovely here. They want to build on all the green belt now, though.'

'Oh, I think Her Majesty wouldn't be too chuffed with her view of the Craigs being interrupted. This patch of green's safe enough ... Some people in Edinburgh you just don't mess with.'

She didn't register a hit; politely smiled. 'I'm sure you're right.'

'If it was up to me I'd be building on all the golf courses. Not that we need more developments in Edinburgh, but we do need fewer golf courses ... everywhere. Do you play golf, Mrs Crawford?'

A wide smile. 'Yes, a little. You can call me Katrina.'

We schlepped on, sticking to the path. Had a feeling we were being followed but there was no sign of it. I hadn't met the plod yet that could manage to tail me without making himself known, so I put it down to paranoia, or the fact that I was getting jumpy.

My mind had been on Moosey. Swung the pendulum from being pissed off for getting me wrapped up in another below-radar city killing to something approaching sympathy. The more I imagined what must have been going on, the more I saw Moosey as a pathetic pawn.

Katrina took a seat on a bench by the side of the loch. 'Here will do.' A smile; fine lines formed at the sides of her mouth. She put her bag over her shoulder, asked me to sit.

'I'd sooner stand.'

She didn't respond, looked ahead.

The wind came sharp below the Craigs, whistling down over Saint Margaret's Loch and smacking the senses. Made me feel like a drink, said, 'Why don't you tell me about Christine.'

She lost her composure, seemed less communicative. The strap of her bag fell from her shoulder. She watched it rest on the crook of her arm but didn't move to correct it. 'I wasn't expecting that.'

I wasn't either. I felt an inward wince that I'd raised the death of this woman's daughter so abruptly. 'I'm sorry ... it must still be very painful for you.'

A weak smile. 'No, it's all right ... I mean, yes, it's still a fresh wound but I can talk about her. I loved my daughter.'

She seemed to suddenly tense up; her jawline firmed and tight muscles showed in her neck.

I said, 'I understand.'

'Do you?'

She turned to face me but I couldn't hold her gaze. I dropped my eyes and ferreted for my cigarettes. I lit a tab, offered, but got a shake of the head.

'We all know about loss, don't we?' I said.

'After a certain age, Mr Dury . . . Christine was three years old when she was murdered.' Katrina crossed her legs away from me, watched as a van from the SSPCA pulled up. Two workers got out and headed for the swans. It was business as usual whilst we delved into this woman's hurt.

'The man who killed Christine was a common criminal. How can you defend him?' She put the emphasis on 'common'. I didn't like the way she used the word.

'I'm not defending him. But if I was, I'd remind you murder is murder, Katrina . . . Your husband knows the law of this land better than me. Hasn't he pointed that out to you?'

She looked offended, eyes widening. 'I'm sure I don't know what you mean by that remark.'

I put a foot on the bench, leaned over her. 'Well, let me spell it out for you . . . I saw Mark at the murder scene and I wasn't the only one.'

'What?'

'The police had a witness, an old derelict who was living on the hill, who saw Mark there too. I found him and he was ready to make a statement when he was run down in the street like a dog. Someone killed him, and I've good reason to believe that someone is connected to your son.'

She turned on me; her eyes darkened. She spat, 'That's crap!'

I let down my foot, flicked the ash from my tab, said, 'I think you and I both know it isn't, Katrina. I think you and your husband should think very carefully about how you are protecting Mark.' I showed her my back, started off in the direction I'd come from. The SSPCA lot had been joined by a pumping lorry from Scottish Water.

'Wait,' called out Katrina.

I halted.

She came running. 'What do you mean by that?'

I looked down the road, then at my watch, said, 'Time's running out for your son . . . He's up to his neck in the murder of two men and one way or another the truth is going to come out.'

Katrina lost some colour from her face, dropped her gaze, fiddled with the rings on her fingers, said, 'You're wrong.'

'Well, let's see.'

As I walked to the edge of the road I was stopped by one of the SSPCA guys. 'Got a light, pal?'

I produced a box of matches, handed them over. 'What's with the loch?'

'Some idiot's dumped a load of car batteries in there. Killing off all the swans it is.'

Over his shoulder I could see a colleague bagging up a dead swan. Said, 'Another casualty?'

'That's the fifth one . . . They'd all be dead if it wasn't for that.' He pointed to the palace. 'Can't have Herself looking out on piles of dead swans. That would never do.'

Chapter 33

I KNOW WHY MY WORDS with Katrina Crawford dredged all
of this up, but I didn't want to face it. Sometimes, though, there's
just no escaping the past. I guess there's just no way I'm getting
free of this stuff, ever . . .

We can't afford anything flash, so it's a register office do. Hod's
helping out: hired the kilts, put Debs in a decent dress. Nothing
fancy – she doesn't need it. I can hardly stop staring at her as she
appears, walking down the row of cheap plastic chairs they're still
laying out in a makeshift aisle. They play 'Teenage Kicks' by the
Undertones, our wee joke; it's a moment like no other.

We're too young for this. Everyone says so.

'Should be playing the field, Gus,' Hod tells me. He's done this
a million and one times already.

'Debs is all I ever wanted,' I tell him back. I see it doesn't
register. It's my first inkling that this day isn't exactly blessed.

My heart's beating so hard I wonder if it'll burst out my chest
and onto the floor. As Debs reaches my side she smiles. Not a big
smile. Not even a natural smile. Nervous. She's trembling. I don't
know if I'm allowed to look, never mind touch her, but I want to
scoop her up in my arms and say, *It's okay. It'll all be okay.*

I freeze as the registrar speaks. She's an old woman, steel-grey hair and specs. Small round ones like John Lennon's. I like them because the fashion right now is for great big ones in bright red or green. She looks – what's the word? – *schoolmarmish*.

It's a joy to hear Debs say 'I do'.

I'm so choked I can hardly manage to get my own words out.

When the ceremony's over there're calls for Debs to throw her little bouquet into the crowd. She doesn't want to, says, 'I'd like to hold on to it.'

It's only a £1.99 job from the garage at the supermarket.

'Well, don't do it then. Keep it,' I say.

'That wouldn't be fair.'

I know this is Debs all over – putting others first. She turns her back, throws the little bunch over her shoulder. I'm so glad to see the scramble for the flowers, the smiles and the heartfelt joy. I look at Debs and she's smiling too. Maybe everything will work out okay, I think.

Hod has a camera. We go into the street. We have sunshine, a rarity.

An old woman wrapped in a blue scarf walks past and puts her hand on Deborah's elbow, says, 'My, you're a beautiful bride, love.'

Debs smiles, thanks her.

I see cars slowing down to check us all in our best gear, happy. Rice and confetti go up and Hod hollers on us to get in a row in front of the register office.

We line up; there's joking and fun all about. Debs reveals her garter; people applaud.

'Gus, what's worn under that kilt?'

That I *don't* reveal. An old joke: 'Nothing, it's all in perfect working order!'

Hod clicks away. I imagine we'll have quite an album. I'm growing used to the idea that we've made the right decision. Even after all that's happened, all the pain. The heartache. The tears. The bloodshed. I forget the days before, when Debs begged her parents to give her another chance, to come to the wedding, give their blessing. I forget what I know people will be saying about why we're here. We want to show the ones who said we were just stupid kids. To show the ones who said I'd amount to nothing. To show the ones who called Debs a silly wee cow. A hing-oot who got what she deserved.

We made a mistake. We know it. But this is putting it right, isn't it? This is showing them.

Hod yells, 'That'll do . . . It's a wrap!'

There're laughs all round. People applaud.

The old woman with the blue scarf has stayed to watch. 'You'll have some lovely, lovely pictures, dear!'

Debs smiles. 'Thank you.'

The old woman has a tear in her eye, a croak in her voice when she says, 'You can tell the ones that are in love, you know . . . You can tell, for sure you can.'

I take a hankie out of my sporran, hand it to her. 'I hope they're happy tears, now.'

She wipes her eyes, says, 'Och yes, och yes . . . I'm just so happy to see a young couple so in love.'

Debs reaches in, places a hand on her shoulder. 'Oh, that's so sweet of you. I'll remember this moment for ever.'

I'm so filled with pride. I know what we've done is right now. Not because of what the old woman said, but because I see Debs believes her. She knows what she said is true. We have something special.

The old woman dabs at her eyes and, as she turns, says, 'Cherish each other.'

I watch Debs's lip tremble. I believe we both see decades of life together for us. We see each other growing old and grey. I know I feel sad, but I know it's because the situation is such a happy one. It's a complex feeling that I can't explain. And then it vanishes.

There's a kerfuffle. A struggle in the crowd.

I see Hod put down his camera bag, drop the tripod. He's running towards the crowd, but it's too late. A figure has pushed through; people step away.

Deborah's mother appears.

Her face is a war mask. Dark. Angry. Violent.

She moves quickly. Not a run. But a purposeful stride. I grab Debs's hand, move in front of my wife. I know what's coming.

There're words yelled. I only pick up a few of the familiar ones. The hatred in her voice is drowning the others out.

She reaches over me, tries to claw at Debs. Her own mother, clawing. Not a slap. Not a punch. Real, vile hate. Directed at her daughter.

I hold her away. She doesn't land a single blow.

She tires herself out and stands back.

I release my grasp.

'Shame on you,' she says.

I raise my arms.

She speaks again: 'Don't touch me, you fool boy.'

I hold firm.

Debs is shaking with fright, tears, her face a red mess.

'Why, Mum? Why? . . . I'm still the same person.'

Her mother steps forward. I'm surprised by her strength, power. She says, 'You're no daughter of mine.' She spits in Debs's face: 'You whore!'

That's it for me. 'You don't talk to my wife like that.' I'm ready to slap her. I'll kill her, I know it. Hod sees the fire in my eyes, steps in. He puts an arm round the mad woman's waist, carries her away, kicking and screaming.

I turn to Debs. She falls into my arms. I have to hold her up.

Over her shoulder I see the old woman with the blue scarf standing open-mouthed. As she walks away, she drops the hankie I gave her. I want to tell her, but I'm too far gone from this world for words now. I wonder: Will I ever come back?

Chapter 34

I HAD MORE PRESSING MATTERS to attend to, but I couldn't put this off a minute longer.

My mother's street was crammed with cars. When I was a boy, I played kerbie here, raced bikes with my brother Michael. Now there wasn't a single child. Hot-hatches lined both kerbs. The yuppie tideline had risen again.

My mother's front lawn – if you could call it that; barely a patch, really – had grown to a depressing height. Some litter blowing about, old Maccy D's boxes and kebab-shop containers. I'd never seen the place neglected like this. For a moment I wondered if I had the right house.

'What a tip,' I mouthed.

The window in the front door looked filthy. This was something my mother usually took such pride in. I could still remember her scrubbing the step the last time I visited. What the hell was up here?

I rapped on the door.

Nothing.

Another rap.

Movement, voices.

I opened the letter box. The place looked like a dosshouse. Three or four sets of dirty trainers lying in the hallway, a pile of mail and a new Yellow Pages stacked up on the telephone shelf.

I yelled in, 'Hello . . . hello?'

'Who the fuck's that?' came back.

I didn't know that voice: a male, young.

I dropped the letter box, stepped back. What the hell was going on here? The place a cowp, a young lad cursing like a trooper – in my father's house only one person was ever allowed to speak like that.

I stepped back from the door. My heart pounded ferociously. I was about to put a boot through the frosted glass but thought better of it. I edged up to the front window, peered through a gap in the filthy, stained-yellow net curtains. Inside two youths in Adidas trackies and baseball caps sat on the couch, one of them crouched over, trying to light the bong in his hand. I couldn't believe my eyes. Who the hell were they? What the hell was going on here?

I ran back to the door. I was ready to kick the lock off. Had a boot aimed when suddenly a key turned.

My mother peered out through a slit of light.

'Mam?'

A shriek.

She shut the door quickly. Slammed it on me.

I knocked on the glass. 'Mam, it's me . . . Gus.'

'Angus, go away.'

I heard some voices raised – the youths', carrying out into the street.

I thumped on the door. 'Mam, what the hell's going on?'

Behind me a neighbour appeared at her gate, lugging two bulging Iceland carriers. 'Oh, it's you . . . Hope you're there to sort that pair of wee bastards out.'

I turned. 'What?'

'Those little shits have been nothing but trouble since they moved in. You should be ashamed to have your own mother live like that, drug dealers round every other night, police cars. It's a disgrace!' She scowled at me, then marched indoors.

I went back to the letter box.

'Mam, open this door now or I'm putting my foot through it.'

The key turned in the lock again. When my mother appeared I got the shock of my life – she looked drawn and pale, close to collapse. But the heart-stopper was her split lip, a cut that looked like she'd been batted one. I put a hand on her face and she started to cry.

'Mam, what's this?'

Two yobs in trackies came into the hall, stooped over her. One of them had a five-skinner in his hand, toked away whilst listening to every word I said.

'Mam, is this Catherine's boys?'

My mother sobbed, nodded.

I looked at the pair of them. They had dopers' eyes, ringed in red.

'Come on, Mam . . . let's get you upstairs, have a nice lie down.'

She was in pieces, exhausted. I put her into bed, said I'd make her a cup of tea once she'd had some rest.

She smiled, said, 'They were such lovely laddies . . . once.'

'Shhh, get your head down. I'll see you in a while.'

I closed her bedroom door.

It was only once I was in the hall that I realised the last time I'd been in there was to watch my father die.

Should I feel a flicker of sympathy for the man?

Nothing came.

I descended the stairs, slowly.

My heart calmed. Pure anger, white rage, doesn't pump hard. I've felt it many times before and it's always surprised me by its methodical calm.

At the foot of the stairs I removed my coat.

Chapter 35

I OPENED THE LIVING-ROOM door slowly. Inside, *Chuckle-Vision* blared. I switched the telly off. Put my folded coat on the chair beside the mantel.

'I was fucking watching that,' said one of my nephews from the couch; I couldn't tell which. This lot all sounded the same to me.

'Not any more you're not.'

'Y'what?'

'Let's say you've lost your privileges.'

The pair laughed, hacking coughs like chucking-out time at the bingo.

I started to take off my watch, roll up my sleeves. Said, 'How did my mother get that lip?'

'I don't fucking know,' said one.

'Maybe she walked into a door,' said the other.

They both laughed, high-fived.

I picked up an ashtray, said, 'Put that out.'

'What if I say no? . . . You gonna smack me, eh?'

'Put it out.'

'Fuck off . . . You'll no' touch me.' He rose, fronted me. 'You're family so you are – you can't.'

I grabbed his face in my hand. 'You think that counts for fuck all?'

The other one rose too. 'Hey, fuck right off! You're supposed to be our uncle.'

They both laughed, it was all a joke to them.

I said, 'Let me tell you, blood never protected me from my own father in this house and it's not going to protect you.'

I saw the swing for my head with the heavy bong about ten minutes before I walked in the room. His reactions were slow. I caught his arm while I still held the other's face. 'Now, lads, that's not very clever.'

I yanked them together. They were weak, emaciated.

I cracked one with a right and his head fired back into the other's.

Blood gushed from an eye and a nose simultaneously.

'I told you, you've lost all privileges.'

Looks, first to each other, then to me. 'What you saying?'

'Do I need to spell it out?'

'We're set up here ...'

'Not any more you're not.'

A chest got stuck out, a white baseball cap went back as a headbutt was aimed at me. I saw it in slow-mo. There's only one way to deal with a nut-job. I dropped my own head; he smacked his nose off the top of my skull, fell to his knees. Blood oozed. His brother tried to raise him.

'Are you both entirely stupid?'

'What about our stuff?'

'I'll put it all in a bag and chuck it the fuck out ... You want to argue?'

They turned, walked to the door. I went with them, watched them open up.

They said nothing as they got to the gate. Left it flapping. I called them back. 'Close it.'

They complied.

I saw the neighbour's curtains twitching. 'One last thing ... I hear either of you have been within a country mile of this place again, I'll find you.'

Stuttering: 'And then what?'

I looked that one in the eye, said, 'If I find you there's no "and then what".'

I let my mother sleep for a couple of hours or so. Tried to tidy the place up. Roach dowps scattered everywhere. Found a bag of skunk – pocketed that. The rest I binned. Took down the net curtains, put them in a basin of bleach. It looked like the first time the windows had been open in weeks. With some fresh air the place brightened a bit. Ceiling had turned yellow, though; would need repainting.

When my mother appeared I was stood with a duster in my hand. She laughed, 'Och, Gus, that's some picture.'

I raised the duster. 'Well, glad I can amuse you.'

She came in, sat down, looked about. 'You have the place lovely.'

I put down the duster, fitted the cap to the Mr Sheen furniture polish. 'What happened here, Mam?'

She shook her head, looked out the window. 'I don't know, Gus . . . They were such nice laddies once.'

I didn't know what to say. Anything I trotted out would sound like a *Daily Mail* editorial . . . blame the parents, breakdown of society, yob culture. 'What about Catherine?'

'What do you mean?'

'Why aren't they with her?'

'She turned them out . . . Had enough.'

Where the hell had I been? Had I lost touch with my whole family? 'I don't understand, Mam . . . If they were so bad their own mother turns them out, why would you pick them up?'

My mother grabbed her wrist, squeezed. 'You can't turn your back on your own . . . I might be old-fashioned, but it's just not what you do.'

I thought of Katrina Crawford – did she have that notion?

'But Mam, look what they did here.' I pointed to her lip. 'Look what they did to you.'

My mother put her face in her hands. I knew I'd pressed her too hard, too soon. I went to her side, placed an arm around her. 'Hey, never mind, eh.'

She started to shake, sob.

'Mam, c'mon . . . you did your bit. You can't change what they've become.'

'Och, Gus, it's so sad. I feel so responsible for you all.'

I wondered what possible reason my mother could find to blame herself for what I'd become.

'Mam, no. That's not true. People go their own way. You have to let them make their own mistakes and face the consequences.'

She trembled some more, grabbed her wrist again. I placed a hand over hers, said, 'C'mon, I'll make you some tea.'

She smiled, brightened. 'That would be nice.'

In the kitchen I put the kettle on.

As I stood staring out the back window I felt such an emptiness. There was so much hurt and disappointment in my mother's eyes. I wanted to have been able to provide her with some happiness. I knew if I'd made more of a success of myself she would have had something to latch on to. The list of people I'd failed and disappointed hung round me now like a darkness.

I poured myself some Black Bush from a half-bottle I carried. Brought my mother her tea; sat down.

'Thanks, son.'

'No bother.'

Awkward silence.

'How's things going with the writing?'

'Och, y'know . . . it's going. Working a story.'

She looked embarrassed. I wanted to say something, anything, just to give her some iota of hope. 'I saw Deborah again.'

Her eyes lit. 'You did?'

'Well, we went for a walk.'

A full-on smile. 'That's wonderful . . . I always knew that girl was the right one for you.'

Hell, I'd said too much. But could I take it back? Not ever.

'Well, it's early days.' I was leading my mother astray. My mouth was wandering – what had I said? I just so wanted to give her one thing to feel good about. One good thing that came from me.

191

'I'm so pleased, Angus. Really, so pleased.'

I drained my mug, jumped up. 'Look, Mam, I have a little bit of business to attend to so—'

'No, you go, son. You have your life to lead.'

'I'll come back soon. I'll mow that lawn when it's dry. And the ceiling – it'll need painted again—'

She raised a hand, cut me off: 'Angus, I don't need any looking after.'

'No, Mam. That's one thing I *will* be doing now. I'll be keeping a closer eye on you, I promise.'

She smiled sweetly, drew her cardigan around her.

I headed out the door. She followed, waved me off as I passed into the same street I'd known since I was a boy.

The second I saw the Mondeo stuffed with suits I knew I'd made a mistake visiting my mother.

Chapter 36

A WHITE POLICE CAR, SIRENS blaring, pulled up behind me and mounted the kerb. The four doors of the Mondeo swung open. A cocky-looking wido fronted me. 'Get in the car, Dury.'

As he spoke, I recognised him at once. 'Fuck me, it's the cludgie cop . . . Never made the dumpster, then?'

I was grabbed from all angles, arms up my back, cuffed. As they threw me in the back of the van I managed a glance at my mother's window. Thanked God there was no sign of her.

My mind raced. Only the effects of the Black Bush kept me together.

We drove in silence.

At the nick they checked me in.

In a police cell, facing a murder charge – was this really what my life had come to?

I paced.

My heart rate increased.

Nerves shrieked.

If they were hoying me in again, it could mean only one thing: bad news. I tried to play over what Fitz had said. Nothing sparked. Then I remembered something: I'd removed Moosey's wallet. I'd tried to wipe it clean but if they had my prints that wouldn't look good. I was ninety-nine per cent sure they didn't. It was the one per cent that put the shits up me.

Adrenaline rushed in.

I felt primed. Fight-or-flight instinct kicking in again. Were flight still an option, I'd be happy to take it. Mac's advice battered me over the head again.

Scolded myself: Dury, what the fuck were you thinking?

I'd achieved little more than zip with my efforts to find Moosey's killer. All right, I'd had some issues to wade through, but when did I never? The verdict on my being in a police cell, once again, about to have my arse well and truly caned, was 'Gus, you fucked up.'

The door swung open.

Uniform, young lad. Chest like a bull on him. He tipped the visor down on his hat and turned up the lights. Thought: Here we go.

Behind him walked in a character straight out of *LA Law*. Did they still make that show? If they didn't, nobody had told him. Light-grey suit, pale purple shirt and a navy silk tie with white diagonal stripes. If he was conscious of my being in the room, he didn't let on. I watched him position himself at the table, straighten out his cuffs and run a tanned hand over his head. From where I stood I could see there was some male pattern baldness creeping in, but there'd been some considerable skill applied to compensating for that with the old blow-dryer.

He took a silver pen from his pocket, made a show of pressing the button to release the tip. Said, 'Sit.'

I stayed put.

He let a good minute drag out before turning to the door pug. Only took a nod. The big lad hollered at me like a staff sergeant going for a squaddie, lunged over and put an arm round my neck. 'You want me to throw you against the fucking wall?' he said.

I played it cool. 'Why? Think I'll bounce?'

He threw me. My shoulder caught the cell wall. Pain shot down my backbone, then seemed to retrace its steps and settle at the original point of impact.

I felt my whole arm turn to cork. Tried to move it, couldn't, cradled it with my other arm.

'Bring him over here.'

A fist in my back. Felt the imprint of every knuckle.

At the table I saw three folders had been laid before me. Two were closed. On top of one sat sheaves of paper.

'Right, Mr Dury . . . settled down now, have we?'

I rubbed my elbow.

He spoke again, 'Glad to hear it. Now, I'm quite certain you know why we've invited you here today.'

'Help with your inquiries,' I tutted.

'Indeed.'

I leaned forward. 'Which I am more than happy to do.'

From behind him, the door opened.

I said, 'DI Johnstone enters the room . . . That's what they say on *The Bill* isn't it?' A wide smile. '"For the benefit of the tape", that's the other bit.'

Jonny Boy hid hands in his pockets, strolled over to the desk and stared at me.

I said, 'Hello there, Jonny. Looking well . . . My ex must be taking good care of you.'

LA Law spoke: 'DI Johnstone is assisting me; a mere observer.'

I flicked my index finger, said, 'Gotcha!'

Jonny lunged, grabbed the digit, said, 'Don't get fucking smart, cunt . . . We're putting you away.'

He had a firm hold on me. I reached out with my other hand to work on his grasp, but the pain in my shoulder was too great. Couldn't have been a good look – verged on capitulation.

'Keep that look, Dury, that's the one we want you to show when they throw away the key.'

As he let my finger go I gasped uncontrollably, said, 'This would be playing hardball, I guess?'

LA Law answered, 'No, Mr Dury, this is checkmate.'

'Come again?'

He flicked on the tape recorder, made his spiel, announced himself as McAvoy. He raised a polythene bag from the sheaves of paper. Inside was the skunk I had taken from my nephews. 'Yours, I believe, Mr Dury.'

I said nothing. Shrugged.

'Oh, it is. Let me assure you.'

I looked at the bag, said, 'You're seriously doing me for a bag of puff?'

McAvoy looked to Jonny. The pair exchanged thin smiles.

'Oh aye, Dury,' said McAvoy, 'there's laws against this kind of thing.'

'How about I take the caution and go back to my life?'

McAvoy's smile faded. He tipped himself back in his chair; the legs creaked on the tiled floor. As he shuffled his feet I saw his socks. They matched the colour of his shirt. He read out the charge.

I looked to the ceiling, scratched my head, said, 'Fucking hell.'

McAvoy switched off the tape, threw himself at me, brought his dart of a nose to within an inch of my face. 'I'm just getting started on you . . .' he bellowed. I felt my ears throb. 'I'm watching you very closely, Dury, and if I hear you've been near the Crawfords again you'll have plenty to worry about.'

I held up a hand. Had seen this done on *Oprah* – knew it would get a reaction.

'Whoa! Who's pulling your strings? You have precisely fuck all on me, McAvoy. Jonny couldn't fit me up, so you're having a go now, is that the game?'

'This is no game, laddie . . . A man's dead.'

'I make it two . . . one a witness who confirmed to you I was nowhere near the scene when Moosey was killed.'

McAvoy gave a silent laugh, pointed to me as he winked at Jonny. 'You hear this shite? That fucking jakey was away with it. He was off his nut on meths.' He laughed louder this time, shook his head.

I wanted to put a boot in his teeth. 'He might have been a jakey but he wasn't a ponce, and he had more of a clue about this case than you.'

He waved to the pug, who raced to the desk and put me in a headlock as McAvoy yelled in my ear. 'Listen to me, you scrawny little shitkicker. If I say you killed Tam Fulton then that's the way it's going to be and you'll be begging me to take a confession so's to keep Rab Hart from chopping you into fifty grand's worth of tiny fucking pieces.'

My head felt about one hundred degrees Fahrenheit. There was no way I could form words.

'Aye, that's better, adjust your attitude . . . We know you're short of cash, Dury. Now, the missing money might get you out of a big hole – that's some incentive, is it no'?'

I still couldn't speak.

McAvoy continued, 'You see, these days evidence can be made to tell any fucking story you want. You've seen *CSI* . . . a fingerprint here, blood smear there, it's magic! But things like motive, that's what can't be faked – and that's what gets folk put away.'

I went for a gob in his face. Fair sprayed out, caught some of his shirt.

The pug squirmed. 'You dirty prick.' He lost his grip on me.

I roared, 'Mark Crawford either killed Moosey or knows who did and you fucking know it too! . . . He's been running with the young crew and playing the dog-fighting scene to get his chance and he took it.'

'You're off your scone, Dury,' said Jonny. 'He's the son of a fucking judge!'

'So what? You're both law and as crocked as all fuck.' I was still roaring, banging my chest with one hand and fingering the air with the other. 'Someone's got you pair told to look the other way and you think I'm gonna let you put me in your sights. Fuck that! Fuck the lot of you . . . You want a fight? I'll give you one.'

I saw Jonny Boy make a lunge for me, but I missed the pug

trailing him. As I dodged Jonny's blow the hefty biffer caught me above the eye. With the shortness of my breath it was more than enough to call lights out.

The floor swallowed me.

Chapter 37

IT FELT LIKE BEING DROPPED from a cliff into the ocean.

The pug leaned over me after throwing the bucket of water in my face. I could tell that the sight of my eyes flickering felt like incitement to him. He was stupid enough to confirm it, said, 'You want me to give him a slap, guv?'

McAvoy intervened: 'No I bloody don't . . . Get him back to the table.'

He lifted me by the collar; this guy had been working out. Although the weight of me, I'd guess I was the lower end of his warm-up reps.

The chair skitted across the floor as I was flung into it. I got a size ten in the back to push me under the desk.

McAvoy perched over, poised to strike like a cobra. He grabbed me by the ear. 'You listen to me, Dury . . . You are a washed-up piece of shit.'

Like I could argue that, said, 'Tell me something I don't know.'

'You think you're it, think you're a name cos you brought that grief on this place.' He raised his other arm to the roof, waved it around. 'Well, let me correct your thinking, cockhead: you are nothing. Less than nothing.' He twisted my ear harder, brought my head down to the tabletop, pointed to the skirting. 'See that? See down there, where the roaches and the vermin crawl about?

199

That's your home. That's where you belong. Down among the filth and the scum of the earth.'

'The filth?'

That got him – knew it would. He released my ear, slammed his fist into the side of my head. My vision blurred. Room spun. As I tried to focus, to see what was coming next, I caught sight of him looming over me, yelling. Shit knows what he said. He was mad angry. Going Lou Ferrigno on me. I imagined a tear ripping down the back of a flannel shirt. Eyes bulging. Bottom row of teeth on show. Fury wasn't in it. This was beyond rage.

I reined it in, stood up. Faced him. Jonny Boy and the pug lunged for my arms. I pushed all the buttons. 'C'mon, then, let's fucking have ye, McAvoy.'

Meet rage with rage. Always seemed to work in my boyhood home.

I struggled. Put my jaw out. 'You think you've got something on me? Let's fucking have it.'

He looked shocked. Slunk back. His face changed shape.

'I said, let's fucking have it, McAvoy . . . Give it your best shot. You want to put me away, you better be fucking smarter than the other pigs that came before you.'

He drew a fist. Launched it in my gut.

I buckled over. Wheezed. 'I said "smarter". Not every bit as pig-shit thick.'

He drew his fist again. Planted it back in my gut.

I grinned at him.

The days of me taking this kind of punishment were well over; I'd be crumpled on the floor in no time. But something – stubbornness, bitterness, whatever – kept me sticking my hand in the fire.

'Like I thought: you're all the same. Dumb as fuck.' I knew I was risking a booting to end all bootings, but I also knew this guy's anger would be his undoing. If I could get him noised up enough, he'd balls up. How I knew this, well, it takes one to know one.

It was Jonny Boy who surprised me. Called five. Gathered up the papers and evidence. They left me alone, to catch my wind.

My head throbbed. My body felt hollow, empty. Like there was nothing from my chest to my groin. It felt so numb, until I touched it, then every muscle and sinew in me shrieked in agony.

Inside ten minutes the three returned.

McAvoy looked as if he'd combed his hair, straightened his tie. I'd have guessed maybe mopped his brow with a towel. He spoke with a different voice entirely now, the one I presume he reserved for brown-nosing his superiors. It put the shits up me. There was a grin delivered on every word.

'All right, Dury . . . get out my sight.'

'What?'

'You heard. Shift it. I don't want to see your skanky arse round here . . . today.'

I opened my arms wide, turned up my palms. 'Finally – some common sense.'

Jonny walked over to McAvoy's side, whispered in his ear. McAvoy's eyes shot left, caught the Boy Wonder's gaze. For about a minute they played this over between the pair of them, then the cobra was back.

'Just one more thing, Dury. Tread very carefully with your press friends.'

I went for cocky. Scrub that: cocksure. 'Yeah, well, you work your side of the street, I'll work mine.'

Another glance shot at Jonny Boy.

Tension.

McAvoy's face hardened. 'Out! Get fucking out of here!' He jumped up so hard his chair left the ground, smacked off the cell wall. Jonny ran at his heels, clipping them like a gundog. The pug's lower lip drooped in utter confusion.

'What?' I said.

'Shut yer yap!' the pug barked, then he followed the others.

The door closed tightly behind them. Keys in the lock. An hour later I was given back my bootlaces and belt. Pointed to the front desk by a uniform.

'No more cosy chats with Detective Inspector McAvoy?'

A shove towards the door.

I collected my things from a dour thirty-something with tied-back dirty-blonde hair. She looked unfussed who she offended. Thrust the lot at me, pointed a chipped pink fingernail to the box I should sign, said, 'Off to get blootered, are you?'

I looked her up and down. This one wouldn't need a mask to do ET in fancy dress. Said, 'Jealous?'

She snatched back the clipboard. 'Don't make me laugh.'

Hit back: 'Do I look like a fucking magician, love?'

Outside, the rain was coming down in sheets. Edinburgh rain falls straight as stair rods and is liable to do as much damage. I hunkered in the doorway, fed my belt through the loops, laced up my Docs. My stomach turned over in agonies with every move. I wondered how many others they put through that treatment. Was it just me, or all those they knew wouldn't stand a chance of carrying a complaint?

I was about to move off when:

'You are piss weak, Dury.'

Jonny Johnstone stepped beside me, hands in his pockets. He looked out into the rain. He waited for a response. I gave him none. He turned, looked me up and down, said, 'Piss weak.'

'I heard you the first time.'

'So bad hearing's not one of your flaws, then?'

I knew this was going somewhere, only Jonny's little intimidation didn't wash with me. I saw through him. He was a type I'd turned up too many times before. Shiny-arse on the make. Loose-moralled little brown-noser with an eye on the big office, the Beemer, the whole ball of wax.

'Pal, I'd take my flaws over your virtues any day.'

I let that fry a few brain cells.

He ruffled. 'Look, shithead, I'm warning you . . .'

I squared up to him, met his eye. 'What are you warning me?'

'I'm on your fucking case.'

'Yeah, well, I know that already . . . Do I look frightened?'

'You look like a fucking nobody.'

I laughed. This from *him*. Went with, 'A tip, Jonny Boy . . . Glory is fleeting, but obscurity is for ever.'

He turned down the corners of his mouth, mumbled, 'Is that supposed to be like a quote or something?'

'Napoleon. You should look him up, you share some . . . traits.'

Guess he didn't take it as a compliment. He put his finger in my chest, was close enough to smell the – what was that, Obsession?

'Know this, Dury: Debs is with me. I'm the one she comes home to every single night.'

I felt my facial muscles tightening. He had some moves after all.

'Every single *fucking* night . . . and that's how it's going to stay, you get me?'

I said nothing.

He went on, 'I have Debs. You don't. And I am going to give her everything you never could – the big house, the two cars parked out front, the foreign holidays, the kids – we're gonna be living happily ever after and you . . .'

He trailed on for so long I lost interest. My mind was stuck on the little dream scene he'd created for him and Debs. It didn't square with the facts. Either he was totally deluding himself, or Debs was doing it for him.

I turned to walk away.

'Hey, I'm talking to you.'

'No you're not.'

I took a few steps, turned to see Jonny spraying Gold Spot on his tongue. He looked smug; I'd be wiping that look off his chops before long.

I trudged off, collar up, into the rain.

Got as far as the Tesco Metro on the corner when I noticed two raincoats following me, making it all too obvious what they were about. I stopped and pretended to read an ad in the window for Nigella Lawson's latest cookbook. The raincoats stopped behind me, stamped their feet.

Thought: Fuck me.

Chapter 38

SPARKED UP A BENSONS, MY last one. Scrunched the pack, dropped it in the bin. Made a show of looking up and down the street. I darted for a newsagent's across the road. My fan club followed suit while I smoked the cig near to the filter.

Outside the shop, I stubbed my tab. Went in.

'Twenty Marlboro, mate . . . red top.'

Paid the man, then made a call on my mobi.

'Hod, you about?'

'Fucksake, Gus . . . where you been?'

I stalled him, 'Around.'

'Don't give me that – where?'

'Does it matter?'

'Well, yes, actually . . . we've had a bit of a stroke of luck.'

Luck. What was that? 'Do tell.'

'Well, my dog-fighting contacts came up trumps.'

'You what?'

A sigh on the other end of the line. 'We have a pit fight on.'

I knew where he was going with this: catch Sid in the act, see who was pulling his levers. But I also needed to grab hold of the dog-torturing wee bastards. Things were getting desperate.

I played Hod along: 'Good.'

'"Good". That it?'

'Well, I've kinda got a fair whack on my mind right now, Hod.'

'What's up?'

It was time to spill. 'I had my collar felt again. Now I've got two of Lothian's finest clocking my every move.'

'*Christ.*'

'What's he got to do with it? Although they do look a bit like Jehovah's on the door-to-door.'

'Where are you?'

'Just out the nick.'

'Got any ideas?'

'You know me – Mr Creative.'

'Well, c'mon, let's hear it.'

I filled Hod in. Told him to jump in his motor and wait for me outside the Cameo cinema. I tucked away my mobi, hit the street again.

I took plod onto Lothian Road. At St Cuthbert's Church I stalled, took a deck at the graveyard. They have a watchtower in there, a remnant of Burke and Hare's grave-robbing antics. I always stop to stare at it – reminds me there's more to this city than most people imagine.

Made for the Lavazza coffee stall and bought up a large black. Kept my shakes at bay till I could get hold of something stronger.

A Romanian beggar approached me. She carried a cardboard sign that read: PLEASE HELP ME FEED CHILD. GOD BLESS YOU. I looked at her. Her face was dark, heavily lined. She wore a red shawl; intricate stitching and beads fell all the way round the edge of her face. Below she seemed to be wrapped in a blanket. Popping out beneath were a set of Nikes, the swoosh on show.

She made to open her mouth, brought pinched fingers up. Thought: The international symbol for *I'm friggin' hungry*, right?

I said, 'You want a feed?'

She looked at me, put out her hand.

I'd read a story in the local paper recently, said people had reported seeing vanloads of these Romanian beggars being dropped off at strategic locations around the city. I thought it sounded like a typical slow news day beat-up. This woman looked dirt poor, starving.

I pressed: 'Look, you want food? I'll buy you something to eat.'

She put her hand out, ran a finger over the palm. 'Money. Money.'

I shook my head. 'No. I'll buy you food.' Slit the air between us with my palms. 'No money.'

Her face turned, twisted. The teeth gritted as she ranted at me in Romanian, a hail of curses, then she spat at my feet. Could have sworn I heard laughter following me; turned to check my stalkers were still on plan.

Guess she wasn't so hungry after all. Was that me cursed now?

I made my way up to the top of Lothian Road and followed the dog-leg round to the Cameo cinema. It is one of the few remaining places in the city you can go that hasn't been taken over by one of the multinational chains. Still looks like a cinema – cornicing, old-fashioned balconies, ornate plasterwork. Not a hint of plastic cup-holders. It still has chairs that feel like they're stuffed with horsehair.

The Cameo is said to be Quentin Tarantino's favourite picture house in the world. I would have thought Grauman's Chinese Theatre in Hollywood might have the edge, but what do I know? That's the thing about your home city: you lose sight of its charms. It takes the tourists, the visitors, to point them out to you sometimes. I know one thing for sure – we lose the Cameo, this place would be poorer for it. We've lost too much of the old stuff already.

I ordered up a ticket to the matinee: *3:10 to Yuma*. Was a remake starring Russell Crowe. Christ, have they made an original film in the last ten years? Still, wasn't intending to watch the thing anyway. Would serve my purposes.

I got myself settled in the very last row. End seat, nearest the door.

Watched as plod came in. There was some confusion.

Heard, 'Shit.'

Some tutting.

They opted for the same row as me. Other side of the cinema. What choice did they have? Sit in front of me? Unlikely.

The dodgy cinema ads were mercifully short. Must save the long-play ones for the later shows. Trailers for a few soon-to-be-released films, then we were into Crowe strutting his stuff. Carrying a few more pounds, I thought. His co-star was Christian Bale. Obviously going for the Antipodean crew; probably shot in the outback too. Was looking to be not too bad a flick, quite getting into it when I remembered why I was there.

My first move was to loosen my belt.

Had the entire length wrapped round my hand when I stood up, stretched. Saw plod get jumpy at my side. Shifted uneasily in their seats. I was about, say thirty or forty yards from them. Maybe another twenty to the doors. Figured that gave me a bit of time to get a start on them.

I sat back down.

Fired off a quick text to Hod. It read: *You set?*

He replied: *In place. Outside Cameo.*

In a second, I vaulted the back of the chair, made for the doors. As I ran, I unfurled my belt, caught the buckle in my hand.

On the other side of the doors, I fed the belt through the handles, drew it together, fastened it on the last notch. It held tight.

I was off, chanking it for the street.

I could hear the thumping on the cinema doors as I got to the foyer.

Outside, I flashed my eyes left, right.

A blast of horn. Hod's tyres screeched.

I jumped towards the road.

The car just about mounted the pavement, then, 'Get in!'

I wasn't about to argue.

Chapter 39

HOD BURNED RUBBER DOWN Lothian Road, spun at the lights and snaked round the castle. Pedestrians flagged us to go slow. I thought they had a point.

'Hod, there's no benefit dumping plod to get done for sixty in a thirty zone.'

He settled. 'Right, where we going?'

'What do you mean *we*?'

He lifted hands off the wheel, slapped them back down. Gripped tight. 'Gus, c'mon, we're a team, right?'

'Uh-uh, buddy. Teams I don't do.'

'But I thought—'

'Hod, whoa-whoa! . . . Let me do the thinking, eh?'

He drove on, occasional scratch at his thickening beard, and soon we were on South Clerk Street, heading for North Bridge. At Hunter Square there used to be a heavy-duty drinking school. Had attracted protests from the retailers. The police had promised a clean-up. At the high point, upwards of fifty jakeys were seen in the square at any one time, pished up and ready to rumble. Not a pretty sight. Not good for the tourists. And *that* would *never* do.

I said, 'Where's the jakey brigade?'

'On the square? Gone.'

Last I looked, they were still in full attendance, said, 'How did they manage that?'

'Simple, really.'

He was playing coy. I said, 'Nothing in this city is simple. C'mon, spill it.'

'Well, y'know they tried just about everything – locking them up, arrests, bans, warrants ... even a twenty-four-hour police presence, just about.'

'Yeah, and none of it worked.'

'Until some bright spark had a brainwave.'

'Which was?'

'Why don't we start pouring their drink away in front of them?'

I looked out at the square: not a jakey in sight. 'Worked like a charm, Hod.'

'Well, you think about it – what's the one thing that's gonna put the frighteners on a jakey?'

I got the point.

'By the way, you didn't—'

'Glovebox.'

I opened the panel in front of me. A half-bottle of Grouse stared back. Said, 'Thanks, Hod.' Added, 'Yer all right, yer all wrong.' Real Scottish wisdom; defies explanation.

We crossed the bridge. Hod took the lights, headed round to George Street. Place was heaving – lot of French Connection bags, some Prada. Hard Rock Cafe doing a bustling trade; doorman putting up the stanchions with the red ropes already. Man, it was boom time in Edinburgh.

'So where to?' asked Hod. A set of shades and he could have been Teen Wolf.

'From the sublime to the ridiculous.'

'Come again?'

'Sighthill.'

'You're shitting me.'

I turned, pointed to my chops. 'Does this face lie?'

He drove on.

I changed the station on the radio, got some shock jock ranting about Polish plumbers. Apparently there were two busloads of Poles turning up in St Andrew Square every week. The homeless hostels all had to have a full-time Polish speaker on every shift now. Not all Edinburgh's streets were paved with gold.

'Bring 'em on, bring 'em on . . .' went the shock jock. 'My brother's a plumber, and he's never had it so good, cleaning up after the mess these unlicensed, unregulated, untrained, *unreal* Polish plumbers are making in our homes . . .'

Hod laughed. 'It's true . . . they're all shite!'

Couldn't all be bad, said, 'Well, why do they hire them?'

'Same old, same old . . . they're cheap!'

Made sense, of a sort.

I flicked. Found Thin Lizzy doing 'Jailbreak'. Would do for me.

I changed tack, 'So, dog fights . . . what's the rundown?'

'I have a pick-up.'

'You what?'

'A point of contact – we go there on the night, we get given the location and follow on.'

'Right, like a convoy.'

Hod raised a thumb, made to pull an imaginary truck horn. 'Bang on.'

'Bit organised for yobbos.'

'Gus, none of these boys are lightweights. Your little schemie skanks are likely up to their nuts in some dirty business. Whoever's stamping their meal ticket ain't gonna be a pushover. The whole pit-fight scene is serious, serious hardcore shit.'

I got the picture. I saw it had changed a little, but only a little. The fact remained: I wasn't getting answers from the young crew without some persuasion.

Took out my mobile. 'Turn down the radio, Hod.'

'Who you calling?'

'A contact.'

I dialled Fitz's number. Got right to the point: 'Fitz, it's Gus.'

211

'Dury, by the holy, that was some stint ye—'

'Fitz, later, later . . . I need to know about that stuff I asked you about the Corrado.'

'Dury, 'tis not news ye'll like.'

'Try me.'

'Well, hold on . . .' I heard rustling; he moved some papers on his desk, opened a drawer, closed it again. 'Right, here we are.'

'I'm waiting.'

'Well, there's twenty, no, twenty-plus, in the immediate vicinity.'

'You shit me?'

'Popular car.'

'Fucking hell. They've stopped making them – how popular can it be?'

'Ah, now, 'tis what ye might call popular with a certain *section* of the community.'

'Fucking boy racers.'

'Ye wouldn't be far wide of the mark there, Dury.'

I rested my head on my hand. I didn't have the time to check twenty addresses for these little pricks. 'Fitz, any listed in Sighthill, or Wester Hailes?'

I heard pages turning, then, 'Not a one.'

'Tell me you jest.'

'Would I ever?'

I didn't answer.

On a hunch I wondered if Mark Crawford was connected, said, 'What about Ann Street?'

'You kidding? Fuck no, there's none in Ann Street.' He changed tone, seemed almost smug. 'By the way, I hear that was a fine performance ye pulled off earlier.'

'Which one?'

'Would be the whole thing.' A laugh. 'Haven't ye McAvoy running about with a face like a Halloween cake!'

'That would be bad, right?'

Laughter. Uproarious. 'Oh, feck yes, Dury . . . Did ye ever, when ye were a chiseller, catch a wasp in a bottle? Well, isn't that the

212

spit of his like this afternoon, man. I'd say ye had him rattled! Rattled indeed, no mistake.'

I thanked Fitz for the 3D image, even though it was well and truly the last thing I wanted to hear right now.

'Well, Dury, I will tell ye this: McAvoy is no man to cross . . .'

'You said that already.'

'From what I'm hearing about him now, I didn't know the half of it.'

'Go on.'

'No danger . . . not on the line. We'll talk soon.'

He hung up.

We were pulling off the last road from civilisation, into the badlands.

'Where to?' asked Hod.

I pointed to a shop. Outside there was a girl, must have been no more than fifteen. She wore a bright pink boob tube and a black leather mini. Her face was aflame with acne, still visible through layer upon layer of slap.

'You sure?'

'Oh, yeah. You better take off too.'

'You what?'

'I mean it, fuck off home. I want peace from you. Prepare yourself for the pit fight. Conserve your energy.'

He shook his head. 'Right, okay.'

Hod revved the engine, clocked the girl walking over.

I joked, 'Your luck's in, you might have company.'

He wound down the window, hollered, 'Fuck off, you! Now. Back the way you came.'

The girl raised a single digit, fired it at Hod.

I had to smile as I saw him furiously wind up the window, mutter, 'Dirty hoor.'

Chapter 40

I ROCKED UP TO THE shop. Well, it sold stuff; similarities to any other shop I knew ended there. The outside was secured with hardboard and tin sheets. Above the door, razor wire. Inside you'd have to go back in time to Stalinist Russia to get the full flavour. The joint averaged three items to a shelf. Behind a barred-up counter, an old Sikh eyed me with suspicion. I don't believe he thought I was a shoplifter, more like lost.

'How goes it?'

No reply.

'Wonder if you could help me? I'm looking for a few lads, one with a flashy motor, a Corrado.'

Still no reply.

'Do you speak English?'

A sigh, nod.

'Great, we're making progress.' I heard someone scuttle in through the door behind me. 'Like I say, I'm after these boys ... You see, I need them to help me out with a bit of a problem.'

A young girl shoved a bag of dog biscuits under the bars, asked for twenty Berkeley. The Sikh put the lot in a bag, sorted out some change. Never opened his mouth.

The girl stared straight at me. She had a split lip and the biggest eyebrow piercing I'd ever seen. Under her arm was a white poodle, struggling for dear life.

'Can I help you, love?' I said.

She spazzed her mouth at me, said, 'You're fuckin' radge.'

'Yeah, and nice to meet you too.' I turned to the Sikh. 'This car, have you seen it?' I was losing the rag now, slipping quickly beyond frustration. 'It's white and it has these really unusual wheels, they're gold mags, y'know, like alloys.'

The girl slammed the door and the Sikh turned away from me. Went to sit in the corner of his little cage, topped a Mr Men mug up with Grant's.

I leaned over, yelled, 'Thank you, much appreciated.' I didn't envy the guy his job, or, by the kip of him, his life. I knew Sikhs were supposed to stay on the dry bus, but I suppose out here that was just too tall an order. I turned, gave him a wave, and headed for the door.

The first thing to hit me on the outside was the revving of a seriously high-powered engine. The next was the girl from the shop jumping into a Corrado and throwing the poodle on the back seat. After that something like a baseball bat took the legs off me and I fell to the ground, copping kicks and punches at all angles.

'Can you hear me, Mr Dury?'

I heard the voice, but didn't recognise it. I opened my eyes and latched on to an indistinct set of features, some burst blood vessels on the nose, heavy bags under the eyes.

'Mr Dury, are you with us?'

The paramedic sat me up. Someone else put a red blanket around my shoulders. My head throbbed; I saw some blood on the pavement.

'Quite a doing you got . . . You're lucky Mr Singh stepped in.'

I looked over the paramedic's shoulder. The old Sikh was returning to his shop. 'Him?'

'Oh aye – saw them off, then called us.' He reached in his bag, took out a vial. 'Now, tip your head back. This might sting a bit.'

'Ahh, Jesus Christ.' I jumped back, rocked the ambulance on its wheels.

215

'I told you it would hurt.' A wipe with cotton wool, some gauze attached to my head. 'That's going to need stitching. Come on, let's get you in the back of the vehicle.'

'Eh, no, I'll be fine.'

'You will not, you're bleeding from a head wound and you'll need a scan as well as those stitches.'

'Trust me, I'm fine.'

I stood up, felt a bit woozy. Immediately slid back down the side of the ambulance.

'Mr Dury, you're in no condition to—'

'Where did you get my name from?'

The paramedic handed me my wallet, said, 'I'd be more careful around here, you know.'

'Careful's my middle name. Look, thanks for the patch-up, but I'm fine, really.'

He knelt down, prised open my eyelids and switched on a little torch, 'How many fingers am I holding up?'

'Two . . . just like Churchill.'

A frown, unimpressed. 'The cut needs stitched, there's no way round that. You leave it, you'll have a nasty scar.'

'Nasty I can live with. Just patch me up and let me get out your way. I'm sure you've more deserving cases to get to.'

He shook his head, reached in his bag again. 'This is only a butterfly clip. It'll close the wound, but like I say, it'll scar.'

'Go for it.'

The procedure didn't take too long. Finished up with a bandage around my head.

Paramedic asked, 'Can you stand?'

'Yeah, no trouble.'

'Then we'll take you home.'

My legs felt rubber, but I got moving, said, 'Just a minute – want to say thanks to the shopkeeper.'

A hand on my arm. 'Mr Dury, send him a card. You're going home, or to hospital.'

The road back to Hod's boat seemed bumpy, but the codeine

tabs took the edge off. Was feeling pretty raw after my second doing-over in the last twenty-four hours. Wondered if I would last the next. I knew Mac and Hod would have some sage advice for me too; just couldn't wait to hear it.

Despite evidence to the contrary, I thought I'd had a lucky escape. Another five minutes under the cosh and I'd be taking my meals through a straw for the foreseeable. Then again, given my current diet, maybe I could manage that.

'Is this the place?' yelled the driver.

'Yeah, right out front's fine.'

The wheels came to a halt and then the back door slid open.

'Careful now. You don't want to be doing too much,' said the paramedic.

'I'm fine, really.'

'Well, let's get you inside.'

'Look, would you stop fussing? I can take it from here.'

Had the 'some people' stare sent my way. It wasn't that I was ungrateful for the help, I just hate fussing. I thanked the paramedic again, went inside.

The boat seemed empty until Usual shot out from under the bunk. I'd grown used to him jumping up and down every time I walked through the door but he was going ballistic with excitement. I could have done with more pain relief but had to settle for a bottle of 100 Pipers.

I lay in the bunk slipping in and out of sleep. The usual dreams – or should that be nightmares – came. Moosey's corpse appeared, then Debs on our wedding day.

I rose. My head hurt worse than any hangover but as I started to think about what Jonny had said outside the nick regarding Debs, my heart hurt even more.

Chapter 41

WAS I DREAMING? I DIDN'T think so; this had *happened*, surely. Were I asleep, it would be a nightmare . . .

Debs takes down the pictures of the little yellow hippos. She packs away the cuddly Barney toy, the Elmo from *Sesame Street* and the two-foot-long Doggie Daddy.

I don't like to watch.

I don't know what to say.

She seems so composed. There's an 'at work' look about her. I feel it's wrong. There should be some emotion, surely. But what do I know? I'm a man. This is women's business.

There're two boxes on the floor, one pink, one blue. 'We'll get one of each,' she told me only a week ago in another of our jaunts to John Lewis. 'You never know!'

Now she uses them to pack all this stuff away. She takes down the little blue dresses, the hand-knitted cardigans we seemed to get so many of. The news was such a joy to everyone.

'Debs is carrying,' Hod said. He bear-hugged me. 'God, that's smashing.'

'Yeah, yeah, I know . . . we're made up.'

Of course we were made up. It took us ten years to get to this level. Ten years to get over the thing we would sooner never think about. We just never realised the two events – one so sad and one so happy – could be intertwined. How could they be?

I watch Debs fold more little clothes. The little booties look like Christmas tree decorations. One box is full. She puts the little empty picture frames on top of it, turns to me, says, 'Can you take that down to the garage?'

I nod, lift up the box.

I want to speak now. I hear a voice prodding me: *Say something to her, say something to her. This behaviour isn't natural; she's in shock.*

But I say nothing.

I take the box away. In the doorway, I turn. She's almost filled the second box; a little yellow bath, no bigger than our kitchen basin, is being filled up too.

I walk away.

In the garage I can't bear to look at what I've carried down there. I shove it up against a stack of old tyres. It looks so out of place with the mower and power tools sitting nearby. I'll take it to the charity shop, I tell myself. I want to go straight away, get the next box, fill the car. But I don't. I stay in the garage. I stay in the garage and smoke a succession of cigarettes. Lighting each new one with the tip of the last. Only when the pack runs out do I go back inside.

The place is quiet. Eerily so.

The television is on low, *Antiques Roadshow*'s familiar tune playing. I walk into the room, hoping to see Debs. But she's not there.

I go through to the kitchen. It's empty. The bedroom too.

I know the only place left is the spare room, but I don't want to go back in there. She'll have packed up the place. Stripped the walls and cupboards. It will be a different room now. It's not that I want to remember it how it was, how we set it up. No, I want to forget that. I want to forget it all. Pretend it was never there in the first place.

But I can't.

I hear Debs crying and I know I have to go to her.

I try to edge the door open but there's something wrong. The door's blocked.

'Debs, what's up, sweetheart?' I push the door again, but it's still blocked. 'Debs, babes, I can't get in . . .' I push harder. In panic, I wonder what she's done to herself.

The door gives way and I see her lying on the floor.

I rush to her side. She's tipped out all the stuff from the boxes. All the stuff she so carefully packed.

'Debs, what is it? What's wrong?' It's a stupid thing to say, I know it. But what else can I say? There's no instruction manual for this kind of thing.

I kneel by her side and place a hand on her back. She trembles. I remember the time she trembled on our wedding day and it sends a shard of ice into my heart.

'Debs, please . . . don't do this.'

She's completely lost to me. I wonder: Does she even know I'm here?

I try to rub her back, calm her. She still trembles and then she turns over and curls up like a small child. She looks so helpless, so frail. I feel every shiver that passes through her.

'Please, don't do this to yourself, Debs.' I stroke her head. Her hair is shiny and smooth. It seems unreal to me, like the whole world has become now.

She shakes some more, cries hysterically. Her face becomes a mass of red, her cheeks look fit to explode. I try to stop her convulsing but I can't.

I know no one can.

I do all I can do. I lie down beside her on the floor and hold her. Just hold her. I hold her tight. As she cries and cries into my chest she repeats the same word over and over again: 'Why?'

I know there is no answer.

'Why?'

I wish I knew.

'Why?'

Yes, God . . . why?

220

Chapter 42

I PUT ON MY LONG coat. Crombie, navy blue. Was a remnant from my work days. Cost me a few sheets. I checked myself in the mirror. I'd removed the bandage, gelled my hair flat over my butterfly stitches. Had that gaunt definition going on with my face, bit of breakage in the nose adding some edge. Where I was headed, I'd need as much as I could muster.

'Rutger Hauer, eat your heart out,' I said.

The Hitcher didn't get a look in.

Debs had agreed to meet me. I was taking Usual for support. 'Wanna go for a walk, boy?'

Barks. Loud, one after the other.

I leaned over, could feel my ribs pinch. Must be bruising up nicely now, I thought. 'Well, boy, let's hope this goes better than the last time.'

Usual nuzzled his chops against my leg. His tail wagged, like he was ready to go. I took the hint.

He sat.

'Okay, let's nash.'

As I watched him spring up for the door, I wondered what he had been through. I felt a part of me grow closer to this wee dog every day; we were life's losers together.

We bused it to the South Side.

Set off down through the Meadows. Let Usual take a run over the grass. He seemed to have a route all mapped out for us. He checked on a few trees, sprinkled them, kicked out his back legs.

We left the park, snaked through the streets with Usual tugging on the lead.

A bloke in half-jog for the bus hollered, 'He's a lively one.'

I nodded. 'You bet.'

We were hitting Papa John's Pizza when I felt my pulse quicken. I'd know that walk anywhere. Wasn't exactly an Impulse ad moment, but in the ballpark. Then the image shattered as Debs spotted me too. We were both early.

'It's yourself,' she said.

'Hello, Debs.'

She lowered her head to the street. 'What's that?'

I leaned, patted Usual. 'Eh, my new best friend.'

Debs ventured a giggle. 'Come to that, has it?'

I was grateful for the in. 'Could say so.'

She laughed as Usual raised a paw. Hey, it was a start.

Awkward silence.

Forced herself: 'Look, Gus . . . I don't want to—'

'Debs, whatever you think I'm going to say, I'm not. All I wanted to talk about was how you were coping, and to say . . . sorry.'

She looked back to the dog, played with the buckle on her shoulder bag. A big retro number, said 'Gola' on the side in black and red letters.

'Jeez, they're back.'

'What?'

'Those bags, Gola . . . Remember when we used to do the squash club thing?'

She tapped the bag. 'God, Gus, stop. That was for ever ago.'

She seemed so young to me. Debs hadn't aged a single day since I'd met her. All that exfoliating and hydrating working wonders. She had miracle skin. I wanted to touch her face, just to know it still felt the way I remembered, but more, just to have the connection.

'Will we grab a coffee?' I asked.

She stared up the street, searched for the Peckham's with the chairs outside, said, 'Yeah, c'mon.'

We moved off towards the caf. Usual followed.

They had lightweight chrome chairs on the pavement. It was sunny now, but the last downpour still sat on top of them.

'They're soaked, Gus.'

I put a newspaper down for her. 'There – sorted.'

Was an age before the waitress appeared, hurriedly grabbed our orders. Debs took a pair of sunglasses out of her bag. Big jobs, thick legs. I knew they were the latest thing, not because I followed fashion, but because when you're so far removed from it – in the realms of anti-fashion – you can't miss it.

'You look like Jackie O.'

'That supposed to be a compliment?'

'One of the world's great beauties . . .' I felt a beam rise on my cheeks. Christ, Gus, when did you get to be so nervous around her? This is Debs, I told myself. Remember, your childhood sweetheart. Former wife. Love of your life.

'I'll take it as such, then,' she said.

I waited for the return fire. Normally, in this situation, she'd say I looked like shit. Not from nastiness – from concern. A rod to poke me with; I was used to people trying to motivate me to do things in myriad ways. None worked.

She pointed to my head. 'Been in the wars?'

'Just a scratch.'

Silence. Heads turned away.

The coffees came.

Debs smiled. Sipped, said, 'Mmmh . . . it's good.'

I looked at the bill, wanted to say, *Bloody should be at that price*, let it slide. Went for, 'I've been thinking a lot about . . . you know.'

The sun vanished. Debs lowered her cup. She raised her glasses, sat them on her head. Her hair trapped underneath gave her a sleek look.

'You can use the word, Gus.'

I didn't want to.

'I . . . I don't know why, just the time of year, I guess.'

'She would have been eighteen this year.'

My chest constricted. My throat froze. I knew words were impossible now. Debs had always said it was a girl. We never knew.

'Eighteen . . . I know that's right, only it seems wrong.'

'Too long ago, or too short . . . I can't decide.'

I knew exactly what she meant. It was a long time ago, but yet, at the same time, it seemed like yesterday.

'It never leaves you. It's as if . . . it's as if it's impossible to move on from that time.'

The sun seemed to have left for the day. Debs put back her shades; I knew she wanted to hide the reddening of her eyes. 'Sometimes, I wonder, did we make a mistake?' she said.

I felt I should reach out and hold her hand, but I didn't want to scare her off. I knew this was important; we needed to talk about this, however painful it was for us both.

'Deborah, we were judged enough for that decision . . . Don't be judging yourself now.'

'But—'

'No buts, Debs . . . We were children ourselves; there was no way we could have raised a child. For crying out loud, your mother turned you out the house when she found out you were carrying. There was nothing we could have done different. Nothing.'

She nodded, understood. 'Gus, it was abortion . . . a horrible thing.'

Oh hell. The word.

No other word in the world haunted me like it. It accounted for a million and one miseries I'd seen Debs go through.

'Deborah, don't play that Catholic guilt trip on yourself.'

'I can't just stop, it's—'

'Your programming. It's all just religious mumbo-jumbo, Deborah. Listen to me, you are a good person, don't ever think anything different for a second.'

As she looked at me I realised, without thinking, I'd taken her hand. We sat holding each other's hands for a moment and then it passed. Debs pulled her fingers away slowly. 'Thank you,' she said.

'I don't say it lightly.'

I'd seen the best and worst of her, and I knew there was little difference. Even when she was whipped by the family she'd done nothing to deserve, she held her values in check. She was as good and kind a soul as I had met and I knew it would be a lifetime before I met another like her. As I stared into the depths of her I understood the misery I had brought her. Her time with me was something she could have done without. She had so much to look forward to. She had so much going for her. But when she took up with me all that evaporated. An abortion, then a miscarriage that ruined her chance of a child when we dearly wanted one. I was a plague on this poor girl's life. She had every right to hate me for what I had brought her to. And, worse, denied her still.

'Debs, I don't want to mention this . . .'

'*But* . . .'

'Yes, well, there's always one of those, isn't there.'

'Just spit it out, Gus.'

'I, eh, met Jonny again.'

She didn't flinch like I thought she might. Only the intonation of her voice shifted, became harder. 'And?'

'Well, he said something which didn't quite make sense to me.'

'He thinks you killed a man, Gus.'

That bust my flush.

I threw up my arms. 'There you go, that again. I didn't fucking kill anyone. Though that little bastard gives me any more of an excuse, I might yet!'

Debs sat further back in her seat, pouted. 'Look, what did he say, Gus?'

'He hauled me down the station to tell me fifty grand was lifted from Tam Fulton's corpse and he thinks I took it.'

Debs's mouth widened; she looked as if she'd been slapped. 'Fifty thousand pounds . . .'

'Your prick boyfriend is pinning his hopes on it being my motive.'

'I don't think he'd do that, Gus.'

I tried to rein things in again. 'You don't think, Debs? Full stop you don't think, if that's how you rate the fella.' I'd gone too far. 'Look, I'm sorry. I'm a little on edge.'

'Need a drink?'

Booka-booka. She got me.

I stood up, said, 'Deborah, I think I should go. I've enjoyed being with you again. I really appreciate that you still see fit to give me the time of day and I don't want to get in the way of any happiness that you have found for yourself.'

A cold stare. 'You think he's wrong for me.'

I put a tenner down on the table, moved my cup and saucer over it. 'Debs, I've said too much.'

'You think I'm wrong to marry him.'

The dog sprang to life. Ran to my heels, eyes wide.

'Who am I to say?' I wouldn't be drawn in; I knew I'd said too much already. Debs needed to find some enjoyment in life. She was still young, beautiful. She could move on, put the past behind her.

'Gus . . .' she grabbed my arm, 'I can't bring myself to tell him that I can't have children.'

I was on my knees, holding her tight before I even realised the tears had started all over again.

Chapter 43

PRINCES STREET HAS COME DOWN in the world of late. Once the site of Scotland's most prestigious retailers, now it plays host to pound shops, puggies and, worst of all, Ann Summers. I slunk past the window display of naughty nurse uniforms, dominatrices and – is there a worse euphemism? – love toys. If it made me blush, Christ alone knows what John Q. Citizen thought of it. Back in the day, a window display like that would have the dirty mac brigade scuffling outside clutching brown paper bags – now it's fair play for the Scottish capital's main drag. How things have changed.

I tied up Usual and jumped into a whisky shop. There were less of them, too. Got a half-bottle of Bell's and a full bottle of Glenfiddich in a presentation case; had plans that required a 'bring a bottle' touch.

Outside the shop I unscrewed the cap of my latest purchase, took a good blast. The dog was scratching at my legs to be untied. I let him loose, got strolling again and jumped a bus back to the boat. The slow drive through the city and the mild buzz from the whisky had me thinking about Debs all over again. I couldn't put our meeting out of my mind. There's a streak in me, Presbyterian probably, that moons over predestination at times like this. It's a uniquely Scottish trait. We even have a phrase to live by: *What's for ye'll no' go by ye.*

Rough translation: what's meant to be, will be.

I liked the cut of it. Appealed to my alkie's wisdom. We're all looking for someone to say, 'You're doomed, there's nothing you can do about it.' In such instances, the best course of action is always to say: 'Fuck it, let's get blootered.'

There are some alkies who can separate out the doomed stuff from the everyday disappointments like the shaving cut, the burnt toast, the late bus. Me, I add them up, say, 'There's your proof.'

It's when things go right that I become truly distressed.

When nothing goes wrong on you, when the world conspires to give you calm, it's the drinker's duty to disrupt it. You start to feel the world closing in on you. It's too small a place. Too simple. People, normal people, begin to irritate you endlessly. Your anger knows no bounds. Shouting, ranting, bawling and raging at anything becomes the norm. A DJ's comments on the radio, a chance remark overheard in a shop, and you're off. You want out. Anywhere will do. Just away from this . . . state.

I'd read about famous alcoholics; it had become almost an obsession with me. To a one they all said the same thing: 'I can't imagine a world without drink, it would be too . . . boring.'

When I hear this I know at once that it's the addiction talking. Alkies just can't put up with themselves. To a one they are self-loathing. Days on the dry are endless. Like being locked up with a stranger. A stranger you hate. You drink, and the stranger goes away, leaves you in peace. But more than that, you find another state. Somewhere where you don't need to scream all day and all night like you were in purgatory being poked in the ribs by the Devil.

Rousseau said: 'Man is born free, and everywhere he is in chains.' Alcohol was my key. It unlocked the chains. It set me free – for a little while.

I was back on the boat before I knew it. Hit the half of Bell's again; tanned the lot this time. The dog was watching me. Could have sworn he had disapproval on his face.

'Sorry, boy, got to leave you again.'

I knew I was wrong to stray too far from Hod's boat. What I needed was something like that scene in *Trainspotting* where Renton locks himself away with the tins of soup, goes cold turkey. I also knew, like Renton, there wasn't a chance in hell I was doing any cold turkey.

Anyway . . . *what's for ye'll no' go by ye.*

I flagged a Joe Baxi to Sighthill. When I got out I gave the driver a nod, said, 'Go safe.'

A smile; whole head quivered on his meaty neck.

I could hear trail bikes burning up the park beyond the road. This was the new craze: get a bike and go grabbing handbags. We had them all over the city now, young neds on bikes, could spot them by the bare head. There'd been some bad incidents, folk knocked to the ground and near killed. No one seemed to have any trouble identifying them, except plod. No revenue in it I guess.

I nashed through the streets, over paving flags all cracked to buggery. Round the burning wheelie bins – apparently you can get a buzz off them. I kept my head low this time, avoided any eye contact. Avoided the hails of skag merchants, yelling:

'You sorted, pal?'

'What about some jellies?'

'Bag ay puff?'

Didn't answer, got:

'A shooter ye after, big man?'

'You for a ride? Only top nanny, mind.'

Then:

'. . . *Well fuck ye*!'

'. . . *Homo*!'

'. . . *Fucking bawbag*!'

Was hard to imagine meaner streets. Christ, even I was a tourist here. But if a Corrado skidded into view, I'd be ready for it. Somehow I doubted it, though. Smart money was on that baby being garaged for the foreseeable.

At the boarded-up store I tapped the counter, roused the Sikh. 'How goes it?'

A 'like I care about that shit' stare.

I produced the bottle of Glenfiddich, pushed it through the bars, said, 'I wanted to say thank you . . . for what you did the other day.'

His face lit up. A huge row of teeth, fair dazzled me. He took the bottle, said, 'Thank *you*.'

I shrugged. 'I'm the one giving thanks here, don't be turning the tables on me. I'm serious: what you did, you probably saved my life.'

A wave of the hand. 'No, sir, I do the same for anyone.' He wiped at the bottle with the tips of his fingers. 'Come, a drink, yes?'

Like I'd say no.

The Sikh called through to the back. A young girl in denims came out, slouched at the till and started to chew on red-liquorice laces.

Out back smelled of strong spices, cooking. Made my mouth water.

He put two china cups down on the table, poured. I waited for him to drink first. He raised his cup, clinked it on mine. All the while he smiled like a cheeky child. At first taste, I could see he approved.

'I am Rafi.'

'Gus. Pleased to meet you.'

We shook.

More smiles. Didn't think his English was up to much more; tried anyway: 'I wondered, how did you get those little shites off me?'

A laugh. His head shook on his shoulders. 'Mossberg!'

'You what?'

In a second he was out of his chair, unfurling a chain from his belt with a bunch of keys on the end. He slid one into the lock of a battered old cabinet, popped the door. As he turned he grasped the barrel on a pump-action shotgun. 'Mossberg. Best, yes?'

Somehow, when I see a gun like this, I pinch my lips. 'That's some piece. I'm guessing that'll do the trick.'

He smiled, beamed wide. 'No talkie. No talkie, Mr Gus.' He wagged a finger at me. 'Rafi, no papers.'

I couldn't help but laugh. He laughed with me, poured another cup of whisky.

For an hour we sat, finished the bottle.

'You eat with us, Mr Gus.'

'I'd love to, Rafi ... love to, just love to, mate.' I was feeling a bit tanked, the good stuff mixing with the codeine tabs I'd swallowed earlier on an empty stomach. 'But my wife would disapprove of me imposing on your family.'

'A wife, yes. Good. Good.'

'Sorry, I meant ex-wife.'

'Ah, ex-wife, not good.'

'You got that bang to rights. Let me tell you about the *d-i-v-o-r-c-e* ...'

He knew the song, surprised me, joined in:

'*D-i-v-o-r-c-e* ...' We raised the roof, clutching each other, peals of laughter flooding out of us when the door was flung open and an old woman in a sari pushed in, blasted Rafi with some heavy-duty home language. For that stuff you don't need the lingo, it's the same the world over. He shrank before me, lowered his head. I followed his lead. When she left, slamming the door behind her, I stood up.

'Time to boost ...' I had to meet Hod and make our venture out to the pit fight. 'I've enjoyed your company, Rafi, but I must nash.'

The headlight smile came back on. Handshake. 'Always my pleasure, Mr Gus! Any time, any time.'

As he grasped my hand tightly, I had a thought, said, 'Rafi, y'know, if it wouldn't be stretching the friendship too much, there is one thing you could do for me ...'

Chapter 44

HAD SOME RAIN. LEFT THE streets looking washed. In this town that's something. The council was wrestling with a 'budget black hole', according to the papers. Never ceased to amaze me: any other city you visit in the world, they manage to empty the bins, tend the parks, clean the streets. Edinburgh, unless there're developer kickbacks or a massive tourism pay-off, forget it. Daily the population gets one in the coal-hole from the mob in the City Chambers. Really boils my piss. Such a scenic town. A World Heritage city. But in reality, just a jam pot for the few with their hands on the levers.

I jumped into the nearest newsagent's. Ordered: 'Twenty, nah, make that forty Rothmans.'

They had a collection of bottles behind the counter, up on the shelf. Lambrusco on offer, great fluorescent orange star stuck to the side saying £1.99. Wasn't tempted. But after starting on the whisky with Rafi at Sighthill, I wasn't stopping. Said, 'Oh and chuck in a couple of quarter-bottles of that.'

I pointed to the vodka. Was overtaking scoosh in the convenience stores now; the first choice of our influx of Polish immigrants.

The newsagent put the bottles before me. I looked at the label – name I'd never heard of. Pocketed them. On the street I stood waiting for Hod, wrestled the cellophane off my tabs, sparked up.

The smoke cancelled out the smell of dampness rising from the paving flags. It was like an old memory being shoved to the back of my mind: dampness, wet, rain . . . When I look back these are the background images in every scene. My life has been lived in the tones of Van Gogh's early paintings, grey and greyer. The few moments of colour all involved Debs; but she featured in a lot of the grey days too.

I had a Mossberg pump under my Crombie that Rafi had sold to me; kept a firm hand on the barrel. As I schlepped over the road, the shooter rammed into my ribs with every step. Knew it pulled my coat south. I felt lopsided, but in this rain, who was looking?

I wasn't messing about. End of.

The night was cold. Dark clouds gathering at the edges of a red sky. As I waited at the roadside I powered through my Rothmans King Size. The sharpness of the air seemed to take the hit out of the cigarette so I stubbed it. For some reason I thought of Debs again. It was on nights like this we'd begun to bond. Freezing half to death on park benches, sharing ten Regal on a roundabout in some skanky playground.

The reverie was soon interrupted as Hod's car screeched up; a yell, 'Get in.'

I opened the door. 'Fuck me, it's Chewbacca!' I sat down and buckled up. All the while trying to disguise the shooter. He wouldn't approve.

'What's with the faraway look?' said Hod.

'No look.'

'Bollocks . . . Is it Debs?'

Jesus, did it still show? 'No, no way.'

'C'mon, you can't kid me, I was your best man, remember. I know that look.'

I took out my smokes again. Sparked another one. 'I saw her earlier,' I said.

'And?'

'She told me Jonny Johnstone has it set in his mind that I'm going down.'

Hod pulled around a red Micra, waved a hand to let out a bus. 'Hasn't she been speaking up for you? Can't she set this arsehole straight? I mean, she should be our inside track here, no?'

I wound down the window, flicked ash. 'Hod, she's not my wife any more. She doesn't owe me anything and besides . . .'

I trailed off mid-sentence but Hod was listening, a gap appearing in the fuzz of his face. 'Besides what?'

'I think she'd be too frightened to speak up for me. Not because she's shitting it from J.J., but because she wouldn't want to rattle him any more. Like Fitz said, the man has a boner for me.'

Hod fired up: 'I thought plod was supposed to be professional about these things. Fucksake, what's his problem? I just don't get this.'

'Jonny Boy's young and insecure, Hod. That's what it boils down to. He wants to obliterate Debs's past, completely own her – with this murder case he's found the perfect way to do it . . . And there's more to it. He's up to some kind of shit I can't quite get a handle on.'

'But how? He's off the case.'

'Bollocks to that. McAvoy's working the case for him: a man desperate for a collar, any collar – what a gift!'

'Bad boys stick together.'

I frowned. 'I'm not sure about that. I mean, I don't know how much McAvoy is interested in J.J. as a partner, even a junior one. The pair struck me as both a little too self-interested to get along . . . D'you know what I mean?'

Hod revved the engine, dropped a gear; in second he beat the lights. He didn't need to answer my question, I could see he understood where I was coming from – the pair would cut each other's throats to get ahead.

'Anyway, things might change tonight,' said Hod.

I had my doubts but I was willing to give it a go. 'You think the wee bastard with the Corrado will be there?'

'There's every chance. They don't put these sort of gigs on every night of the week.'

'I suppose.'

'Look, be positive . . .'

I saw Bell's books again – reran 'Techniques for positive visualisation'.

'Positive – that's horseshit. You'll be telling me to keep my fingers crossed next.'

'Gus, we have a chance here, slim as it might be, to track down the little fucker that killed Tupac, maybe even link him up to Mark Crawford. Let's not balls it up is all I'm saying.'

'Okay. Okay.' The point was taken. Stay off the sauce. Keep the head. Don't, under any circumstances, lose it.

'At the very least we get to see that slimy fucker Sid in action. Keep a close eye on him – whoever he's mixing it with might be useful to us.'

I took a grip on the shooter. I had a handful of cartridges in each pocket of my Crombie. Felt comforting. Like insurance.

'And anyway, it's not the end of the world if we don't grab us a gimpy boy tonight,' said Hod.

'How come?'

'Well, we have some leads now, right?'

'*We*?' I wasn't getting this Hod seeing himself as my partner business one iota.

'Yeah, well, I'm on the team, right?'

'Hod, there is no fucking team . . . there's me versus the world. I wouldn't be opting for a side so quick if I were you.'

Hod pelted the accelerator, hit the bypass. 'C'mon, don't mark me for a wuss – I'm in, all right.'

An artic pulled out from a slip road. Hod had to floor it to get past.

'Hod, watch the road, eh?'

'Gus, my man, relax there. With me on the team you have an extra pair of hands, eyes, and that's not to mention my brain and brawn.'

I laughed. 'You put it like that . . .'

'How else would I put it?'

'Well, there's no question you can be a help. What I'm having trouble with is the whole babysitting aspect.'

'Oh . . .'

'Yes, *oh* . . . Hod, I know you and Mac and maybe one or two others are scheming to get me off the sauce, sorted, into, I dunno, the poor man's Priory. Hear me now: it'll never happen.'

Hod put on the indicator, pulled off the bypass at the Loanhead roundabout.

Just before the village was a row of abandoned terrace cottages, old-style red-brick jobs. All boarded up. Like a post-apocalyptic Coronation Street. How, in the city's mad state of overdevelopment, these had not been snapped up was beyond me. A few flat-pack kitchens, plasterboard walls, we were talking a quarter mil for one of them.

'You're not scoping new property, are you?' I said.

'Fuck no – Loanheid!'

'Well, why you slowing down?'

'This is the first part of the trip, my son.'

'You what?'

A skinny lad in a blue Lonsdale hoodie came scurrying out of the backyard of the nearest boarded-up terrace. He looked down the street, left to right, then seemed to take a note of the number plate and check it against a list.

'Here we go. Let me do the talking, Gus.'

'Go yerself.'

The lad lolled up to Hod's window, leaned over. He spoke, 'You know the big man, eh?'

'Yeah, I know the big man . . . he likes his fishing.'

'That'll be *fly* fishing?'

'He's a *fly* man.'

The lad unzipped his Lonsdale top, tucked a hand in and brought out a bit of paper, handed it over to Hod. 'That's yer map there. Have a good night, eh, mate.'

'Oh, I think we will . . . I think we will.'

Chapter 45

THE MAP TOOK US BEYOND the city boundaries, deep into the countryside.

'We're gonna be in fucking Glasgow soon, Hod.'

'I'm following the map.'

'You sure about that?'

He thrust the piece of paper at me, said, 'Check if you like.'

I didn't bother.

I had a quarter of vodka in my inside pocket, cracked it open, tipped back a few mouthfuls. Then a few more.

Seemed to settle the thrashing in my stomach.

'You're not gonna lash that, are you?' said Hod.

I held up the bottle; seemed pathetically small, said, 'Could I? Is it possible?'

'You could have half a dozen of them stashed about you, I wouldn't know . . . I mean, what's with the coat? It's hardly the weather for it.'

I let that slide, tucked away the bottle.

We took the M8 for about six miles before hitting the side roads. Lots of brown-backed signposts appeared declaring we were on a 'Tourist Route'. Official: this entire country is not for those who live in it.

After a mile or so, Hod chucked a hairpin right, hit dirt track.

Heard David Byrne wail, 'We're on a road to nowhere' . . . except maybe the dark heart of the forest. Light overhead became thinner and thinner, until it was time to flick the headlamps on.

'This is spooky shit,' said Hod.

'Man, not the time to be bottling on me.'

'Bottling? Me?'

'You just said you were spooked.'

'I was scene-setting.'

'Oh yeah.'

Through the forest and out the other side we hit a clearing, another dirt track. In the open I could see it had been churned up quite a bit. Deep puddles and a mush of black earth indicating some heavy traffic had passed this way recently.

'Looks like we're getting close.'

'According to this,' Hod waved the map, 'we should be just about there.'

'Hold up . . . what's this?'

A big biffer in a black leather jacket, shaved head, unshaven face, approached. He had a moustache that would put Harley handles in the shade. As he got closer I saw he looked like the late Ollie Reed, matched him for size and sheer shit-stopping radgeness.

A hand went up. Hod braked, wound down the window. 'All right, mate.'

Not a flicker; cold eyes. 'What you up tae?'

'We're, eh . . . friends of the big man.'

'Aye, spare me that shite . . . You got Hosie's map?'

'Hosie . . . oh, right, the wee hoodie.' Hod held up the map.

The biffer stuck a hand through the open window. Four sovereign rings played for attention with some nasty spider's-web tats. One inky near the wrist read CUT HERE. He grabbed the map, tucked it in his pocket then pointed out to the left: 'Take the motor over there, by that wee clump ay trees. You can park in front ay the barn. Pit's on the inside.'

Hod put the car in gear, raised a little wave in gratitude, then drove for the barn. 'You see his face?' he said.

'The scar . . . fucking deadly.'

'Never seen a Mars bar like that before.'

I knew what he meant: it wasn't a clean cut, it was jagged. 'What do you think, a bottle fight?'

'Maybe a dog attack . . . or maybe someone just wanted him to look carved up good and proper.'

I didn't like to think about it. I touched the barrel of the Mossberg for reassurance.

As Hod parked the car I got out, hit myself up with another blast of vodka. The bottle near emptied on me. I held it in my hand, staring at it until Hod appeared at my side and said, 'What's up?'

'Nothing.' I raised the bottle again, finished the dregs.

'Got you in some shit that stuff, hasn't it.'

It was a low blow, but could I fault him? It was perfectly pitched.

I threw the bottle, watched it smash on a tree, said, 'C'mon, let's do this.'

I put my collar up as we strode towards the barn doors. There were angry pit bulls chained to car axles that had been staked into the ground. Every one of the dogs strained to break free and attack its nearest neighbour. An Irishman stood pointing to one of them, highlighting each of its scars and regaling a slope-shouldered yoof in trackies with tales of the fights it had won.

Inside the place was hoachin. Like a cattle auction. Men stood three, four deep around the centre of the barn. Light was poor, save at the midpoint, where some old storm lanterns were suspended from the roof beams.

We edged our way closer. Suddenly the crowd seemed to disperse.

'Are we too late?' I asked Hod.

An old gadgie, baseball cap turned round, answered for him: 'Utter fucking shite pagger that was. Where they got that useless wee cunt in there I've no idea.'

Hod smiled. 'A mismatch?'

'Mismatch? Fucking bloodbath – look at it.'

I got to the front of the crowd to see what he was on about. A ring, maybe fifteen feet wide, had been set up. Inside was a forty-pound snarling pit bull shaking the virtually lifeless body of what looked like the same breed. The near-dead animal had remarkably similar markings to Usual. I felt my heart pound.

I turned away. My hand raised automatically to my mouth.

From nowhere, I felt my arm knocked down. 'Don't make that face, Gus,' said Hod.

The stench of blood was everywhere. I felt my guts heave. 'Hod, this is foul.'

'Keep your voice down.'

They separated the two dogs and the victor was raring to go again. The loser merely lay down. Exhausted and unable to move, it stared at its handler. The ground was a blanket of blood. The handler – a hardy neckless type – picked the animal up by the scruff and hauled it to a barrel in the corner of the barn.

'What's he gonna do with it?' I asked Hod.

Under breath: 'Shut up, Gus.'

I watched the guy lift the dog into the barrel and hold it down in there for a few minutes. It was only when the dog was removed, dripping with water, that I realised its reward for fighting to near-death for its handler was to be drowned.

The crowd started shouting for more, baying for blood.

'I don't think I can watch this,' I said.

Hod started to get rattled. He placed his hand on my elbow. 'You don't think what?'

I saw another vicious pit bull – this one must have weighed fifty pounds – being led from the front of the barn. He struggled and clawed to get to the ring. His handler, a teeny lightweight in head-to-toe Adidas, struggled to hold on to him. He jerked the choke chain, yelled at him. The dog ignored all of it. He was ready to kill. Primed.

In the ring another pit was already waiting, similar size, raring to go. All around us grown men were roaring.

A loud call went up: 'Release the dogs.'

In a second the two beasts were unleashed; they collided like the bottle I'd just smashed on a tree. The noise of their skulls connecting hurt my ears. They were both thrown in the air, a shower of teeth spraying the crowd.

'Hod, this is sick.'

'Dury, get a grip.'

I turned away. At the other end of the barn I saw a flash of white. I thought I'd seen a ghost. Then I saw it again. The shape was more visible this time. I recognised it as a dog. But not a pit bull, or anything like it. It was a white poodle. Somehow the dog had evaded its handlers. My guess, it sensed its fate.

I knew this dog was the intermission – some very light entertainment between bouts. I followed its attempts, running frantically the length and breadth of the barn, looking for an escape; it couldn't find one. Suddenly it was grabbed by the scruff. Jostled about a bit, yelled at. It turned its little snout away from the lad doing the yelling. I clocked him at once: it was our Corrado driver.

'I'm sorry, Hod.'

'What do you mean you're sorry . . . sorry for what?'

I opened up my Crombie. Felt for the handle of the Mossberg. 'I'm sorry for this.' In a second I raised the shooter.

The sound of the gun's discharge made everyone in the room duck in unison. A few turned skywards as they crouched, expecting to see the roof come down. I cut a path through the crowd, pushed people aside left and right. No one seemed too bothered to stop me.

A voice yelled out, 'Police, stay where you are!' It was Hod. Self-preservation or initiative, I didn't care which – it did the trick. The place emptied with a stampede.

In a few seconds I was on the yob with the poodle. He saw me heading his way and dropped the dog, scampered.

'Fuck . . . Hod, get that fucking dog!'

I watched Hod lower his arms, call to the dog, but it was all over the place.

'Get fucking after it!'

The barn emptied in a hurry, people running for the hills. This shit you don't want to get hoyed in for.

I set off after the yob. He was dressed all in white, trackies and top to match. It made my job easier. 'I'll blow yer fucking head off!' I yelled.

He was fast, through the back of the barn and the path skirting the trees to the clearing. I tried to catch him but my lung capacity had been seriously reduced by years and years of full-on tab usage.

'Stop, you little prick!'

At the clearing where the cars were parked, I caught sight of him sliding across the front of a bonnet, *Dukes of Hazzard* style. I raised up the shooter, but he was gone behind another car, ducking and weaving for dear life. 'Shit, this fucker's fast.'

Everywhere cars pulled out, screeched tyres. Engines revved all around, was like the starters' line-up at the Indy 500.

As I got to the first row of cars I heard an engine roar, then coming straight for me, right down the middle of the road: it was the Corrado.

I raised the gun.

I shouted, 'I'll fucking use this!'

My warning didn't register. Driver went straight for me.

I'd no choice, dived out of the way. As the car screamed past, I got to my feet, fired off a round. It put out the back window. Glass exploded all over the dirt track, settled for a second, then was mashed in by the flood of fast-moving cars.

As I stood up I caught sight of a brand-new Audi being driven like it was a Knockhill wrecker. Behind the wheel was a face I recognised, but the one sitting next to it told a whole other story.

Chapter 46

THERE WAS NO SIGN OF the resident plod lurking outside so we washed up back at the Holy Wall. Mac had a pint of Guinness ready and waiting for me on the bar. I knocked the head off it quick smart. Soothed like an old friendship. Felt like medicine.

The white poodle played on the floor with Usual. Hod laughed. 'Christ, it's a hard dog that you've got, lads – mates with a poodle.'

Mac went off, 'Get that dog down to the fucking pound. It's someone's pet – they'll be looking for it!' He pointed Hod to the door, puffed his chest. 'And get a fucking shave, ye gypo!'

Not biting, Hod moved off. 'I was only joking. I'm going. I'm gone already.'

Mac walked behind the bar, picked up a bag of KP nuts, raised another bag for me. I declined. As he munched away he let his thoughts escape. 'Well, that sounded like it was all a complete fucking farce.'

'How do you gather that?' I said.

'They got away.'

'Ah but . . .' I got out of my stool, reached over for a bottle of Haig, poured out a wee goldie, downed it.

Mac grew impatient. 'But *what*?'

'We got a direct hit on the car . . . and I caught sight of a very cosy scene that will take some looking into.'

'What?'

'Sid the Snake and Jonny Johnstone sharing a motor.'

A head-shake, rapid eye movement, a swallow. 'I'm gonna stretch that wee cunt's neck.'

I raised my pint, pointed a finger. 'Hold that thought.'

I left Mac in the bar, went out to the hallway to make a phone call. My mind was on one thing, and one thing only. In the midst of such an overwhelming crisis, I couldn't believe I was focusing on this.

By the back door sat a cardboard box. Inside were old pictures of my father in his playing days. By the look of it, old Scottish Division One. I remembered a row with the Wall's original proprietor, Col, about these very pictures. He'd taken them down so as not to offend me. As I looked at them now, I wished he'd thrown them out altogether. I laid a kick into the side of the box, heard a loud crack from the glass.

'The fucking last I want to see of you.'

I dialled up Debs's number.

Ringing.

An answer: 'Hello?'

'Hi, Debs, it's—'

'I know who it is.'

Well, that was something. 'Are you all right now?'

'Gus, I'm always all right.'

I knew what she meant: there is *all right* and there is *well* – the two aren't the same thing.

'I wondered if you were still, y'know . . .'

'Gus, you don't need to worry about me.'

'Debs, c'mon, you were in bits when I saw you. I don't stop caring just because you're out of sight. You know that.'

Silence.

The gap on the line stretched out.

'Debs . . . Debs, you still there?'

I heard her begin to cry down the line. 'Gus, I'm sorry . . . I just can't play the hard bitch any more.'

'You were never that, ever.'

Sobs. 'I just feel like it's all getting to me now.'

'What, Debs, the baby thing?'

'Gus, it was a fucking abortion – can't you say the word?'

I could say it; I just didn't want to. And moreover, I knew she didn't want to hear it. 'Stop it, Debs. Just stop torturing yourself.'

'Why? Have you got the monopoly on that?'

'No, I—'

'Gus, why did you call?'

Why did I call? I wondered that myself. Did I want to help her? Was I being selfish? 'I don't know.'

'Neither do I, Gus . . . This is all pointless. You know we're not going to get back together, don't you?'

I felt wounded. I had no hopes of us getting back, no real ones anyway. But to hear her say this cut deep. 'Of course not, Debs . . . I only wanted to . . . Christ, do I need a fucking appointment now to check on you?'

Silence again.

'Debs. *Debs*.'

'I'm going to go now, Gus.'

'What have I said?'

'Nothing. Nothing. I'm just going to go.'

'Debs, just tell me you're okay.'

I heard her voice start to quiver; her words struggled to get out. Tears, more this time. 'I told him, Gus.'

So Jonny knew. I wanted to ask how much he knew. 'You told him everything?'

'I told him why I can't have children, Gus.'

Debs's voice came clouded in sobs. I wanted to be there for her now, put an arm around her, tell her it was all going to be okay. Tell her it was better out in the open. Any old cliché, just to make her feel better.

'You did the right thing, Debs.'

She yelled down the phone, 'No, Gus, I didn't! I never do the right thing. Never. I never do that.'

245

'What do you mean, Debs? What do you mean?'

'I can't save you this time, Gus . . . I just can't.'

I didn't understand. 'I'm not with you . . .'

'Gus, I'm not able to . . . I just can't do it. I don't know what you expect me to do. Jonny isn't in my control, you know.'

This was out of left field. 'Debs, I don't want you to do anything for me.' I didn't want her to put herself in any danger; I'd go down for Moosey's murder before that happened. I couldn't believe I'd given her any other impression. 'Debs, I only want you to be happy. I'm sorry if I— Debs, Debs . . .'

She'd hung up on me.

Chapter 47

SID THE SNAKE'S STREET WAS quiet, maybe too quiet. After the raid we'd staged on the pit fight Hod had word that certain folk were none too chuffed. I anticipated another howk from Rab's pugs but was more concerned with some rasslin' of my own.

We sat just up from Sid's gaff and waited. He had to emerge sooner or later and when he did I'd be there. And more worryingly for him, so would Mac the Knife.

'You look pumped.'

Mac squeezed the steering wheel. 'That wee prick's gonna be pumped.'

'You're remembering your record, of course.'

A laugh, cut in half, replaced with a smile. 'I'm playing my record!'

There was some movement down the street; Sid's door opened. Two skelky yoofs stepped out and slouched themselves into the wind. I couldn't see their faces hidden behind hoodies. I let them traipse along the pavement. When they passed the van I saw one of them had a bag over his shoulder.

'What you think's in there?' I said.

'Fuck knows . . . Skag? Could be anything. They're in with Rab and he's into it all.'

I thought about going after the yob for a look, but then Sid's door opened again and I was harshly thrown back in my seat.

As Mac brought the van to a halt there was a screech of tyres. A gust of black smoke lingered in the air as I pulled open the slide door. Sid stood on the pavement wide-eyed, his mouth drooping like a feedbag above his scrawny neck. I reached out and grabbed him by the collar. He was surprisingly light as I threw him into the back. Mac spun the wheels again as the door slammed shut.

I said nothing, let Sid wonder.

I kept eyes on him as he jittered before me, wiping a dribble from the side of his mouth.

He looked like a cornered rat, hunched over and ready to bound away first chance he got. His thin knees poked through his keenly pressed denims like tent poles. In the van there was an atmosphere you couldn't mistake. Sid was shitting himself. Not literally, but if he was you wouldn't catch it over the reek of Blue Stratos he was wearing.

'What the fuck is this?' he said finally.

I blanked him.

'C'mon, this is out ay order. I've told you all I know before.'

I rubber-eared him again.

He banged on the side of the van, yelled, 'Hey, let me out!'

He'd pushed his luck. I leaned forward and grabbed Sid by the neck. He squirmed; hands shot up as he tried to speak. His voice came like a croak, but there were no words he could form.

I watched Sid struggle before me, slap my hands pathetically, then I smacked his head off the side of the van.

He slumped, hands clawing at his collar, gasping for air.

Mac shouted to us, 'What the fuck's going on back there? . . . If I've to stop this van I'll do the cunt here and now.'

Sid's feet paddled on the floor of the van as he retreated from me in blind panic.

I said, 'He's settled now. If he moves again, I'll do him myself.'

We drove for an hour.

Mac had obviously done this before; he knew how to stretch out the tension.

None of us spoke, though I swore I saw Sid mouthing the rosary. His complexion had gone from the natural schemie grey to white as a maggot. He sat with his knees folded under his chin and his arms wrapped around his shins. Only occasionally did he look in my direction and if he caught my eye he'd divert his gaze promptly.

I saw through the front windscreen that Mac had driven us out into the country. We were coming off a B road and heading down a dirt track. I saw trees. Don't ask me what kind – I'm from Leith – but they were lined up along the banks of a little burn. They had thick branches, kind you could get a rope over; more than strong enough to hold a skelf like Sid.

Mac brought the van to a halt. Turned off the engine and put the keys in his pocket. He made a great show of hunting under the front seat for the rope, shouted, 'Gus, where the fuck's that rope?'

I was watching Sid. He dropped his hands, pushed himself up on his palms. 'The noose?' I said.

'Aye, the fucking noose,' said Mac.

I reached behind me, opened the tool carrier fitted into the van and took out the rope. Mac had tied the slip knot. The sight of it made Sid start to whimper, spout nonsense I couldn't make out.

'Give us it here,' said Mac.

I passed the rope and Mac left the van to throw it over a branch.

I leaned towards Sid. He shrieked. I opened the slide door behind him and he fell backwards into the daylight.

Mac already had the rope in position as I raised Sid by the scruff of his neck to the edge of the burn. Mac took Sid from me as though I was passing him a bag of trash. 'You are a slimy little fucker, Sid, y'know that?' he said.

'What? What the fuck have I done?'

I moved forward. 'You know why you're here, Sid. Don't shit us.'

He was staring at the noose. Couldn't take his eyes away for a second. 'Nowt. I've done fucking nowt. What have I done? What have I done?'

Mac looked at me. He was ready to pound into Sid. I raised a hand. As Mac walked away to the front of the van, I looked at Sid. His glasses were held together in the middle by a strip of Elastoplast – my doing. But beneath the big lens of the left eye there was a shiner coming up. He had a cut lip and some scratches on his temple. 'Who gave you the doing, Sid?'

'What? What doing?'

I half turned, enough to throw a windmill right. I decked him. As he lay pegged out on the ground I told Mac to come back and pick him up. He held Sid; I tried again.

'Rab's boys have paid you a wee visit, haven't they, Sid?'

He was looking at the noose again. A nod. 'Aye, aye, they came round.'

'Why?'

'I don't know, I don't fucking know.'

Mac tightened his grip on Sid, said, 'Let me string the cunt up. I can't be doing with this.'

Sid hollered, 'The other night at the jolly house.'

I turned to Mac. He explained, 'The pit fight.'

I faced Sid again, squeezed his hollow cheeks in my hand. 'I saw you there with Jonny Johnstone . . . Very fucking cosy with the filth you are, Sid.'

He stuttered, 'I'm not, I'm not.' He started to fluster, whimper. 'He was just after a bit ay sport.'

Mac lost it: 'I'm not being fucked about any longer.' He dragged Sid into the burn. The gimp was crying now, what we call *greetin' like a wee lassie* in Scotland. I let Mac get the noose around Sid's neck then start to tighten it.

'You better talk fast, Sid . . . Mac the Knife's not happy.'

I saw the name tip more fear into Sid's eyes. He spluttered, gripped at the noose with his fingernails and yelled, 'Pay-off! He was there for his pay-off!'

'What pay-off?'

Sid's fingernails were all that was keeping the rope from strangling him. 'Rab feeds Jonny a wedge to turn a blindy to the dog fights.'

It made perfect sense to me. 'How long's this been going on?'

'I don't know, I promise I don't. Moosey used to pay him . . . It was my first time.' Sid kicked out at Mac, tried to push him away. 'Call him off! Call him off, for fucksake!'

I nodded to Mac. He let down the rope.

Sid collapsed in the burn, panting.

'Speak,' said Mac. 'I can easy fucking string you up again.'

Sid tried to get up. The stones underfoot were slippy and he fell again and again. I walked into the burn, placed my hands on his neck and belt loop – threw him onto the bank.

I followed him out and placed my foot on his shoulder as he tried to get up. I pushed him down again. Mac joined me. We towered over Sid, put the heavy threat on him as I said, 'Speak.'

'I don't fucking know any more, I promise I don't. That's it, man . . . Jonny Boy's Rab's fixer with the polis.'

'Who else?'

'What do ye mean?'

'Who else in the filth is Rab paying off?'

'I-I don't know. I swear, I only do the books on the dogs.'

I looked at Mac. His face was non-committal. I turned back to Sid. 'Who's the little fucker in the white Corrado?'

'What?'

'The little bastard that ran over Tupac.'

Sid was gathering his senses, his breath returning to normal. 'It's Gibby – top man with the young crew . . . He's a wee fucking Jack the Lad.'

I could tell he knew more. 'You know who told him to kill Tupac, so don't make me knock it out of you.'

Sid looked at Mac. 'It was Jonny . . . But that's all I know, I swear. I don't know why but he told him to fucking do it. Gibby told me himself – he's a boasting wee cunt.'

'Is this Gibby pally with the Crawford kid?'

251

Sid nodded. 'I've seen them going about together.'

I got Gibby's address out of Sid and then Mac picked him up by the ponytail, dragged him screaming to the edge of the burn and kicked his arse back into the water.

As we got in the van, I rolled down the window, yelled to Sid as he schlepped out of the water, 'That rope's staying up there . . . and if one word of what you've told us is bullshit, by Christ, you'll fucking swing.'

As we pulled out, I could hear Sid yelling, 'Hey, you can't leave me here! I don't know where the fuck I am!'

Thought: Welcome to my world.

Chapter 48

MY MIND WAS BUZZING WITH thoughts; hacked up a line from Aristophanes: 'A man may learn wisdom even from a foe.'

Mac was a bit too primed. Any day of the week, Mac was a bit too primed. I couldn't trust he wouldn't go radge and carve up this Gibby kid. Like he hadn't the form.

It was working against my better judgement to take Mac along, but it was either that or go alone and it seemed the lesser of two evils. Desperation had a hold of me now.

'You ready for this?' said Mac.

'Look, just cool the beans, okay.'

Mac floored it, spun through the lights. An old giffer with a walking stick raised it above his head. Mac was holding the wheel at ten to two, gripping tight. Add the black leather gloves and he did a fair impression of a post-raid wheelman.

'Mac, I have to tell you right off, this isn't your fight.'

'I know, I know.'

'Do you?'

He turned to me, smiled. 'Look, I'm Mr Frosty here, okay?'

'You better be. I don't want you being put away again on my conscience.'

'Sure.'

He settled some. Relaxed back in his seat, put a hand on top of the dash, cruised. Sighthill was its normal burnt-out self. I could hear the tyres going over broken glass every fifty yards.

'Fucksake,' said Mac.

'You're worried about punctures? What makes you think you'll still have tyres when we get back to the motor?'

The address we had was for a high-rise. Mac didn't flinch, even though we were going right into the heart of the war zone. I pointed the way through the winding streets littered with deros, trash and more than a few needles.

'The state of this place,' said Mac.

'Not exactly primo real estate.'

'You can say that again.'

We found our block. Outside a mattress had been set alight. Two kids in trackies chucked branches on the flames. I'd love to have known where they got them – didn't look like any vegetation for miles around.

Mac parked; we stepped out.

The kids left the fire, turned to the new addition to the landscape. 'Hoy, mister . . . want us tae mind yer motor?'

I looked at Mac. He smiled at me. 'What you think?'

'I'd say make them an offer they can't refuse.'

'And that would be?'

I called the pair over. 'You the local heavies?'

In chorus: 'Aye. Aye.'

'What do you pay for a heavy round here these days?'

Laughter: 'Fifty quid an hour, man.'

'Fuck off.'

'All right, twenty.'

'Tell you what.' I took out a skydiver, handed it over. 'This van's still in one piece when we come back, I'll give you another five.'

They took the five-spot and ran off laughing.

'Wee bastards.'

Mac patted me on the back. 'What did you expect – a receipt?'

We took the stairs. The flat was only two flights up, but as I knocked on the door, nothing.

'Empty?'

'I'd say so.'

I peered in the window where Mark Crawford's young crew partner in crime stayed. Place was definitely habited: Chinese takeaway boxes on the window ledge and a couple of plates on the table. 'Looks like they were at dinner not so long ago.'

Mac was peering out over the balcony. Thought he was checking the van. 'Is it still in one piece?'

He mumbled, 'I'm not looking at the van.'

'What, then?'

He pointed. 'Take a deck at that.'

Down below, in full view of every flat in the street, a pagger was in progress. Two burly roided-up types with pit bulls straining at the leash had a lanky streak of a lad pinned to a wall. He cowered, hands out; took off his Burberry jacket to whip back the dogs.

'Does that look like our boy Gibby?' said Mac.

'That's the little wanker from the pit fight. Our Corrado man, for deffo . . . Saw him on the hill with the Crawford kid the night Moosey was killed.'

'Then this'll be his payback for fucking up.' Mac crossed his arms on the rail, settled into spectator mode.

'You just gonna watch?'

Mac laughed. 'Think we could do anything?'

The big lads didn't take too kindly to the jacket being aimed at the dogs: grabbed it off the wee yob and watched the pits pull it apart. The jacket soon turned to threads and the dogs kicked off, snarling, went for each other. Took all their handlers' strength to keep them apart.

The string bean Gibby screamed like a loose fan belt.

'Christ, they're vicious,' said Mac.

'No kidding.'

The next move was an obvious one. A knock to the jaw for String Bean and down he went. The pugs stepped back, let the pits off the leash. They went for the throat. A huge arc of claret sprayed out of the yoof's neck as one of the dogs hit the jugular. One of the big lads took a direct hit, his white T-shirt copping for an enormous splash of blood.

'Holy fuck.' For a moment I couldn't look, turned away. Some wailing called me back. It was the girl, the one I'd seen in Rafi's store with the poodle.

'What's she gonna do?' said Mac.

'Run, if she's smart.'

I thought I should too. Was pure instinct – I dived for the stairs.

Mac grabbed me; we struggled. 'Where you going, Gus?'

'Someone's got to do something.'

'Like what?'

I tried to free myself. 'Anything – they're gonna kill him.'

Mac put a bear hug on me. 'Gus, get a grip . . . I'd say they've already done that.'

I saw the girl slapped down, carted away up the street by one of the spectators to the scene. The dogs were led away too as the big biffers got into a Toyota pick-up and sped away. From the truckbed the pits barked as if it was a job well done.

A lifeless pile was all that was left of Gibby on the street.

Blood pooled on the pavement, ran into the gutter.

We took the stairs back down to the van. The sight of the yob's remains up close was enough to have me holding back some chuck. I started to retch. The people who had come to watch while the murder was in full swing, however, seemed to have disappeared altogether. I understood why as a blast of sirens was swiftly followed by flashing blue lights from a trail of police cars.

Three of them blocked in Mac's van as Lothian and Borders' finest poured out and headed in our direction.

As I stopped retching, Mac turned to me. 'You done?'

I looked up at the uniforms. 'I'd say well and truly.'

Chapter 49

THE POLICE CARS' DOORS HAD barely swung open before plod was reaching for me, with a smile on his face.

'Trust me now, Dury . . . you are well and truly fucked,' said McAvoy. He gave a nod to the uniform to cuff me behind my back, then placed a playful slap on my cheek. '. . . Well and truly fucked.'

'What's it this time? Let's see now. You've already had me for possession of a bit of puff. Maybe jaywalking?'

'Droll, Dury, very droll . . . I think I'll wait till we get you down the station, though, before I fill you in.'

'Is that literally? Cos I'm a bit delicate after the last booting.'

He firmed his gaze, pointed to the street, said, 'Get this clown out my sight.'

I watched Mac being led away too. Could see people appearing at the windows of homes, but nobody came out to help the police get their story straight.

'Aren't you going to go house to house?' I bawled out.

I got a knee in the back for my trouble, thrown in the cart.

I spent my time in the back of the meat wagon wondering what the filth had in mind for me this time. I knew it wouldn't be pretty. Somehow, all I could think about was how Debs might get dragged into all of this. I didn't want that. She'd suffered enough. I'd let them throw the book at me, and catch it square in the coupon before I'd let Debs be harmed again.

The booking-in went by in a daze. Handed over: belt, shoelaces, lighter and wallet.

Said, 'Can I hold on to those?' nodding at my pack of Marlboro.

Desk sergeant raised a dark eyebrow towards a white mop of hair, said, 'What do you think?'

He didn't want my answer to that.

The cell was cold.

For about seven hours the cell was cold while I sat there on my own without so much as a knock at the door. At eight-thirty a uniform brought in a tin tray containing two scoops of mashed potato, a greasy pile of mince and some carrots, diced. I looked at this, said, 'No afters?'

Uniform pretended to stifle a sneeze, then let rip, spraying the tray. 'You hungry, are you?' he said, putting the food on the table before me.

I wanted to say, *You filthy pig bastard*. What I went with was, 'No, not so much.' Rubbed my stomach. 'Had a good feed before I got here . . . but thanks for asking.'

He left the mince and tatties. Fucked off.

It took reserves of calm I didn't know I had to stop me lifting the tray and battering it off the back of his head. I wasn't for playing games any more. I'd be telling it straight and McAvoy could get as rough as he liked. I had my version of events to play with and it would make better reading in the paper with some police corruption allegations thrown in. Let him deny it. *Veritas* is an absolute defence.

Another half-hour or so passed. The uniform came back for the tray. I tried him with, 'Look, is anyone going to come in here to interview me? I'm kinda keen to get this over with.'

'Shut yer fucking yap!'

'Is that a no, then?'

He lifted a fist, showed me his bottom row of teeth – grey and jagged; reminded me of a graveyard.

'Careful – you'll spill the mince.'

He fucked off again.

I got the message: they were keeping me waiting. I figured on a morning session. Hunkered down on the cold bench. I ached after the dig to my back earlier. I checked it out: bruising up nicely. The hard bench didn't do me any favours. I turned over. As I lay there, hands tucked behind my neck, I knew this was one of those moments where drink wasn't going to come and fill the void.

I thought of lots of things: Moosey, the life he had led with Rab and the huge sums of money they'd made from the misery of those poor animals. I thought of the Crawfords' loss, how they felt for little Chrissy, how they still hurt. I wondered how these two different worlds had collided. How? How did that happen? I knew that in a city of haves and have-nots it was inevitable: the paths must cross sometime. It was all a bloody mess. I thought of Tupac and Gibby, two more casualties, and I thought of Mark Crawford and the role he played in all of it, but I knew there were parts of the puzzle that were still missing.

I wanted to know the score but, barring a miracle now, I wasn't hopeful.

I felt sweats breaking out along my back. Even though the temperature was plum-clenchingly cold, I had the sweats. I was craving alcohol. On top of the pain in my back it was quite a combination. A night in hell faced me.

I'd read somewhere that Richard Burton, the great Welsh actor, had once gone under the knife for his back. Apparently some fuckwit, jealous of how much Burton could put away and not get drunk, spiked his drink with wood alcohol and he fell down a flight of stairs. Years later, when he needed an operation to repair the damage, as they opened him up his surgeons were shocked to see the entire length of his spine covered in crystallised alcohol. They spent eleven hours scraping it off.

The sweats intensified.

I rolled onto my side. Made no difference.

Oh, shit . . . I saw a face. Debs.

I knew she wasn't there. I knew it was the booze calling, like the bats when they came swooping.

'*Debs*?'

Why was I saying her name? I knew she wasn't there.

I felt a hand on my shoulder. I trembled.

'Oh, fucking hell . . . *Debs*.' I was calling her like a boy calls his mother.

I felt a slap.

I opened my eyes. It was Fitz.

'Jeez, ye were far gone there, boyo,' he said.

I sat up. 'When did you come in?'

'Just now. I thought, well, here's what I thought . . .' He handed me a bottle – said 'VB' on the front.

'What's this?'

'Beer, lager I think. I got it over the road. 'Tis all they had, 'tis a deli really . . . I think it's Australian.'

I looked at the label: VICTORIA BITTER.

'It tastes all right, but have you not got something stronger?'

'Get that down you first.'

I drained the bottle, wiped my mouth. Passed it back, said, 'Done.'

Fitz delved in his pocket, brought out a half-bottle of Grouse, some tabs – Regal, and a lighter. 'Fill yer boots, boyo.'

I ripped into the low-flying birdie, drenched my throat. Tasted like paradise. I kept two-fingers in the bottle; sparked up a tab. 'Fuck, these are the proper lung-bleeders, Fitz.'

He shrugged. 'How they treating you?'

I couldn't help but laugh – like I was staying at the Hilton. 'Oh fine, thanks for asking . . . Jacuzzi's a bit cold, though.'

Fitz pulled over a chair, sat by the bunk. He took a tab from the pack, lit himself up from my tip. 'It's the end of the road now.'

I took back my cigarette. 'Y'think?'

Fitz drew deep on the tab, looked at the ash forming, blew on it. 'You know they'll throw the book at ye.'

I'd expect any less? 'You sound confident.'

Fitz fidgeted, tapped at his watch. 'Well, there's something you ought to know, Gus.'

I was reclined on my elbow but pushed myself up. He never called me by my first name. 'And what would that be?'

He drew on the Regal. Deep lines formed in the edges of his eyes. 'Jonny Johnstone and McAvoy are taking salary from Rab Hart.'

I knew about J.J. but McAvoy was only a suspicion. I played him, 'You're a bit late coming to me with this.'

The tab again, a deeper drag. 'What did you expect? You want me to grass on my own? I'm a fucking Irishman, I can't do that.'

I didn't buy the patriotic bullshit. Fitz was filth, if he was shitting on Jonny Johnstone and McAvoy then he was working an angle. 'Then why are you now?'

He threw down the cigarette, stamped it underfoot. 'Fuck off, Dury. You think I have some grand play lined up? . . . Do me a favour.'

'That's exactly what I have been doing all along, isn't it? . . . Stirring up shit for that pair was like a fucking godsend to you, wasn't it? What the fuck's your angle here, Fitz? You better spill it now or it's blood I'll be spilling and you know I'm good for it.'

It was all stage pacing, improv. Fitz had information to lay on me; he just didn't want to make me think he was giving it out for free. I'd worked him enough. 'Okay, well, you listen up here and remember I never told you any of this.' He moved towards me, pulled the whisky bottle from my hand and took the last belt. Said, 'McAvoy is in deep with Rab.'

'How deep?'

'As deep as it gets, but that's not the issue here.'

'Then what is?'

'Judge Crawford.'

The name wasn't one I expected to hear spoken in the same

breath as Rab Hart and McAvoy. This stalled my thought process; I went onto auto. 'The judge?'

Fitz turned to face me. I was close enough to see the cracked veins in his red cheeks. 'Look, Crawford is hearing Rab Hart's appeal, don't you get it? Fuck me, Dury, don't you fucking get it?'

I rose, walked to the other end of the cell. My head hurt with the possibilities. I couldn't fathom what Fitz was telling me. Somehow my thought processes had seized up.

'Don't you fucking get it yet?' said Fitz.

I flagged him quiet. 'I get it. I get it.'

'Johnstone and McAvoy have been taking Rab's cash for months, years even, but this is a whole other payday for them.'

My cigarette had burnt down to the filter. A long grey slew of ash fell to the floor. I dropped the filter after it. 'They're working me to get Mark Crawford off the hook.'

Fitz slapped his palms on his heavy thighs, stood up to face me in the narrow cell. As I looked at him I didn't know where my mind was. I felt lost in some rage, some bitterness, some misdirected hatred . . . He was nearest to hand, so copping for all of it.

Fitz spoke, 'I did my best for you, Dury.'

Still he played me. 'Anything you did for me, Fitz, was either to put the boot into McAvoy and Jonny Boy or to keep me from blowing the whistle on how you came by some of your previous collars, so don't come acting the big benevolent with me. You're filth, like the fucking rest of them.'

He straightened himself, pulled at the belt loops on his trousers and fastened his coat. His face flushed red, the whites of his eyes glowing with rage. He held out a hand for the cigarette packet. 'Come on, then, get that over. I'll be on my way.'

As he walked to the cell door, Fitz turned briskly. 'One more thing, Dury . . .'

'What?'

'That's us even.'

'Fuck off, Fitz.'

'No way, laddie. I want to hear you say it.'

I walked over to him, said, 'We will never be *even*, Fitz . . . but if it makes you feel better, we'll call it quits.'

As he walked out of the cell, he spoke in a near whisper: 'And you are well and truly on your own now, boyo.'

Chapter 50

MCAVOY FAVOURED an early start.

Lights flashed on; must have been all of six in the a.m.

He came in battering a steel tray with the heel of his hand. 'Rise and shine, cocksucker,' he yelled. Leaned in close to my ear, added, 'Today's judgement day.' A laugh. Uproarious. The full demoniac head-tilt to follow.

Was I rattled? Past caring? I couldn't judge.

Flung my legs over the side of the bunk. Too slow for some: a pug in uniform grabbed my shirt, led me to the interview room.

McAvoy sat, crossed his legs. His socks caught my eye – black with red and green argyle diamonds down the sides. His hair seemed to be carefully gelled into place, but no amount of combing was going to disguise the bald patch.

As I took my chair, McAvoy pulled the cuffs of his shirt beyond the limits of his jacket. The cuffs, white like the collar, were fastened by black onyx links; gold arrows pointed at me from each of them. I'd seen them somewhere before, those arrows . . . Oh yeah – on the old prison uniforms.

McAvoy twiddled with the cufflinks, smiled like a car salesman. 'Here we all are again,' he said.

'The gang's all here.' A pack of smokes, John Player Specials, sat between us. I reached out for them. From nowhere the pug slammed down his hand, crushed the smokes underneath his giant mitt. I looked at him, said, 'Little jumpy, are we?'

McAvoy laughed. 'Oh, Dury, you kill me. You really do.'

Wanted to say, *I'd fucking like to*. Somehow thought it wouldn't quite fit the situation; went with, 'You know, you crack me up too.'

The pug retreated. McAvoy took the packet of tabs, removed the cellophane, smoothed out the crushed edges. He opened the top on the cigarettes, pinged the base until two or three tabs popped up, offered me one.

I accepted. Put it in my mouth. 'How about a light?'

'Sure, sure.' He leaned back, ferreted in his jacket pocket, produced a silver, soft-touch lighter. Flame shot up about an inch high.

This was going too well. I felt unsettled. That was the aim, right? I tried to focus. Remembered I had right on my side. Of course I'd done wrong, many times, but not this time. This time I was in the right. It would take a hell of a lot more than placing me at the scene of the crime with a dodgy motive to get me put away for a man's murder . . . wouldn't it?

McAvoy watched me, curiously. Let me get halfway down the tab, then spoke: 'You get about, Dury.'

'You mean the Gibby thing . . . Not gonna try hanging that on me too, are you?'

A smile. Wry one, maybe. 'No, definitely not. We have that little, *ahem*, incident tidied up already.'

'Clean-cut, was it?'

A laugh. 'Let's say we got an early lead on it.'

'Wonders never cease.'

McAvoy sighed, weary of me already. He leaned in. 'Your involvement is still something of a mystery, but I've bigger plans for you, Dury.'

I raised an eyebrow. 'Have ye now.'

Didn't register a hit. He reached below the desk, took a sheaf of papers from his briefcase. He shuffled them a while. Hummed, hawed. Pointed his tongue to the inside of his cheek, then, 'Ah, here we are. Now to other matters.'

He placed two sheets of paper before me. Both held graphs: identical red lines highlighted on each of the two pages. McAvoy peered at them, twiddled with his cufflinks again, made sure they were on show. Said, 'Why don't you take a look at those, Dury? A close look.'

I picked up the pages. They were fingerprint analyses; seemed to indicate a match for the two. 'Okay, you have two charts, matching prints for something,' I said.

McAvoy looked pleased. Too pleased. He smiled, almost giggled, leaned forward. He removed a silver pen from his top pocket, pointed, said, 'Now, see here . . . where the two red lines peak?'

I nodded.

'That's a definite match – one hundred per cent – that can't be faked.'

I drew on my tab.

He pointed with the pen again. 'And here . . . and here . . . and here . . . and here.' He kept pointing to similar peaks and troughs on the two charts.

I cut him off, 'You've made your point.'

'Have I? Have I really?'

'Yes, I think so.'

He looked at the pug, smiled. The pug smirked back like an inbred farmer's son who'd just received a pat on the back for fucking his first sheep. 'Are you sure you understand, Dury? I mean really understand?'

I stubbed my tab. Leaned across my side of the desk, blew out the last of my smoky breath in his face as I spoke. 'You have my fingerprint from the murder scene.'

McAvoy's face changed shape, and colour. His brows drooped. He said nothing, sat back and waited for me to speak.

I said, 'I'm guessing you found this on Moosey's wallet.'

McAvoy was speechless. I wanted to plug his mouth. He checked to see the tape was running as I spoke. I wondered what his pulse

rate was sitting at. He was as psyched as a Formula One driver in
the pits, raring to go.

I played it cool – what had I to lose now? 'Yeah, I guess I must
have left my prints when I took out his wallet.'

McAvoy couldn't hold back, 'You removed the victim's wallet?'

'Yes ...'

'So, you admit you were on the scene at the moment of death?'
He grabbed his notes. 'You are telling us you were at the murder
scene on Corstorphine Hill on May fifteenth, and removed Thomas
Fulton's wallet ...'

'I called you in, if you remember.'

McAvoy nodded rapidly, said, 'Yes ... you admit being on the
scene of the murder, we can place you there. We have your dabs
on the corpse. What were you after in his wallet – money?'

I felt my mouth narrow to a small aperture. 'Fuck no.'

'You weren't looking for more money ... like you knew Fulton
was carrying?'

'What money? First I heard he was carrying money was in
here.'

McAvoy swept a hand over his hair. 'How did you know him?'
he said.

'I didn't.'

He looked up, flashed eyes on me, then returned to his notes
and produced a set of photographs. They were pictures of me talking
to Moosey's wife, with Sid at his house, and with Rab Hart in
Saughton Prison. 'You are one of Fulton's known associates. Why
else would you be seen with this lot?'

I tapped the table. 'McAvoy, my next answer might confuse you
... I was doing something known as *detective* work.'

That put the needle in him. He placed down his pen. Suddenly
he seemed to remember he was here to hitch my arse to the flagpole.
He lost it. 'Right, Dury, why did you kill him?'

I laughed in his face. 'You think I killed him ... ? You're dumber
than you look.'

He stuck a finger in his collar, undid his top button. 'Stop messing me about. We have you on the scene, the victim was fifty thousand pounds lighter after you left and you are roughly that amount in hock for the pub. I think that's enough of a reason for me to say we have you bang to rights.'

I took the cigarettes up. His lighter was still resting on the pack.

'What you have, McAvoy, is no fucking clue.'

'*What*?'

'I didn't kill Moosey – I stumbled across his corpse. He was gutted before I got to him.'

'Oh, I see, you were just in the wrong place at the wrong time?'

'Something like that.'

'And you'll be able to corroborate this, will you?'

'I can go one better . . . I can hand you the real killer.'

He sighed, shook his head. 'And that would be?'

I blew smoke. 'Well, if you and Jonny Johnstone weren't taking a nice slice of Rab Hart's activities, you'd have him in here by now.'

Someone had obviously been listening, through the way the door was flung open and Jonny Boy strode in. 'Now I am fucking warning you, Dury, about your allegations!' He was – what's the phrase – fit to be tied.

McAvoy's eyes widened as J.J. entered. He firmed his shoulders; for a moment I thought he would speak, but he scratched his ear instead. He rose, came round to my side of the desk, said, 'You are wrapped up in one world of shit, Dury.'

I spun in my chair, said, 'So, what's new?'

'What's new is I'm now arresting you for the murder of Tam Fulton.'

Chapter 51

I HEARD THE WORDS BUT they didn't register for a few seconds.

'You're what? . . . Are you serious?'

'Oh, yes,' said McAvoy. He shuffled his papers again, gave me the 'you do not need to say anything' spiel.

I jumped out of my seat. The uniform pug approached but I flung off his arm and put a halt to any idea that I was taking his shit. 'Now look the fuck here, McAvoy . . . I know your game. You are setting me up to take the fall for Judge Crawford's son.'

Laughter from Jonny and McAvoy.

'Oh, funny is it? Not so funny that Crawford's hearing Rab Hart's appeal, is it? How do you think the courts will look on that when I blow it all wide open?'

More laughter. The tape was off now.

'Dury, who the fuck do you think is going to listen to a washed-up old soak like you? You're finished. I am going to put you away and that's an end to it.'

Jonny joined in, 'Get used to the idea, Dury. It won't be good for your mental health to be so angry when you're in stir and I'm in my comfortable home banging your ex-wife every night of the week.'

I lunged at him. My fist got halfway to its target before the uniform pug stepped in and grabbed me round the throat.

McAvoy backslapped Jonny. He was still laughing when his mobi went off. As he answered it his face changed quickly. 'Whoa, back up . . . What the fuck do you mean Complaints are on the way down?'

The smirk suddenly left Jonny's coupon. 'Who's that?'

McAvoy flagged him down, listened to the caller more intently. 'Who told them this? Where did they get the money from?' As the information was relayed to him, McAvoy's face firmed – his jaws seemed to pop as he clenched his teeth – and then he turned to Jonny and threw the mobile at him. 'You fucking silly cunt!' He ran towards him, roaring, 'You fucking daft fuck!'

Jonny backed up, took a pelt in the puss. It was enough to put him on the floor. McAvoy weighed into him with his fists. 'You fuck, you cunt . . . you fucking took it, did you?'

'*What? What?*' Jonny was sliding along the ground, the trousers of his Boss suit creasing up.

The pug holding me suddenly became confused and let his grip slip. He freed me so he could go to the door and call for back-up.

McAvoy hit his stride. He had Jonny by the throat, strangling him on the floor. 'You thought fifty Gs was too big a fucking payday to pass up so you stiffed me and took it for yourself!'

Jonny's face was reddening. His arms flapped wildly at his sides as he tried to get a hold of McAvoy, but he had no chance. McAvoy was going like ten men, ready to kill. 'I'll fucking do you worse than you ever dreamed of doing me.'

I was ready to take a seat and wait for McAvoy to finish him as a dozen or so uniforms piled in and dragged the pair apart. The door was left open and I contemplated slipping out while the going was good but as I edged closer I was rumbled.

'Sit the fuck down, you're going nowhere,' yelled a uniform.

I did as I was told. The frantic mass left.

The interview room seemed much quieter.

I was alone again.

They gave me a few more hours to sweat. I imagined rows of drink, strung the length of a bar, singing to me. Bottles, barrels, warehouses wouldn't be enough. I pined for the oblivion it brought.

I imagined myself walking into the rain, rattling from bar to bar. I didn't even bother to shield myself from it. I wanted to be soaked, wet through. As I paced, my imagination fed hallucinations. There were people all around me, scurrying on either side, but none could touch me. Where I was, there was room for only one. Did I face a life of pacing like this? Pacing an empty flat, listening to music, alone. Fearing the future, alone. Eating frozen dinners, carry-outs, alone. And the worst: watching television, seeing people enjoying themselves before your very eyes, taunting you. Christ, comedies, on television, how could I watch them? To watch a comedy, laugh, escape yourself and then hear the sound of your own laughter and know there was no one there to share in it. Would there ever be?

A key turned in the door.

Pug yelled, 'Get out.'

'That it?'

Fat fingers grabbed my shirt, a yank. 'Move yer fucking arse.'

In the corridor I caught sight of a familiar face shaking hands with Fitz the Crime. Judge Crawford had his hand on his son's shoulder as he led him from the interview room. The boy looked fraught, on edge. I knew Fitz would have another collar to his credit soon enough, maybe more than one.

I muttered under breath, 'Nice one.'

I felt a prod in my back.

'C'mon, move it.'

I turned to face the pug. As he shoved me towards the desk sergeant I managed to straighten my shoulders. As I progressed along the corridor, I came face to face with the judge and his son. The boy's head was bowed, facing the floor. For a second his father didn't register my face. When he did, he followed his son, dropped his eyes.

I tutted, shook my head, leaned into Fitz's lapels, said, 'Kids today . . .'

Fitz glowered at the pug, yelled, 'Get him the hell out of my sight!'

I didn't recognise the plod on the desk. He handed me my shoelaces, belt, lighter and wallet. Said, 'That you off to get blootered?'

I frowned. 'What is it with you lot – is that line in the manual?'

Outside a force-ten was blowing. Rain battering the plastic roof of the entrance. I turned up my collar, lit a tab.

As I started to walk, I caught sight of Debs hunkering down in the driver's seat of a brand-new Audi. She'd spotted me, I could tell, but she didn't know how to react. What the hell was she doing here?

I crossed the street, tapped on the door.

She lowered the window.

'Debs, you're here?'

She seemed agitated, looking round me. 'I, well . . .'

'Tell me you're not . . . Whose car is this?'

She sighed, twice, then, 'It's Jonny's – he only just bought it.'

'Och, for fucksake, Debs . . .'

She turned in the seat. The rain was blowing in; she had to shield her eyes from it. 'Gus, it's not what you think.'

'How have you fucking bought into this guy?' I threw down my cigarette. 'Deborah, I credited you with more sense.'

She shook her head, took the key from the ignition, opened the car door and stepped out. 'Gus, I've been waiting here for hours.'

'Don't waste your time, Jonny Boy's had his collar felt.'

Debs looked confused. 'You don't know, do you, Gus?'

'Know what?'

She smacked her hand off the door. 'Gus, I-I . . .'

'What is it, Debs, you're having a jailhouse wedding?'

She fired up, 'Fucking shut it and listen . . . I shopped him.'

I stared right at her. 'You what?'

Debs poked me in the chest with the car key, yelled, 'You know, Gus, it's not all about you and your childish fucking one-upmanship. I did the right thing for once in my life. I found the money, Gus. Jonny had a carrier bag full of used tenners stuffed away in the back of the wardrobe . . .'

I kicked a car tyre. 'It was you . . . all the Complaints stuff in there was down to you?'

She calmed, nodded. 'I called Fitz.'

I looked back at the station.

I knew I should be smiling, laughing, but I felt a cloud of Presbyterian gloom rising. I heard the old predestined apophthegm – 'Man plans, God laughs'. Somewhere in the back of my mind, as I watched Debs, I felt sure she'd only one reason for doing this, but I needed to ask her: 'Why?'

The rain and the wind lashed us as she spoke; the gale was getting worse. 'For you.'

I put my arms around her. She smiled, nuzzled into me. I felt the car key press into my chest again. I took it from her. 'You won't be needing this.' I ran the key along the side of Jonny's new car, then I dropped it into a drain.

'Gus, that's shitty.'

'I know.'

She laughed and we set off into the rain, together.

By the time we got back to the Wall we'd been drenched, sodden as dock rats. But somehow it didn't seem to matter to either of us.

Mac had Usual resting on top of a bar stool. The dog launched himself at me as I appeared.

'Down, boy. Down.'

'Someone's glad to see you.'

I took off my jacket, took up a bar towel to dry my hair, handed one to Debs.

I pointed to the Guinness tap. Mac got the message, started to pour. My mobi was dead, needed charged. I plugged it in and sat at the bar. Usual came and scratched at my legs.

'Down, boy. Later, I promise, we'll go to the park.'

'Oh, don't say that,' said Mac.

'Say what?'

'That word.' He spelled it out slowly: 'P-a-r-k . . . He knows it

273

now. Smart animals, dogs, picking up stuff all the time. Like children.'

I saw Debs look at me. She grabbed my hand, squeezed.

I ruffled Usual's ears, patted him on the head. As I did so I felt a coldness suddenly come over me, like when people say the old phrase *Someone just walked over your grave*.

Mac placed my pint before me, then nodded to the rear of the bar. I turned and saw Katrina Crawford stood behind me, looking like a woman who had recently collapsed in shock. She had holes in her stockings, both knees scraped. Black mascara ran beneath the eyes.

I stood up. Words wouldn't come.

Chapter 52

KATRINA CRAWFORD POINTED A BROKEN fingernail at me. 'You have no idea what you've done . . .'

Debs stood up, said, 'Who's this?'

I waved her away. 'It's okay. Katrina, would you like to sit down?' I walked over to her. Her eyes were distant, a faraway glaze on them. 'Come on, let's sit in the snug.' The poor woman was in bits. I felt a heart scald to think of what she'd been through already with little Chrissy, and now her only son would be locked up. I called out to Mac, 'Bring her a brandy.'

All the way to the snug, she shook her head, again and again. Her lip trembled as we sat down. I saw her grip the arm of the chair tightly. 'You don't understand.'

I took out my cigarettes and lit up. I offered one to her but she just stared at it as though it was an alien artefact. She was lost, in a dark, dark place. I wondered, would I, or anyone, be able to reach her?

Mac brought the brandy and she threw it down in one desperate gulp. Her hair trailed into her mouth, stuck to her wet lips, but she seemed oblivious. I saw the empty glass held so firmly that I thought it might shatter in her hands; I took it from her, placed it on the table. There was an awkward silence between us for some moments, then her eyes rose, and slowly, she began to talk. 'You don't understand.'

I spoke softly, 'Then tell me, Katrina.'

A smile played on her face. She registered amusement at the sound of her name. 'I'm not her any more.'

'I'm sorry, I don't . . .'

Her smile strayed as she looked to the ceiling. 'I stopped being her a long time ago . . .'

I knew this was a human being in a place of absolute hurt. I had covered the territory a few times myself, but something about her assured me I'd never been this far gone. I watched her through the rising cigarette smoke. Her grasp on reality seemed every bit as tenuous as the thin wisps of grey floating around us. As I stared at her she seemed to sense my gaze, turned and brought my eyes into her view. 'I remember the strangest things . . . the strangest things.'

I nodded, sensed she felt encouraged to go on.

'When she had just turned three we gave Chrissy a little tricycle. It had a bell the shape of a ladybird. She loved that little tricycle; the bell followed us everywhere. For weeks we heard that bell about the house . . .' She dropped her gaze towards the table, laced her trembling fingers together. 'We thought about disconnecting it, you know . . .' A tear fell down her cheek. 'What I'd do to hear that bell now.'

She removed her hands from the table, gripped tightly once again on the chair's arms. Her knuckles turned white. But still there wasn't a flicker in those eyes. Her gaze held firm. She was lost in thoughts, reveries, barely with us. I had no words that could comfort her, asked, 'Is there someone I could call?'

'No!' She was harsh, indignant, gripping harder on the chair. 'There's no one.'

I could feel my heart freezing over at the sight before me; the woman was in bits. She needed some help, medical attention, sedating probably. I wasn't fit for the task of comforting her, said, 'I just think that, you know—'

She cut me off, lunged forwards: 'Mr Dury, I have to tell you—'

I didn't know what to say, mumbled, 'About what?'

'About Mark.'

'Look, you can't hold yourself responsible.'

She dropped back into the chair, started to weep. Deep, pained sobs from a part of her no other person would ever want to witness. As I watched her shoulders shaking, I laid a hand on her arm. 'Come on now.'

She grabbed her head in her hands. 'I couldn't lose another child.' She stiffened. I withdrew my arm. 'I knew he was going to kill him,' she said.

'Katrina, you don't need to do this.'

'I knew when he started to latch on to that gang he wanted to avenge Chrissy.' She turned to me, seemed suddenly animated, gripped my hands in hers. 'Mr Dury, I couldn't lose another child, don't you understand?'

I understood.

She removed one hand from mine and put it in her coat pocket. From inside she withdrew a long bloodstained knife with a serrated blade. The knife was damaged.

She said, 'The tip broke off inside him. They'll be able to match that, won't they?'

'Katrina, is this what I think? I mean, are you saying . . .'

'I killed Fulton . . . I had to, I couldn't lose another child.'

She placed the knife down on the table. I covered it with a bar towel, wrapped it up.

'I followed Fulton for weeks. I knew Mark was planning to kill him. I'm his mother, I could see it, there was a change in him . . . as if his whole life was over.' She spoke so plainly now, so matter-of-fact, as if making this confession to me was the most natural thing in the world. For the first time since she'd walked through the door of the Wall she seemed stilled, calm. She knew exactly what she was doing, perhaps she had all along. She went on, 'I watched Fulton with those morons, those little shits . . . and Mark. I watched them for weeks. I knew Mark was just biding his time, waiting for the right moment when he'd have Fulton alone and then he'd . . .' Katrina stopped flat. She started rocking to and fro in the chair. 'I followed Fulton, onto the hill.' She stopped again.

I prompted, 'On the night he was killed?'

She didn't look at me, just kept staring into the distance. 'Yes. At home I overheard Mark on the phone. He said he was going up there. I panicked because I knew what he'd become capable of . . . The change in him, Mr Dury, he wasn't himself any more . . . I took the knife and I drove fast. I got there before him . . .' She suddenly snapped back to reality, faced me. 'I couldn't lose another child, you must understand.'

'Go on.'

'Fulton had those little white headphones in, he didn't hear me till I caught up with him on the trail. My heart was pumping and pumping. All I could think of was Mark coming and of Chrissy . . . Fulton killed Chrissy, he killed my lovely daughter. When he turned, the knife went cleanly in his side. It was easier than I ever imagined.' She spoke briskly now, animating her actions with thrusts of arms. 'He wasn't a very big man; I was taller. He had his hands up but the knife kept slicing through his palms. He fell back, I think he must have been dead already, but I dropped on top of him. I couldn't stop. I was in a frenzy, pure rage . . . I'd never felt such strength in me. I kept going long after he was dead . . . He killed Chrissy, he wasn't taking Mark.'

I found myself nodding, but I couldn't form words.

She went on, relaying the full gory account, 'The knife got stuck, the blade broke in his ribs, I had to heave to get it out his chest . . . The tip will be in there, won't it?'

'I should think so.'

She went on some more. I switched off. When she was finished, I spoke. 'Did Mark witness any of this?'

'No.' She seemed relieved to have given her account. 'No, he wasn't even there by the time I left . . . I quickly covered the body with branches and went home to clean myself up.'

She seemed so cold now; I asked, 'And your husband?'

'No, never . . . but . . .'

'Yes? What is it?'

Katrina slouched back in her chair, subdued once again. 'He told me . . . he confided . . . that he thought our son . . .'

'Your husband suspected Mark?'

A nod. But no more words.

As I stood up Katrina Crawford's eyes flitted back to reality, just for a moment, but it was long enough. 'You'll have to tell them they've got it all wrong,' she said.

I nodded; I was trembling now.

I went through to the bar. The place was in silence. I broke the reverence, said, 'Go sit with her.'

Debs took one look at me and didn't question.

'Gimme the phone, Mac.'

I dialled.

My heart was beating so strong I could hardly speak, managed, 'Police.'

A pause.

'I want to speak to Fitzsimmons.'

He answered on the third ring. 'It's Dury . . . I'll keep it short: you have the wrong man. It was Katrina Crawford . . . the mother killed him.'

'What?'

'She's at the Wall. I think you better come for her now.'

I gave the phone to Mac. My hand was shaking too much to put the receiver in the cradle.

As I sat at the bar my Guinness had settled nicely.

I raised the glass; beads of moisture shone like jewels down the side. The first taste felt like my *Ice Cold in Alex*. Had I ever waited longer for a drink? I savoured every drop.

Mac stood silently, knew better than to ask.

I called for another drink. As I did so, Hod walked in. He'd lost the beard, but I didn't comment on that.

'It's yours,' I said.

'What is?'

279

'This place . . . the bar.' My eyes were still burning. I could feel them, saw their fire reflected in Hod's. He said nothing.

Mac put three shot glasses in front of us, poured a Talisker bottle over them. He didn't make a toast.

Hod was the first to speak, said, 'Gus, I've been thinking . . .'

'Oh yeah.'

'If you write this up, you could make some serious cash.'

'And?'

'It could be your salvation.'

I felt my heart sink. 'That's what you've been thinking, is it?'

'I have, yeah.'

I stood up, shoved in my stool, beckoned the dog. I could see Debs patting Katrina's back as she sobbed. 'Know what I've been thinking?'

'What?'

'I've other plans.'

Hod spun as I walked for the snug. 'You're not serious . . .'

'*Deadly.*'